YIWEN EDU

英语详注读物

GOOD-BYE, MR. CHIPS

James Hilton

再会，契普斯先生

[英] 詹姆斯·希尔顿 著　葛传槼 俞亢咏 注解

上海译文出版社

写在前面的话

再会，葛传椝先生

朱绩崧

上世纪末，我本科读所谓英文专业，苦于课堂所得支离破碎，难以应用，不禁幻想：有没有什么人、什么书，像风清扬的独孤九剑那样，助我迅速提高英语战斗力？

不久，“葛传椝”进入了我搜索的视野。其实，我高三时已注意到。到底何许人也，竟能位列《新英汉词典》编纂者之首？这部工具书对高考语法题简直无疑不解。

复旦外文系颇有几位老师，是葛先生的学生，课余会讲起Prof. Hertz C. K. Ke 的传说，譬如过目不忘、心细如发。

很快，《英语惯用法词典》成了我寤寐思服、渴盼一窥的武学秘笈。此书六十年代后未见重印，我在号称收藏宏富的文科图书馆也遍寻不得。只好在几柜子检索卡片中，找找葛先生其他著作。

于是，在书库进门左手边的架子上，我翻开了那本封面破破烂烂的《再会，契普斯先生》……

十八年后，我没有忘记掩卷的心情。用武侠小说里常见的一则成语来形容，就是“醍醐灌顶”。仿佛是这条自修成精的老书虫遥遥地在另一个世界，逐字逐句领着我啃完这部小说。或者，那就是张三丰正向张无忌传授太极拳?

呵呵，是我想多了。很惭愧，不学无术、英文勉强入门的我竟也成了大学教员。常遇人问：如何提升阅读技能？我总是劝他们下一番死硬功夫，精读《再会，契普斯先生》，精读葛先生、俞亢咏先生共同注释的另一部文学作品：萧伯纳的《卖花女》。“每本读三遍，一个月里读完，再读前言——十遍！”我对他们说。

他们一定以为我是信口胡说吧。他们会想，老掉牙的书，孔网都难找，果真这么好，为何不重印?

重印《再》《卖》，是我近年向译文社编辑们唠叨不完的话题。现在，这两本书真的再卖了。

翻着责编金宇女士电邮来的 PDF 样张，版式、字体稍易，风貌依稀当年。面对屏幕，我心里说不出地欢喜——葛先生，我们终于再会了。

前　言

读什么？怎样读？——这是我们经常听到的英语学习者提出的两个问题。学习英语，除阅读之外，当然还有听、说、写、译。这五者是相辅相成、不可偏废的，但阅读是基础。尤其在应用方面，我国极大多数涉及外语行当的工作者最需要的还是阅读。阅读，对于自学者来说，更是学好外语的重要途径。

读什么？读现代英美人写的英语。作为精读材料，最好选择一些现代英美作家的作品；要新而不“怪”。就是说：语言既不陈旧，又没有很多奇怪的句子结构和俚语、方言之类；艺术表现手法新，又必须是现实主义的，既不是传统小说的平铺直叙，纯粹的讲故事，又不是“新”得出奇，变成了梦呓式的“天书”。总之，选择读物要着眼于最能收到学习英美语言（进而研究英美文学）的实际效果。我们选择这本《再会，契普斯先生》（*Good-bye, Mr. Chips*），就是试图拿出一个比较理想的实例，来回答“读什么”的问题。

怎样读？读有精读和泛读之分。两者也是相辅相成、不可偏废的，只是要求有所不同。泛读从“量”来要求，广泛浏览，达到见多识广，可以容许“不求甚解”；精读则从“质”来要求，务必一词、一句都弄得清清楚楚：每个词的正确发音，它的词性、在文中的意义、色彩、搭配、用法以及在句子中的作用；每个短语、每个从句在文中的作用和相互关系；每个句子的语法结构，有否倒装或省略等，句型有无习惯上的特殊之处，以及句子的精确含义。这一切都弄清楚了，才能弄清每一章节的意思和各章节之间的联系。这才算是语言方面真正读懂了，才能理解全文讲的是什么，是怎样讲的，才谈得上文艺欣赏、文艺评论和翻译。

这本**注解本**是为精读而编写的，也可以说是试图回答“怎样读”的问题的一个探索性的答案。

精读读懂以后，还希望能反复诵读，因为对于外语学习来说，懂和熟是两回事；懂而不熟，可以说并没有完成学习任务。“熟读唐诗三百首，不会吟诗也会吟。”熟读不但可以加深理解，提高阅读水平、鉴赏水平，而且直接有助于写和译，间接有助于听和说——达到全面学好英语的目的。

作者介绍 本小说作者詹姆斯·希尔顿（James Hilton）1900 年 9 月 9 日生于英国兰开夏郡（Lancashire）利城

（Leign）。他在剑桥大学学习期间就开始为报刊写稿。第一次世界大战后，他遍游欧洲，一度寄居维也纳。他的第一部长篇小说《凯瑟琳自己》（*Catherine Herself*）出版时，他才十八岁。1933 年出版《失去的地平线》（*Lost Horizon*），同年冬天发表《再会，契普斯先生》，轰动一时。1939 年，他去美国，1941 年出版《无心的收获》（*Random Harvest*）。这三部小说都曾拍摄成电影，颇为成功。英语词典中有“Shangri-la”（[ˌʃæŋgrɪ'lɑː] 香格里拉）一词，原作“世外桃源”解，后又衍生出其他意义，并一度在俚语中被用来指“厕所”，——这个词就出于希尔顿的《失去的地平线》。契普斯（其实是小说人物契宾先生——Mr. Chipping——的绰号）也已在英语国家很大一部分人中间像亲人、老朋友一样熟悉，一样亲切。

希尔顿后来的作品有《记忆犹新》（*So Well Remembered*），《奇异无比》（*Nothing So Strange*），《早晨的旅程》（*Morning Journey*）和《再三再四》（*Time and Time Again*）等，他还为好莱坞写过不少剧本。1954年12月20日，希尔顿在美国加利福尼亚州长滩（Long Beach）逝世。

作品介绍《再会，契普斯先生》原先是希尔顿为英国《不列颠周刊》（*British Weekly*）的圣诞节增刊所写的，时在1933 年。翌年重新在美国《大西洋月刊》（*Atlantic Monthly*）上发表，随后美国和英国相继出版单行本，英国广播公司（BBC）还曾连续广播，后来又拍摄成电影，曾在我国放映，片名《万世师表》。1938 年，俞亢咏将小说开头四章详加注释，在葛传椝主编的《竞文英文杂志》上连载介绍，颇受读者欢迎。

小说用极其生动、轻快的笔调描绘契普斯一生在布鲁克菲尔德（Brookfield）公学的教书生涯和他的恋爱、婚姻和为人，情意悱恻，妙趣横生。同时，从布鲁克菲尔德这偏僻的一隅反映出英帝国在19世纪末、20世纪初开始没落的情景，反映了当时社会的动荡和人们思想的变迁。艺术风格和语言都是我们上面所说的“新而不怪”，是学习现代英语和英国文学的一本好书。

《再会，契普斯先生》在许多国家都有译本，并广泛被学校用作教材或课外读物。

关于注解 我们是从语言角度进行注解的，力求详尽。如果你觉得有些讲解是多余的，那就说明这些你已经懂了，可以跳过去。相反，如果这样详尽地讲解了，你阅读还有困难，那说明这本书也许暂时对你还太深了些，可以先读一些简易读物，作为一个阶梯。注解的详略要正好符合所有读者的要求是不可能的。我们希望读者们能够看得出，我们是认认真真地做了这本书的注解工作的，煞费苦心地总想切实有助于学习英语的读者，尤其是自学者。书末附了一张“契普斯先生年表”，也正是为了帮助读者弄清小说叙事的脉络；否则为小说人物编年表，岂不滑稽？

这样详尽地注解英语，还是一个尝试。这一做法是否能收到预期的实际效果，还有待实践证明。注解中存在的问题和错误，恳切希望各界学者和读者批评指正，以利于再版时改正。

葛传槼 俞亢咏

1982年12月

Good-bye, Mr. Chips

第一章

内容提要

人到老年，常日夜梦想着往事。

契普斯（其实是契宾先生的绰号）生于1848年，终身在布鲁克菲尔德公学任教。他在最后辞去教师职务后，寄居在学校对面的维克特夫人家，已经十几年了。他虽已年老，但并没有什么毛病；然而毕竟年老，风霜雨雪都要时刻当心了。

他回忆起二十二岁时初到布鲁克菲尔德来任教时的情景。第一个被他惩罚的学生叫考利。后来考利的儿子、孙子他都教过。他曾对小考利说："你爷爷是笨蛋，你爸爸也半斤八两，而你则是全家中最大的笨蛋。"引起哄堂大笑。

现在契普斯老了。幽默和哀伤的回忆潮水般向他涌来。他常潸然泪下，自己也不知道是在哭，还是在笑。

1

When you are getting on in years[1] (but not ill, of course), you get very sleepy at times[2], and the hours seem to pass like lazy cattle moving across a landscape[3]. It was like that for Chips[4] as the autumn term progressed and the days shortened till it was actually dark enough to light the gas before call-over[5]. For[6] Chips, like some old sea-captain, still measured time by the signals of the past; and well he might[7], for he lived at Mrs. Wickett's[8], just across the road from the School[9]. He had been there more than a decade[10], ever since[11] he finally gave up his mastership[12]; and it was Brookfield far more than Greenwich time that both he and his landlady kept[13]. 'Mrs. Wickett,' Chips would sing out[14], in that jerky, high-pitched voice[15] that had still a good deal of[16] sprightliness[17] in it, 'you might[18] bring me a cup of tea before prep[19], will you?'

1 **getting on in years** 渐渐老了；上年纪

2 **at times** 时常；是习语

3 **a landscape** 一片风景

4 **Chips** [tʃɪps] 契普斯，本书主人公，其实这是他的绰号；他姓Chipping ['tʃɪpɪŋ]，但学生们都称他 Chips。

5 **the days shortened till it was actually dark enough to light the gas before call-over** 白日一天短一天，短到在点名之前已经暗得要点煤气灯。it 指天色；gas 指煤气灯。**call-over** = roll-call 点名。日长的时候当在点名之后才点灯。

6 **For** 并列连词，引起一个全句。

7 **well he might** = he might well measure ['meʒə] time by the signals of the past. well = reasonably.

8 **at Mrs. Wickett's.** ['wɪkɪts] = at Mrs. Wickett's house or home.

9 **across the road from the School** 在这所学校对面。across the road from 也可作 across from。**School** 专指 Brookfield ['brʊkfi:ld] 公学，所以用大写开首，参见下文。

10 **decade** ['dekeɪd] 十年

11 **ever since** 自从；比 since 语气重，有"自从……以来一向"的意思。

12 **give up** ['gɪv 'ʌp] **his mastership** 放弃他的教员职位。

13 **it was Brookfield far more than Greenwich** ['grɪnɪdʒ] **time that both he and his landlady** ['læn'leɪdɪ] **kept** 是 both he and his landlady kept Brookfield far more than Greenwich time 的强调句，意思是说"他和他的女房东所遵照的时间，与其说是格林威治（世界标准）时间，远不如说是布鲁克菲尔德时间。" **Brookfield** 英国地名，也是当地的学校名，这里指 Brookfield time。 **Greenwich** 在英国伦敦附近，为本初子午线经过的地方。

14 **would sing out** 时常高声喊道。would 表示过去惯常的行为。

15 **jerky, high-pitched** ['haɪ'pɪtʃt] **voice** 断断续续的，音调高的声音

16 **a good deal of** 许多（后面接不可数名词）

17 **sprightliness** ['spraɪtlɪnɪs] 生气勃勃

18 **you might** 意思相当于 I request you to，是一种客气的祈使句式。句末附加疑问 will you，也是客气的语气。

19 **before prep** 在上预备课之前。 **prep** 学生用语，是 preparation 的简写。

When you are getting on in years it is nice to sit by the fire[1] and drink a cup of tea and listen to the school bell sounding dinner, call-over, prep, and lights out[2]. Chips always wound up the clock[3] after that last bell[4]; then he put the wire guard[5] in front of the fire, turned out the gas[6], and carried a detective novel to bed[7]. Rarely did he read more than a page of it[8] before sleep came swiftly and peacefully, more like a mystic intensifying of perception than any changeful entrance into another world[9]. For[10] his days and nights were equally full of[11] dreaming.

He was getting on in years (but not ill, of course); indeed, as Doctor Merivale[12] said, there was really nothing the matter with[13] him. 'My dear fellow, you're fitter[14] than I am,' Merivale would say, sipping a glass of sherry[15] when he called every fortnight or so[16]. 'You're past the age when people get these horrible diseases; you're one of the few lucky ones who're going to die a really natural death[17]. That is[18], of course, if you die at all[19]. You're such a remarkable old boy[20] that one never knows[21].' But when Chips had a cold[22] or when east winds roared over the fenlands,

1 **sit by the fire** 坐在火炉旁边。**fire** 火炉中的火。

2 **the school bell sounding dinner, call-over, prep, and lights out** 学校的钟声响起，通知吃晚饭、点名、上预备课和熄灯。 **dinner** 正餐，一般是晚上的一顿主餐，不是 supper。

3 **wound** [waʊnd] **up the clock** 给钟上发条；开钟。wound 是 wind [waɪnd] 的过去式。

4 **after that last bell** 最后一次敲钟（指熄灯钟）之后

5 **wire guard**（放在火炉前的）金属丝安全罩

6 **turned out the gas** 关掉煤气

7 **to bed** 就寝；并不着重“到床上去”。这里的 bed 带有抽象的意思。

8 **Rarely did he read more than a page of it** = He rarely read [red] more than a page of it. 因略有否定意味的副词 rarely 放在句首，所以句中主谓倒装。

9 **more like a mystic intensifying of perception than any changeful entrance into another world**（修饰 sleep）更像是一种神秘的感知强化，而不像是任何变幻莫测的世界切换。因 Chips 年迈，醒时所见反不如梦中所见的清楚。

10 **For** 并列连词，引起一个全句。

11 **full of** 充满

12 **Doctor Merivale** ['merɪveɪl] 梅里韦尔医生

13 **the matter with** = amiss with，wrong with，对于……失常的。the matter 有形容词的作用。

14 **fitter** 更健康的

15 **sherry** ['ʃerɪ] 西班牙等地产的葡萄酒；雪利酒

16 **called every fortnight or so** 每（隔）两星期左右来访一次

17 **'re going to die a really natural death** 将真正自然地死去。 **die a natural death** 指因年老或疾病而死，有别于因事故、遇害、自杀等而死。

18 **That is** 那就是说；即

19 **if you die at all** 承接上句，省去主句 you're going to die a really natural death。

20 **old boy** 老头儿，也作对男子的昵称

21 **one never knows** 人们无从逆料（他究竟如何）。这里有“也许他竟会不死”的含义。 **one** 泛指“人们”。

22 **had a cold** 伤风

Merivale would sometimes take Mrs. Wickett aside[1] in the lobby[2] and whisper: 'Look after him, you know[3]. His chest ... it puts a strain on his heart.[4] Nothing really wrong with him[5] — only anno domini[6], but that's the most fatal complaint[7] of all, in the end[8] ...'

Anno domini ... by Jove[9], yes. Born in[10] 1848 and taken to the Great Exhibition[11] as a toddling child — not many people still alive[12] could boast[13] a thing like that. Besides, Chips could even remember Brookfield in Wetherby's time[14]. A phenomenon, that was[15]. Wetherby had been an old man in those days — 1870 — easy to remember because of the Franco-Prussian War[16]. Chips had put in for[17] Brookfield after a year at Melbury[18], which he hadn't liked, because he had been ragged[19] there a good deal[20]. But Brookfield he *had* liked, almost from the beginning.[21] He remembered that day of his preliminary interview[22] — sunny July, with the air full of flower scents

---

1 **take Mrs. Wickett aside** 把 Mrs. Wickett 拉到旁边

2 **lobby** 前室；门廊

3 **you know** 你该知道（谈话中常用的口头语）

4 **His chest ... it puts a strain on his heart.** 这里 it 是赘词。作者用省略号表示医生说了 His chest 后停顿了一下，再接下去说时，插入一个 it 代 his chest。**put a strain on his heart** 增加他心脏的负担；压迫心脏。

5 **Nothing really wrong with him** = There is nothing really wrong with him 他并不真有什么毛病。 **wrong with** = 上文的 the matter with。

6 **anno domini** ['ænəʊ 'dɒmɪnaɪ]（口语）老年；一般用大写，原义是“公元”。

7 **fatal complaint** 致命的疾病

8 **in the end** 到底；究竟

9 **by Jove** ['dʒəʊv] 一种口头禅，有赌咒的意思，表示“真的”、“不是胡说”等。 **Jove** = Jupiter ['dʒuːpɪtə] 罗马神话中的主神。

10 **Born in** 前面省去 He was。

11 **the Great Exhibition** [eksɪ'bɪʃən] 1851 年英国伦敦举行的第一次大展览会

12 **alive** [ə'laɪv] 活着的，只能用作表语或后置修饰语。

13 **boast** 夸口说

14 **Wetherby's** ['weðəbɪz] **time** 在韦瑟比（任校长）的时候

15 **A phenomenon** [fɪ'nɒmɪnən], **that was** = That was a phenomenon。**phenomenon** 稀有现象。

16 **Franco-Prussian** ['fræŋkəʊ'prʌʃən] **War** 普（鲁士）法（兰西）战争（爆发于 1870 年）

17 **put in for** 请求加入

18 **Melbury** ['melbərɪ] 梅尔伯瑞，英国地名，也是那地方的校名。

19 **ragged** [rægd] rag 的过去分词，“被人作弄”的意思。注意不要与形容词 ragged ['rægɪd]（破烂的，粗糙的）混淆。

20 **a good deal** 许多，这里作状语。

21 **But Brookfield he *had* liked, almost from the beginning.** 这句中把宾语 Brookfield 放在句首，是强调 Brookfield；*had* 印成斜体，也表示强调，要重读。上句说他不喜欢 Melbury，这句说“可是 Brookfield 是他几乎一开始就确实喜欢的。” **from the beginning** 从一开始就……（有“始终”的意思）。比较：**at the beginning** 在开始的时候(开始时候如此，后来未必如此)。

22 **preliminary** [prɪ'lɪmɪnərɪ] **interview** ['ɪntəvjuː] 就职前的面试。雇主在雇用新人之前，往往要先经过一次面试，对雇员进行一些了解或交待一些情况。

and the plick-plock[1] of cricket[2] on the pitch[3]. Brookfield was playing Barnhurst[4], and one of the Barnhurst boys, a chubby little fellow, made a brilliant century[5]. Queer that a thing like that should stay in the memory so clearly.[6] Wetherby himself was very fatherly and courteous[7]; he must have been ill then, poor chap[8], for he died during the summer vacation, before Chips began his first term. But the two had seen and spoken to each other, anyway[9]. Chips often thought, as he sat by the fire at Mrs. Wickett's: I am probably the only man in the world[10] who has a vivid recollection of old Wetherby ... Vivid, yes; it was a frequent picture in his mind, that summer day[11] with the sunlight filtering through[12] the dust[13] in Wetherby's study. 'You are a young man, Mr. Chipping[14], and Brookfield is an old foundation[15]. Youth and age[16] often combine well. Give your enthusiasm to Brookfield and Brookfield will give you something in return.[17] And don't let anyone play tricks with[18] you. I — er[19]— gather[20] that discipline was not always your strong point at Melbury[21]?'

---

1 **plick-plock** 劈里啪啦的声音

2 **cricket** ['krɪkɪt] 板球（盛行于英国的一种球类运动）

3 **pitch**（板球的）两个三柱门（wicket）之间的球场

4 **playing Barnhurst** ['bɑ:nhɜ:st] 和巴恩赫斯特校队比赛

5 **made a brilliant century** 得到个漂亮的一百分。 **century**（板球比赛中的）一百分 (100 runs)。

6 **Queer that a thing like that should stay in the memory so clearly.** = It is queer that ... should .... should 有"竟然"的意思。

7 **fatherly and courteous** [kɜ:tjəs] 慈祥和殷勤的

8 **poor chap** 可怜的家伙（对人怜悯或同情的称呼；这里是称 Wetherby。）

9 **anyway** 无论如何；= anyhow

10 **the only man in the world** 这里 in the world 是习语，并不着重 world 这词的实义，有"天下；毕竟"的意思，如：What in the world is it?（这到底是什么？）

11 **it was a frequent picture in his mind, that summer day** 那年夏季的这一天是他头脑里时常出现的一幅图象；即那天的情景常萦绕在他脑际。这里 it 是虚词，实际的主语是 that summer day; that summer day 后面的话只是它的修饰语。同类的句子如：it is important, education。

12 **filtering through** 滤过；透过

13 **dust** 一片灰尘

14 **Chipping** 是 Chips 的正式姓氏，见前注。

15 **Brookfield is an old foundation** 布鲁克菲尔德是一所（建立已久的）老学校。

16 **Youth and age** 指 Chips 和 Brookfield，参看上句。

17 **Give your enthusiasm** [ɪn'θju:zɪæzəm] **to Brookfield and Brookfield will give you something in return.** = If you give your enthusiasm to Brookfield, Brookfield will give you something in return. **in return** 作为报答。

18 **play tricks with** 对……恶作剧；对……耍花招

19 **er** [ə] 在断续的说话中无意识地发出的含糊音

20 **gather** 推想

21 **discipline** ['dɪsɪplɪn] **was not always your strong point at Melbury?** 你在梅尔伯瑞管学生的纪律并不怎么好吧？（全句用陈述句的形式，句末用疑问号，读时带疑问口气，相当于疑问句。always 没有具体意义，只是使语气婉转些。**strong point** 优点；特长。

'Well[1], no, perhaps not[2], sir.'

'Never mind; you're full[3] young; it's largely a matter of experience[4]. You have another chance here. Take up a firm attitude[5] from the beginning, that's the secret of it[6].'

Perhaps it was.[7] He remembered that first tremendous ordeal[8] of taking prep[9]; a September sunset[10] more than half a century ago; Big Hall[11] full of lusty barbarians ready to pounce on him as their legitimate prey[12]. His youth[13], fresh-complexioned[14], high-collared, and side-whiskered[15] (odd fashions people followed in those days[16]), at the mercy of[17] five hundred unprincipled ruffians[18] to whom the baiting of new masters was a fine art[19], an exciting sport, and something of[20] a tradition[21]. Decent little beggars individually[22], but, as a mob, just pitiless and implacable[23]. The sudden hush[24] as he took his place at the desk on the dais[25];

---

1 **Well** 语助词（谈话时常用）

2 **perhaps not** = perhaps discipline was not always my strong point at Melbury.

3 **full** 十分，极（是副词）

4 **it's largely a matter of experience** 这主要是个经验问题。 **largely** 主要地。

5 **Take up a firm attitude** ['ætɪtjuːd] 采取强硬态度

6 **that's the secret of it** 这个 it 说不出它的先行词是什么，有的语法家称之为"it 的含糊用法"（the vague use of *it*）。

7 **Perhaps it was.** = Perhaps it was the secret of it.

8 **tremendous** [trɪ'mendəs] **ordeal** [ɔː'dɪəl] 可怕的磨难

9 **taking prep** 主持预备课（prep 见第 5 页注释 19）

10 **sunset** 日落时

11 **Big Hall**（Brookfield 学校中的）大礼堂

12 **lusty barbarians** [bɑː'beərɪənz] **ready to pounce on him as their legitimate** [lɪ'dʒɪtɪmɪt] **prey** 强壮的野人们（指学生们，说他们的粗野）准备随时向他扑击上来，当作他们合法的猎物。（用 legitimate 是说学生认为作弄新教师是理所当然的，有讥刺的意思。）

13 **His youth** 他的青春（这里用抽象的"他的青春"指青春时代的他）

14 **fresh-complexioned** 神清气爽的

15 **side-whiskered** 两颊有须的

16 **odd fashions people followed in those days** = odd fashions which（或 that）people followed in those days

17 **at the mercy of** 在……掌握之中；任……处置

18 **ruffians** 流氓们（指那些捣蛋学生）

19 **the baiting of new masters was a fine art** 作弄新教师是一种巧妙的艺术。a fine art 有"拿手好戏"的意思；比较：**the fine arts** 美术，或泛指艺术。

20 **something of** = in some sense or degree

21 **tradition** [trə'dɪʃən] 传统的风气

22 **Decent** ['diːsnt] **little beggars individually** [ˌɪndɪ'vɪdʒʊəlɪ]= They are little beggars individually 他们一个个分别而论都是些循规蹈矩的小家伙。little beggars = youngsters，是戏谑语。

23 **implacable** [ɪm'plækəbl] 无法使其镇定的

24 **The sudden hush** 和后面 the scowl，the smells，the last blood-red rays 一连串名词后面都只有修饰语，没有谓语。这种以名词或名词词组构成的单部句（one-member sentence），在文艺作品中很多，可称为"名词句"。

25 **took his place at the desk on the dais** ['deɪɪs] 在讲台上的书桌前就位（不一定是坐是立）

the scowl he assumed to cover his inward nervousness[1]; the tall clock ticking behind him and the smells of ink and varnish; the last blood-red rays slanting in slabs through the stained-glass windows[2]. Someone dropped a desk lid. Quickly, he must take everyone by surprise[3]; he must show that there was no nonsense about him[4]. 'You there in the fifth row — you with the red hair — what's your name?' — 'Colley[5], sir.' — 'Very well, Colley, you have a hundred lines[6].' No trouble at all after that[7]. He had won his first round[8].

And years later[9], when Colley was an alderman[10] of the City of London[11] and a baronet[12] and various other things[13], he sent his son (also red-haired) to Brookfield, and Chips would say: 'Colley, your father was the first boy I ever punished[14] when I came here twenty-five years ago. He deserved it[15] then, and you deserve it now?' How they all laughed; and how Sir Richard[16] laughed when his son wrote home[17] the story in next Sunday's letter!

And again, years after that, many years after that[18], there was an even better[19] joke. For another Colley[20] had just arrived — son of the Colley who was a son of the first

1 **the scowl** [skaʊl] **he assumed to cover** ['kʌvə] **his inward** ['ɪnwəd] **nervousness** 为掩盖他内心的紧张而做出的皱眉的样子。the scowl 后省去 which（或 that）。

2 **the last blood-red rays slanting in slabs through the stained-glass windows** 一片片血红的残阳穿过彩色玻璃窗斜射进来。

3 **he must take everyone by surprise** 他定要使人人都吃一惊。**he must ...**（Chips 想）他必须……（用 must 而不用 had to...，表示 he 当时的想法。下面的 he must 也是这样。）

4 **there was no nonsense about him** 他（Chips）不容胡闹

5 **Colley** ['kɒlɪ] 考利，姓

6 **you have a hundred lines** 罚你抄一百行拉丁文（英国学校的一种罚则）

7 **No trouble at all after that.** = There was no trouble at all after that. 在那以后就没有麻烦了。

8 **won his first round** 胜了第一个回合。 **round** 一局；一场。

9 **years later** 若干年后。years 修饰 later。

10 **alderman** ['ɔːldəmən] 英国的市政官，次于市长（mayor）

11 **the City of London** 伦敦市区（比通称的 London 范围小）

12 **baronet** ['bærənɪt] 从男爵

13 **and various other things** 还有各种其他头衔

14 **the first boy I ever punished** = the first boy that I ever punished

15 **deserved it** 应得处罚。it 指上句所说的处罚这件事，未必一定要有个名词（如 punishment）做它的先行词。

16 **Sir Richard** ['rɪtʃəd] = Sir Richard Colley，就是上文第一个 Colley。因为他是 baronet，所以称 Sir。注意 Sir 用在 baronet 和 knight（爵士）的姓名或名之前，不可用于姓的前面，和 Mr. 的用法不同。

17 **wrote home** 把……写在家信中

18 **years after that, many years after that** 许多许多年以后（这里，推想起来，当是二十多年之后。）

19 **even better** 甚至更好

20 **another Colley** 又一个姓考利的（他是第三代的Colley了）

Colley. And Chips would say, punctuating his remarks with that little 'umph-um'[1] that had by then[2] become a habit with him: 'Colley, you are — umph — a splendid[3] example of — umph — inherited traditions[4]. I remember your grandfather[5] — umph — he could never grasp the Ablative Absolute[6]. A stupid fellow, your grandfather.[7] And your father, too — umph — I remember him — he used to[8] sit at that far desk[9] by the wall[10] — he wasn't much better, either[11]. But I do believe — my dear Colley — that you are — umph — the biggest fool of the lot[12]!' Roars of laughter.

A great joke, this growing old — but a sad joke, too[13], in a way[14]. And as Chips sat by his fire with autumn gales rattling[15] the windows, the waves of humour and sadness[16] swept over him very often until tears[17] fell, so that when Mrs. Wickett came in with his cup of tea she did not know whether he had been laughing or crying. And neither did Chips himself.[18]

1 **punctuating** ['pʌŋktjʊeɪtɪŋ] **his remarks with that little 'umph-um"** 用那"嗯，嗯"之声（像标点一般）夹杂在他说的话里。umph可读作含糊的[m]，也可读作[ʌmf]；um可读作[əm]。

2 **by then** 到那时候，不迟于那个时候

3 **splendid** 出色的；这里是谐语，有讥刺义。

4 **inherited** [ɪn'herɪtɪd] **traditions** 继承的传统

5 **your grandfather** 指第一个Colley

6 **Ablative** ['æblətɪv] **Absolute** ['æbsəljuːt] （拉丁语法中的）夺格独立结构

7 **A stupid fellow, your grandfather.** = Your grandfather was a stupid fellow. 这种省去连系动词而把主语和表语倒置的句型，口语中常有。

8 **used to...** （过去）常常……。在现代英语中只用过去式used to，不用现在式use to。又，used本当读[juːzd]，但在used to这一习语中读[juːst]。

9 **that far desk** 那个远离讲台的课桌

10 **by the wall** 靠墙的

11 **wasn't much better, either** 也并不好多少。**either** 也；用在否定句中。

12 **the lot** 全体，一批。这里指Colley祖孙三个。

13 **A great joke, this growing old — but a sad joke, too** = This growing old is a great joke — but a sad joke, too 这样一年年变老（的情况）是一个大笑话，……，渐入老境的这个情况既可笑，又可悲。

14 **in a way** 就某一方面而论；多少有些是习语。

15 **rattling** 使震动而发出格格声

16 **waves of humour** ['hjuːmə] **and sadness** 浪潮般的一阵阵幽默和忧伤。humour也读作['juːmə]，那是老式的读法。

17 **tears** [tɪəz] 泪珠；是可数名词复数。注意：动词tear（撕）读[teə]，不要混淆。

18 **And neither did Chips himself** Chips本人也不（知道）。And neither = Neither.

第二章

内容提要

布鲁克菲尔德公学创立于伊丽莎白女王时代，几经兴衰，近年又见低落。正因如此，它才接纳年轻的契普斯来任教。他既没有显赫的社会关系，又缺乏教学经验，学历也平凡，只有个文学学士之类的学位。

契普斯起初雄心勃勃，总想能当上个真正的第一流学校的校长。随着年事增长，经过不少努力和挫折，他终于在布鲁克菲尔德安定下来。到退休的时候，他已成为布鲁克菲尔德的化身。

2

Across the road behind a rampart of ancient elms lay Brookfield[1], russet under its autumn mantle of creeper[2]. A group of eighteenth-century buildings centred upon[3] a quadrangle[4], and there were acres[5] of playing fields beyond[6]; then came the small dependent village[7] and the open fen country[8]. Brookfield, as Wetherby[9] had said, was an old foundation; established[10] in the reign of Elizabeth[11], as a grammar school[12], it might, with better luck, have become as famous as Harrow[13]. Its luck, however, had been not so good; the School went up and down[14], dwindling almost to[15] nonexistence at one time, becoming almost illustrious at another[16]. It was during one of these latter periods[17], in the reign of the first George[18], that the main structure had been rebuilt and large additions made.[19]

---

1 **Across the road behind a rampart** ['ræmpɑːt] **of ancient elms lay Brookfield**

= Brookfield lay（lie 的过去式）across the road behind a rampart of ancient elms. Brookfield 学校坐落在（Chips 寄寓的 Mrs. Wickett 家的）对马路一排古老的榆树形成的围墙后面。

2 **russet** ['rʌsɪt] **under its autumn mantle of creeper** 因在一层秋季的蔓草下面而呈现红棕色。 **creeper** 匍匐植物（不可数名词）。

3 **centred upon** 座落于……中央

4 **quadrangle** ['kwɒˌdræŋgl]（学校里的）方场

5 **acres** ['eɪkəz] 英亩（1 英亩合中国的 6.07 亩）

6 **beyond** = beyond the group of eighteenth-century buildings

7 **small dependent village** 指 Brookfield 地方；其实在 Brookfield 地方设立 Brookfield 学校，学校该是 dependent，但这里反说 dependent *village*，可见学校的声誉和地位高于其所在的地方。

8 **open fen country** 空旷的沼泽地的乡村

9 **Wetherby** 参见第 9 页注释 14

10 **established** [ɪs'tæblɪʃt] = being established

11 **in the reign** [reɪn] **of Elizabeth** [ɪ'lɪzəbeθ] 在伊丽莎白一世女王在位时期（1558—1603）

12 **grammar school** 英国从前以教拉丁文为主的学校，相当于现在的公学（public school）。

13 **it might, with better luck, have become as famous as Harrow** ['hærəʊ] 它（指 Brookfield）如果运气好些，也许已经和哈罗公学一样有名了。（全句含有虚拟的语气；with better luck = if it had had better luck.）

14 **went up and down** 时盛时衰

15 **dwindling almost to** 几乎衰落到（某种状态）

16 **… at one time, ... at another** 有时……，有时……

17 **latter periods** 指 becoming almost illustrious 的那些时期

18 **the first George** [dʒɔːdʒ] = George the First 乔治一世（英国国王，1714—1727 年在位）

19 **It was during ... that the main structure had been rebuilt and large additions made.** 是 The main structure had been rebuilt and large additions made during …的强调句式。 **main structure** 主建筑物。**large additions made** = large additions had been made. **additions** 指辅建筑物。

Later, after the Napoleonic Wars[1] and until mid-Victorian days[2], the School declined again, both in numbers and repute[3]. Wetherby, who came in 1840, restored its fortunes[4] somewhat[5]; but its subsequent[6] history never raised it to front-rank[7] status. It was, nevertheless, a good school of the second rank. Several notable families supported it; it supplied fair samples of the history-making[8] men of the age — judges, Members of Parliament[9], colonial administrators[10], a few peers[11] and bishops[12]. Mostly, however, it turned out[13] merchants, manufacturers, and professional men[14], with a good sprinkling of[15] country squires[16] and parsons[17]. It was the sort of school[18] which, when mentioned[19], would sometimes make snobbish[20] people confess that they rather[21] thought they had heard of it.

But if it had not been this sort of school it would probably not have taken Chips[22]. For Chips, in any social or academic sense[23], was just as respectable, but no more brilliant, than Brookfield itself[24].

---

1 **Napoleonic** [nəˌpəʊlɪˈɒnɪk] **Wars** 拿破仑战争（指拿破仑一世从 1803 年起到 1815 年率领法国与英国、普鲁士、俄国、奥地利之间进行的多次战争，所以用复数形式 Wars）

2 **mid-Victorian** [ˈmɪdvɪkˈtɔːrɪən] **days** 英国维多利亚女王执政（1837—1901）

的中期。 **Days** 时代。

3 **declined again, both in numbers and repute** 在（学生）人数和声誉方面又都下降

4 **restored its fortunes** 恢复它（Brookfield）的地位；使它重新发展起来

5 **somewhat** 多少地；略微

6 **subsequent** ['sʌbsɪkwənt] 随后的（指 1840 年以后的）

7 **front-rank** 第一流的；头等的

8 **history-making** 创造历史的；（干大事业而日后会）被载入史册的

9 **Members of Parliament** ['pɑ:ləmənt] 英国国会议员（简写作 M.P.）

10 **colonial** [kə'ləunjəl] **administrators** [əd'mɪnɪstreɪtəs] 统治殖民地的行政官

11 **peers** 贵族（包括 duke[公], marquis[侯], earl[伯], viscount [子], baron [男] 五等爵位）

12 **bishops** ['bɪʃəps] 主教

13 **turned out** 培养出（某种人）

14 **professional men** 专门职业者（包括教师、律师、医师）

15 **a good sprinkling of**（零零散散的）好些，若干

16 **country squires** 乡绅

17 **parsons** ['pɑ:snz] 牧师

18 **the sort of school** 这种学校。注意，在 sort of 后面的单数可数名词前无冠词。

19 **when mentioned** = when it（指 school）was mentioned

20 **snobbish** ['snɒbɪʃ] 势利的

21 **rather** ['rɑ:ðə] 多少地；有点

22 **if it had not been this sort of school it would probably not have taken Chips** 假如它（Brookfield）不是这样的学校，它也不会聘用 Chips。（这是表示与过去事实相反的虚拟语气，事实上 Brookfield 是这样的学校，所以它聘用了 Chips。）

23 **in any social or academic** [ˌækə'demɪk] **sense** 无论以社会地位或学识而论

24 **was just as respectable, but no more brilliant, than Brookfield itself** 严格说来，这句最好改作 was just as respectable *as*, but no more brilliant than, Brookfield itself。因as respectable不能同no more brilliant合接than；但事实上英美作者的作品中常有这类句子。又，no more brilliant 和 not more brilliant 含义不同；前者有“也不见得高明些”（双方半斤八两，都不高明）的意思，后者就是一般的比较，如说甲高明，乙并不比甲更高明。

It had taken him some time to realize this[1], at the beginning[2]. Not that he was boastful or conceited[3], but[4] he had been, in his early twenties[5], as ambitious as most other young men at such an age. His dream had been to get a headship eventually, or at any rate, a senior mastership in a really first-class school; it was only gradually, after repeated trials and failures, that he realized the inadequacy of his qualifications[6]. His degree[7], for instance, was not particularly good, and his discipline, though good enough and improving[8], was not absolutely reliable under all conditions[9]. He had no private means[10] and no family connections[11] of any importance. About 1880, after he had been at Brookfield a decade[12], he began to recognize that the odds were heavily against[13] his being able to better himself[14] by moving elsewhere[15]; but about that time also, the possibility of staying where he was[16] began to fill a comfortable niche in his mind[17]. At forty, he was rooted, settled, and quite happy[18]. At fifty, he was the doyen of the staff[19]. At

---

1 **It had taken him some time to realize this** = To realize this had taken him some time 他经过一段时间才认识到这一点（“这一点”指上节所说的情况）。 **taken him some time** 费了他一些时间。

2 **at the beginning** 在开始时候（开始如此，以后未必如此）。比较：**from the beginning** 一开始（就如此，有“始终如此”之意）。

3 **boastful or conceited** [kən'siːtɪd] 自夸或自负。boastful 是外露的，conceited 是内心的。

4 **Not that ..., but (that) ...**（作者或说话人所以这样说）并非因为……而是因为……

5 **in his early twenties** 在他二十岁到二十九岁（这一时期）的开头几年里：即二十岁后的开头几年里。

6 **it was only gradually, after repeated trials** ['traɪəlz] **and failures** ['feɪljəz]**, that he realized the inadequacy** [ɪn'ædɪkwəsɪ] **of his qualifications** 是 He realized the inadequacy of his qualifications only gradually, after repeated trials and failures 的强调句型。**qualifications**（担任某项职务等所需要的）资格［用复数］。

7 **degree** 学位

8 **though good enough and improving** = though it (discipline) was good enough and improving. **good enough** 还好。

9 **was not absolutely reliable under all conditions** 并非在任何情况下都是绝对可靠的（间或也靠不住）

10 **private means** 私人财产。means 用复数形式，但说多少财产，用 much means，little means。

11 **family connections** 亲戚

12 **a decade** = for a decade

13 **the odds were heavily against** 形势大不利于……；命运逆着…… **odds** 力量（或有利和不利因素）对比下的差距。

14 **better himself** 提高他自己的地位（或收入）。比较：**improve oneself** 提高自己的学识水平。

15 **moving elsewhere** 迁移到别处去；调个地方

16 **staying where he was** = staying at the place where he was staying 留在他当时所在的地方（指 Brookfield）

17 **fill a comfortable niche** [nɪtʃ] **in his mind** 占了他心中的一个合适的位子；被他认为合适

18 **was rooted, settled, and quite happy** 扎了根，安定了下来，十分快活。

19 **doyen** ['dɒɪən] **of the staff** 全体教职员的头脑

sixty, under a new and youthful Head[1], he *was* Brookfield[2] — the guest of honour[3] at Old Brookfeldian dinners[4], the court of appeal[5] in all matters affecting Brookfield history and traditions[6]. And in 1913, when he turned sixty-five[7], he retired, was presented with[8] a cheque[9] and a writing desk and a clock, and went across the road to live at Mrs. Wickett's. A decent career, decently closed[10]; three cheers for[11] old Chips, they all shouted, at that uproarious[12] end-of-term[13] dinner.

Three cheers, indeed; but there was more to come[14], an unguessed epilogue[15], an encore[16] played[17] to a tragic audience[18].

1 **Head** = Headmaster 校长
2 **he *was* Brookfield** 他（Chips）就是Brookfield；他就代表着Brookfield。
3 **guest of honour** 主宾；宴会上的首席客人
4 **Old Brookfeldian** [brʊk'feldɪən] **dinners** Brookfield老一辈的宴会
5 **court of appeal** 上诉法院；借喻Chips说的话有最高权威。
6 **traditions** tradition作“具体的传统或传说”解时，是可数名词；统称传统或传说时，是不可数名词。
7 **turned sixty-five** 过了六十五岁
8 **was presented** [prɪ'zentɪd] **with** 被赠以……。present和它的同义词give用法不同：give可接双宾语；present不可接双宾语，而须用介词with。
9 **cheque** [tʃek] 支票（美国拼作check）
10 **A decent career** [kə'rɪə], **decently closed** 体面的生涯，体面地结束。这是名词句，closed是过去分词，修饰career。
11 **three cheers for** （对尊敬的人）三次欢呼。three cheers是习语，不能作two cheers，four cheers，注意介词for的搭配。
12 **uproarious** [ʌp'rɔːərɪəs] 喧闹的；兴高采烈的
13 **end-of-term** 学期终了时（举行）的
14 **there was more to come** 还有将发生的事（Chips与Brookfield的关系并不到此结束）
15 **unguessed** ['ʌn'gest] **epilogue** ['epɪlɒg] 意料之外的尾声
epilogue与上文more是同位语，指Chips退休后的生涯。
16 **encore** [ɒŋ'kɔː] （表演完毕后）再演的节目。epilogue和encore同是more的同位语。
17 **played** 被演出；是过去分词，修饰encore。
18 **tragic audience** 观看悲剧的观众

第三章

内容提要

本章描绘了契普斯的退休生活。他常散步到对面学校的操场上去看比赛，又喜欢请新来的学生到他家来吃茶点。学生们都说这老头儿怪可爱的。他也常跟房东维克特夫人谈论这些学生。他说：“小布兰克森告诉我，他舅舅是科林伍德少校。科林伍德在这儿念书的时候，有一次爬到体育馆屋顶上去捡球，被我狠狠打过一顿。”

契普斯也总邀请新来的教师来吃茶点。他们说：“看他手忙脚乱地泡茶的样子——一个标准的独身汉。”这就错了。契普斯结过婚，但那是很久很久以前的事。现在，在布鲁克菲尔德已经没有一个人记得他的妻子了。

3

It was a small but very comfortable and sunny room that Mrs. Wickett let to him.[1] The house itself was ugly and pretentious[2]; but that didn't matter[3]; it was convenient, that was the main thing[4]. For he liked, if the weather were mild enough[5], to stroll[6] across[7] to the playing fields in an afternoon and watch the games[8]. He liked to smile and exchange a few words with[9] the boys when they touched their caps to him[10]. He made a special point of[11] getting to[12] know[13] all the new boys and having them to tea[14] with him during their first term. He always ordered[15] a walnut cake[16] with pink icing[17] from Reddaway's[18], in the village, and during the winter term there were crumpets[19], too — a little pile of them in front of the fire, soaked in butter[20] so that the bottom one[21] lay in a little shallow pool[22]. His guests found it fun to watch him make tea[23]— mixing careful spoonfuls[24] from differ-

1 **It was a small but very comfortable and sunny room that Mrs. Wickett let to him** 是 Mrs. Wickett let to him (Chips) a small but very comfortable and sunny room 的强调句式。这里的 let 是过去式。

2 **pretentious** [prɪ'tenʃəs] 装模作样的，矫饰的

3 **matter** 关系重要。**didn't matter** 无关紧要，主要用于否定句、疑问句和条件从句中。

4 **the main thing** 主要的事

5 **if the weather were mild enough** 要是天气相当温暖的话。were 是虚拟语气，这里指过去的事实，照理这个 were 该改作 was。

6 **stroll** [strəʊl] 散步

7 **across = across the road** 穿过马路（他所寄寓的 Mrs. Wickett 家在学校对马路。）

8 **games** 体育比赛

9 **exchange a few words with...** 和……谈几句话

10 **touched** [tʌtʃt] **their caps to him** 手举到帽边向他敬礼。

11 **made a special point of** 特别注意做到…… **make a point of** 是习语，意思是"注意做到（某一点）"。

12 **getting to**（后接不定式）渐渐达到（目的），渐渐养成（习惯）

13 **know** 认识

14 **having them to tea** 请他们来吃茶点。 **tea** 茶点（名词）。

15 **ordered** 定购；叫店家送来

16 **walnut** ['wɔːlnət] **cake** 核桃糕

17 **icing**（加在糕饼上的）糖霜

18 **Reddaway's** ['redəweɪz] = Reddaway's Shop。Reddaway 是店主的姓（英美人常用店主的姓作为店名）。

19 **crumpets** ['krʌmpɪts] 薄饼

20 **soaked** [səʊkt] **in butter** 浸在（因在火炉面前受热而融化的）黄油中。**soaked** 过去分词，修饰 a little pile of them (crumpets)。

21 **the bottom one**（一叠中）最底下的一个饼

22 **lay in a little shallow pool** 平摊在小小的浅潭里。lay 是 lie 的过去式。

23 **His guests found it fun to watch him make tea** 他的客人们（指学生）看他泡茶觉得很有趣。it是虚词，= to watch him make tea。fun是不可数名词，注意：前面不用a。 **make tea** 泡茶。

24 **mixing careful spoonfuls** 把一匙一匙小心盛装的东西混和起来。

ent caddies[1]. And he would ask the new boys where they lived, and if[2] they had family connections at Brookfield. He kept watch to see that their plates were never empty[3], and punctually at five, after the session[4] had lasted an hour[5], he would glance at the clock and say: 'Well — umph — it's been very delightful — umph — meeting you like this[6] — I'm sorry — umph — you can't stay[7] ...' And he would smile and shake hands with[8] them in the porch[9], leaving them to race[10] across the road to the School with their comments[11]. 'Decent old boy, Chips.[12] Gives you[13] a jolly good tea[14], anyhow, and you *do* know[15] when he wants you to push off[16] ...'

And Chips also would be making his comments[17] — to Mrs. Wickett when she entered his room to clear away the remains of the party[18]. 'A most — umph — interesting time[19], Mrs. Wickett. Young Branksome[20] tells me — umph — that his uncle was Major Collingwood[21]— the Collingwood we had here[22] in — umph — nought-two[23], I think it was[24]. Dear me[25], I remember Collingwood very well.

---

1 **caddies** ['kædɪz] 茶叶罐头

2 **if** = whether

3 **kept watch to see that their plates were never empty** 注意做到碟子永远不空（随时吃完随时添）

4 **session** 指Chips和来访学生的茶会

5 **lasted an hour = lasted for an hour** 持续一小时

6 **it's been very delightful — umph — meeting you like this** = meeting you like this — umph — has been very delightful. **it** 虚词，不仅可以引起*that*-clause和不定式，还可引起名词或动名词。

7 **you can't stay** 你们不能再待下去了（该走了）。

8 **shake hands with** 和……握手

9 **porch** [pɔːtʃ] 门廊

10 **race** （争先恐后地）奔

11 **comments** ['kɒments] 评语。名词和动词读音相同。

12 **Decent old boy, Chips.** = Chips is a decent old boy. **old boy** 见第7页注释20。

13 **Gives you** = He gives you. 口语中有时省去主语。

14 **a jolly good tea** 一顿很好的茶点。**jolly** 是口语，副词，= very。

15 ***do* know** 是know的着重式，*do*要重读。

16 **push off** 离去

17 **And Chips also would be making his comments** 而Chips也常有他的评语。修辞学书中往往说句子不宜用and或but开头，事实上在英美人作品中很常见；这里甚至用And放在一节的开头。would be making = would make，用进行时比较生动；would表示过去经常的行为，已屡见前。

18 **clear away the remains of the party** 收拾掉茶会残留下来的东西。 **remains** 这里指杯盘和吃剩的茶点。party = tea party.

19 **A most — umph — interesting time** = I've had a most — umph — interesting time 我刚才和这些学生谈了一会儿，觉得很有趣。

20 **Young Branksome** ['bræŋksəm] 年轻的布兰克森

21 **Major** ['meɪdʒə] **Collingwood** ['kɒlɪŋwʊd] 科林伍德少校

22 **the Collingwood we had here** 在我们这里念过书的那个科林伍德。we had here前省去 whom或that。

23 **nought-two** ['nɔːt'tuː] 零二年（指1902年）

24 **I think it was.** = I think it was nought-two.

25 **Dear me** 表示惊奇、失望、同情等的感叹词

I once thrashed[1] him — umph — for climbing on to the gymnasium roof[2]— to get a ball out of the gutter. Might have — umph — broken his neck, the young fool.[3] Do you remember him, Mrs. Wickett? He must have been in your time.[4]'

Mrs. Wickett, before she saved money, had been in charge of[5] the linen room[6] at the school.

'Yes, I knew 'im, sir. Cheeky'e was to me, gener'ly.[7] But we never 'ad no bad words between us[8]. Just cheeky-like.[9] 'E never meant no harm.[10] That kind[11] never does[12], sir. Wasn't it 'im[13] that got the medal, sir?'

'Yes, a D.S.O[14].'

'Will you be wanting anything else, sir?'

'Nothing more now[15]— umph — till chapel time[16]. He was killed — in Egypt, I think.[17]... Yes — umph — you can bring[18] my supper about then[19].'

'Very good, sir.'

A pleasant, placid[20] life, at Mrs. Wickett's. He had

1 **thrashed** [θræʃt] 打（尤指用棍棒、鞭子打）

2 **gymnasium** [dʒɪm'neɪzjəm] **roof** 体育馆的屋顶

3 **Might have — umph — broken his neck, the young fool.** = The young fool

might have — umph — broken his neck. 这小傻瓜准会——嗯——折断颈骨（而死）呢。（虚拟语气，含有“如果不是被我发现而打一顿”的意思，但这个条件从句省去了。）

4 **He must have been in your time.** 他（在这里念书）一定是你（在校服务）的时候。 **must have been** 这里是“（过去）谅必是”的意思。

5 **in charge of** 掌管。注意：in charge of 也可作“在……掌管中”解。作后一解时，也作“in the charge of”。因此 B in charge of A 和 A in（the）charge of B 都可以表示“B 管 A”的意思，须看上下文。

6 **linen room** 洗衣室。 **linen** ['lɪnɪn] 用作集合名词，是亚麻布或似亚麻布制的衣衫的统称；这里泛指任何衣衫之类。

7 **Cheeky'e was to me, gener'ly.** = Generally, he was cheeky to me. 总的说来，他就是对我没规矩。上面 him 说成 'im，这里 he 说成 'e，generally 说成 gener'ly，都表示说话人教育不良。

8 **never 'ad no bad words between us** 我们之间从没有吵过嘴。把 had 说成 'ad，以及说了 never 再加上个多余的 no 的这种所谓“双重否定”（double negative），都表示说话人教育不良。 **bad words** 口角。

9 **Just cheeky-like.** = He was just cheeky-like. 他就是有点没规矩而已。

10 **'E never meant** [ment] **no harm.** = He never meant any harm. 他从来不怀恶意（又是“双重否定”）。meant 是 mean [mi:n] 的过去式，“存……的心”的意思。

11 **That kind** 那种人，指 Collingwood 那种没规矩的人。

12 **does** = means any harm

13 **Wasn't it 'im** = Wasn't it he. 比较：It's me = It's I.

14 **D.S.O. = Distinguished Service Order**（英国海、陆、空军的）功勋章

15 **Nothing more now** = I want nothing more now.

16 **chapel** ['tʃæpəl] **time** 做礼拜的时候

17 **He was killed — in Egypt** ['i:dʒɪpt]**, I think.** 我想他（Collingwood）是在埃及被打死的。这句与上一句、下一句都无关，是 Chips 想到就随口插入的。

18 **you can bring** 是“bring”的婉转说法。

19 **about then** 大约在那个时候，在 chapel time 前后。

20 **placid** ['plæsɪd] 安宁的

no worries; his pension was adequate[1], and there was a little money saved up besides[2]. He could afford everything and anything[3] he wanted. His room was furnished simply and with schoolmasterly taste[4]; a few bookshelves and sporting trophies[5]; a mantelpiece[6] crowded with fixture-cards[7] and signed photographs of boys and men; a worn Turkey carpet[8]; big easy chairs; pictures on the wall of the Acropolis and the Forum[9]. Nearly everything had come out of his old housemaster's[10] room in School House[11]. The books were chiefly classical[12], for that had been his subject[13]; there was, however, a seasoning[14] of history and belles-lettres[15]. There was also a bottom shelf piled up with[16] cheap editions[17] of detective novels. Chips enjoyed these. Sometimes he took down Virgil[18] or Xenophon[19] and read for a few moments, but he was soon back again with[20] Doctor Thorndyke[21] or Inspector French[22]. He was not, despite his long years of assiduous teaching[23], a very profound classical scholar; indeed, he thought of Latin

1 **his pension was adequate** ['ædɪkwɪt] 他（退休后）的年金是足够用的；他有足够用的退休金。

2 **there was a little money saved up besides** 另外还攒了一些钱。saved up 修饰 money。

3 **could afford everything and anything** 负担得起一切费用。afford 常与 can 连用。

4 **was furnished simply and with schoolmasterly taste** 这里 and 连接一个副词和一个状语短语。 **schoolmasterly taste** 教员喜爱的风格。

5 **sporting trophies** ['trəʊfɪz] 体育比赛的奖品（如银杯、银牌）

6 **mantelpiece** ['mæntl'pi:s] 壁炉架

7 **fixture-cards** 定期举行的运动会（或庆祝会等）的请帖

8 **a worn Turkey** ['tɜ:kɪ] **carpet** 破旧的土耳其（羊毛）地毯

9 **pictures on the wall of the Acropolis and the Forum** = pictures of the Acropolis and the Forum on the wall. **Acropolis** [ə'krɒpəlɪs] 古代雅典（Athens）的高丘城堡。 **Forum** ['fɔ:rəm] 古罗马的广场。

10 **housemaster's**（学校里）舍监的

11 **School House** 英国公学里的校长住宅或主要宿舍

12 **classical** 希腊、拉丁古典作品的

13 **for that had been his subject**（美国 Little, Brown 版作 the classics having been his subject. 他过去教的科目是古希腊语和拉丁语。后者是独立结构，表示原因。）

14 **seasoning** 原是“调味品”的意思，转义为“增加兴趣的东西”。

15 **belles-lettres** ['bel'letrə] 纯文学

16 **piled up with** 为……所堆满的；堆满……的

17 **cheap editions** 廉价版书刊，普及本

18 **Virgil** ['vɜ:dʒɪl] 维吉尔，罗马诗人（公元前 70—19）；这里指他的著作。

19 **Xenophon** ['zenəfən] 色诺芬，希腊武士兼历史家、哲学家（公元前 435?—355?）；这里指他的著作。

20 **back again with** 回过头来又重读（……书）。上文曾说他爱读侦探小说，所以这里说他读了一会儿古典作品又读起侦探小说来。

21 **Doctor Thorndyke** ['θɔ:ndaɪk] 英国小说家 Richard Alfred Freeman（1862—1943）所著侦探小说中的医生兼律师。

22 **Inspector French** [frentʃ] 爱尔兰小说家 Freeman Wills Crofts（1879—1957）所著侦探小说中的探长。

23 **despite his long years of assiduous** [ə'sɪdjʊəs] **teaching** 虽然他多年勤奋教授（希腊、拉丁语）。这是插入的介词短语构成的状语短语。

and Greek far more as dead languages from which English gentlemen ought to know a few quotations than as living tongues that had ever been spoken by living people[1]. He liked those short leading articles[2] in the *Times*[3] that introduced a few tags[4] that he recognized; to be among the dwindling number of people[5] who understood such things[6] was[7] to him a kind of secret and valued freemasonry[8]; it represented, he felt[9], one of the chief benefits to be derived from[10] a classical education.

So there he lived, at Mrs. Wickett's, with his quiet enjoyments of reading and talking and remembering; an old man, white-haired and only a little bald[11], still fairly active for his years[12], drinking tea, receiving callers, busying himself with[13] corrections for the next edition of the Brookfeldian Directory[14], writing his occasional letters[15] in thin, spidery, but very legible script[16]. He had new masters to tea[17], as well as[18] new boys. There were two of them[19] that autumn term, and as they were leaving after their visit, one of them commented: 'Quite a character, the old boy, isn't he?[20] All that fuss about mixing the tea — a typical bachelor[21], if ever there was

1 **he thought of Latin and Greek far more as dead languages from which English gentlemen ought to know a few quotations than as living tongues that had ever been spoken by living people** 他把拉丁语和希腊语认为是英国上等人应该从中学懂一些语录的死语言，远过于认为是曾经被人们讲过的活语言。

2 **short leading articles**（报刊的）短评；短的社论。 **leading article** 在英国指社论，在美国指报刊上的主要文章。

3 **the *Times***《泰晤士报》（英国著名日报，1785 年创刊）

4 **tags** [tægz] 常被人引用的词句（这里指希腊、拉丁语词句）

5 **dwindling** ['dwɪndlɪŋ] **number of people** 一群数目正在减少的人

6 **such things** 指上句的 tags。

7 **was** 这个谓语动词的主语是不定式短语 To be …

8 **secret and valued freemasonry** ['friːˌmeɪsnrɪ] 秘密而可贵的情投意合（犹之乎“心有灵犀一点通”）。

9 **he felt** 这是插入语。

10 **derived from** 从……中得到

11 **bald** [bɔːld] 秃顶的

12 **fairly active for his years** 拿他的年纪来说，算是相当活跃的了。**for** 就……而论。

13 **busying himself with** 以（事情、工作）使自己忙碌；忙于……

14 **Brookfeldian Directory** [dɪ'rektərɪ] 布鲁克菲尔德人名录

15 **occasional** [ə'keɪʒənl] **letters** 偶尔写的书信

16 **in thin, spidery, but very legible** ['ledʒəbl] **script** 用细小而清楚的字体写成的。**spidery**（字迹）细长的。

17 **had new masters to tea** 请新教师们来吃茶点。

18 **as well as** 在……以外

19 **them** 指 new masters。

20 **Quite a character** ['kærɪktə], **the old boy, isn't he?** = The old boy is quite a character, isn't he? **old boy** 对人昵称，已见前注，这里指 Chips。 **character** 有突出性格的人。

21 **All that fuss about mixing the tea — a typical** ['tɪpɪkəl] **bachelor** ['bætʃələ] 制茶时手忙脚乱的种种样子——一个典型的独身汉。这个句子中没有谓语动词；破折号前后两个名词词组，虽然在语法上没有关系（不能说是省去连系动词的主语与表语的关系），但在逻辑上的关系很清楚。

one[1]'.

Which[2] was oddly incorrect[3]; because Chips was not a bachelor at all. He had married[4]; though it was so long ago that[5] none of the staff at Brookfield could remember his wife.

1 **if ever there was one** 假如世间有个典型的独身汉的话。意即“没有则已；要是有，那就是 Chips。” **ever** 有“在任何时候”的意思。 **one** = a typical bachelor.

2 **Which** 有些语法家认为不能用 which 引起一句句子，更不能用 which 引起一节；事实上英美作家常有这样用的。这里就用 which 代替上节所说 Chips 是 typical bachelor 的话，引起新的一节。

3 **oddly incorrect** 错得奇怪（看下文自明）

4 **had married** 结过婚。marry 和 be married 略有不同：前者指结婚的行动，后者指结婚的状态。

5 **so long ago that ...** 时间如此久远，以至于……

第四章

内容提要

1896年春天，当时契普斯四十八岁，他到英国北部的湖泊区去旅游。在爬山时，看见一个姑娘站在危险的山岩上招手。他以为她在求救，赶去救她，自己却蹩伤了脚踝。姑娘其实是在招呼远处的朋友，并不是求救。结果，反而是她搀扶契普斯回到他借宿的农舍，之后几天又经常骑着自行车来护理他。

姑娘才二十五岁，是当时的“新女性”；契普斯却是个一本正经的老派人。在多次接触后，双方都觉得对方别有可爱之处，逐渐相互了解，产生了感情。一个星期里，他们就订了婚，又过了一个星期，他们到伦敦去结婚了。

姑娘的名字叫凯瑟琳，爱称凯茜。

4

There came to him, stirred by the warmth of the fire and the gentle aroma of tea, a thousand tangled recollections of old times[1]. Spring — the Spring of 1896.[2] He was forty-eight — an age at which a permanence of habits begins to be predictable[3]. He had just been appointed housemaster[4]; with this[5] and his classical forms[6], he had made for himself a warm and busy corner of life[7]. During the summer vacation he went up to the Lake District[8] with Rowden[9], a colleague[10]; they walked and climbed[11] for a week, until Rowden had to leave suddenly on some family business[12]. Chips stayed on[13] alone at Wasdale Head[14], where he boarded[15] in a small farmhouse[16].

One day, climbing on Great Gable[17], he noticed a girl waving[18] excitedly from a dangerous-looking ledge[19]. Thinking she was in difficulties[20], he hastened towards her, but in doing so[21] slipped himself and wrenched[22] his ankle. As it turned out[23], she was not in difficulties at all, but was

1 **There came to him, stirred by the warmth of the fire and the gentle aroma** [ə'rəʊmə] **of tea, a thousand tangled recollections of old times.** There 是虚词；came 的主语是 recollections；stirred by ... aroma of tea 是插入的分词短语形式的定语短语，修饰 him。全句的意思是"炉火的温暖和茶的柔和的芳香勾起他无数纷繁的旧时回忆。"

2 **Spring — the Spring of 1896** 名词句；the Spring of 1896 是 Spring 的同位语。

3 **a permanence** ['pɜːmənəns] **of habits begins to be predictable** 习惯的定型开始可以预言；开始可以看得出固定的习惯。

4 **He had just been appointed housemaster** 他刚被任命为舍监。housemaster 是主语补足语，在 appointed 和 housemaster 之间可以加 as 或 to be。

5 **this** 指舍监的职位

6 **forms** 班级（在英国的公学中，常用 form 代 class 或 grade。一般分六个年级，一年级开始，相当于中学程度。）

7 **corner of life** 安身之处

8 **Lake District** 英国西北部的湖区。柯勒律治（Coleridge）、骚塞（Southey）和华兹华斯（Wordsworth）就因曾居住其间而被称为湖畔诗人（Lake Poets）。

9 **Rowden** ['raʊdn] 罗登，姓氏

10 **colleague** ['kɒliːg] 同事

11 **climbed** [klaɪmd] 爬山

12 **on some family business** 为了一些家事

13 **stayed on** 继续待下去

14 **Wasdale** ['wɒzdeɪl] **Head** 沃斯代尔岬角，地名。 **Head** = Headland 岬角。

15 **boarded** 寄膳宿

16 **farmhouse** 农场里的（主要）住房（别于 cottage）

17 **Great Gable** 大山墙，山名

18 **waving** 挥手

19 **dangerous-looking ledge** [ledʒ] 看上去危险的山岩；险岩

20 **was in difficulties** 处于困难中；有困难

21 **in doing so** 在这样做（指 hastened towards her）的时候

22 **wrenched** [rentʃt] 蹩痛，蹩伤

23 **As it turned out**（待真相大白）原来是

merely signalling[1] to a friend farther down the mountain[2]; she was an expert climber[3], better even than Chips, who was pretty good[4]. Thus he found himself the rescued instead of the rescuer[5]; and neither role was one for which he had much relish[6]. For he did not, he would have said, care for women[7]; he never felt at home or at ease with them[8]; and that monstrous creature beginning to be talked about, the New Woman of the nineties, filled him with horror[9]. He was a quiet, conventional person, and the world, viewed from the haven of Brookfield, seemed to him full of distasteful innovations[10]; there was a fellow named Bernard Shaw[11] who had the strangest and most reprehensible[12] opinions; there was Ibsen[13], too, with his disturbing plays[14]; and there was this new craze for bicycling[15] which was being taken up[16] by women equally with men[17]. Chips did not hold with[18] all this modern newness and freedom.

---

1 **signalling** 打信号示意（指上文 waving）

2 **farther down the mountain** 在那山（指 Great Gable）的更远处的（修饰 friend）。**down** 这里是“过去些”，而不是“下去些”。

3 **expert** ['ekspɜːt] **climber** ['klaɪmə] 爬山老手

4 **pretty** ['prɪtɪ] **good**（爬山的本领）相当好。这里 pretty 是副词。

5 **he found himself the rescued instead of the rescuer** ['reskjʊə] 发觉自己是被

救者而不是救人者。

6 **neither role was one for which he had much relish** ['relɪʃ] 他对这两个角色都没有什么爱好。

7 **For he did not, he would have said, care for women** 因为——他会说——他对女人不感兴趣。he would have said 是插入语，虚拟语气，省去“如果有人问他”等含意的条件从句；“他会说”，实际上并没有说。 **care for** 对……感兴趣；喜欢。

8 **never felt at home or at ease with them** 同她们交往总觉得局促不安。at home 和 at ease 意义相似；仔细辨别，at home 是外表的行动自在，at ease 是内心安宁。

9 **that monstrous creature beginning to be talked about, the New Woman of the nineties, filled him with horror** ['hɒrə]（当时）开始被人谈论的那种可怕的东西——90 年代的“新女性”——使他吃惊。creature 指人，有爱慕或鄙夷的意味，这里有鄙意。 **beginning to be talked about** 分词短语，修饰 creature。 **the New Woman** 19 世纪末要求独立、自由，反对习俗的女性，这里与 creature 同位。**the nineties** 90 年代，这里指 1890—1899 年。

10 **the world, viewed from the haven of Brookfield, seemed to him full of distasteful innovations** 这个世界，在他从 Brookfield 这安宁的地方看来，似乎充满着令人厌恶的新花样。viewed from the haven of Brookfield 是分词短语，修饰 world; haven 原义“港口”，这里是转义，是“安定的地方”的意思。

11 **Bernard** ['bɜːnəd] **Shaw** [ʃɔː] 萧伯纳（1856—1950），爱尔兰戏剧家、评论家。

12 **reprehensible** [ˌreprɪ'hensəbl] 应受谴责的（从思想保守的 Chips 看来，萧伯纳的新奇见解自然不可取。）

13 **Ibsen** ['ɪbsn] Henrik ['henrɪk] Ibsen，易卜生（1828—1906），挪威戏剧家、诗人。

14 **disturbing plays** 使（社会）不安宁的剧本（易卜生的剧本中常提出一些社会问题，在保守的 Chips 看来是扰乱人心。）

15 **craze for bicycling** ['baɪsɪklɪŋ] 对于骑自行车的狂热

16 **being taken up** 被从事

17 **equally with men** 和男子相等地。注意现代英语中 equally 后用 with，不用 as。

18 **hold with** 赞成

He had a vague notion[1], if he ever formulated it[2], that nice women were weak, timid, and delicate[3], and that nice men treated them with a polite but rather distant chivalry[4]. He had not, therefore, expected[5] to find a woman on Great Gable; but, having encountered one who seemed to need masculine help, it was even more terrifying that she should turn the tables by helping him[6]. For she did[7]. She and her friend had to[8]. He could scarcely walk[9], and it was a hard job getting him down the steep track to Wasdale[10].

Her name was Katherine Bridges[11]; she was twenty-five — young enough to be Chips's[12] daughter. She had blue, flashing eyes and freckled cheeks[13] and smooth straw-coloured hair[14]. She, too, was staying at a farm[15], on holiday[16] with a girl friend, and as she considered herself responsible for Chips's accident[17], she used to bicycle along the side of the lake to the house in which the quiet, middle-aged, serious-looking[18] man lay resting[19].

That was how she thought of him at first. And he, because she rode a bicycle and was unafraid to visit a man

---

1 **He had a vague notion** 他有一种模模糊糊的想法。说 a notion，后面却接两个 that- 从句，其实两个 that- 从句所讲的是一个想法的两个方面，读原

文自明。

2 **if he ever formulated it** 这是插入的条件从句，it 代表 notion；假使他曾经把这模糊的想法明确地表达出来（实际上未必明确过）。

3 **weak, timid** ['tɪmɪd], **and delicate** ['delɪkɪt] 娇弱，羞怯，温柔的

4 **polite but rather distant chivalry** ['ʃɪvəlrɪ] 有礼而比较疏远的侠义；（对女人）有礼地保护照料，却不（同她们）亲密。

5 **had not, therefore, expected** 所以事先没有料到（不是"并不希望"）。

6 **having encountered one who seemed to need masculine help, it was even more terrifying that she should turn the tables by helping him**（他）碰到了一个似乎需要男人帮助的女人，而结果她竟反过来帮助他，这才更使他惊骇，照一般语法书说，放在句首的分词短语的逻辑上的主语应该就是句中的主语，如：Having got his pay, he left. 文中 having encountered 的逻辑上的主语是 Chips，而句子的语法上的主语却是 it，不相呼应，这种分词叫做"垂悬分词"（dangling participle）。但实际上在英美作品中常见这样的用法。 **turn the tables** 转变局面，反败为胜；是习语。

7 **did** = turned the tables，也就是 helped him。

8 **had to** = had to turn the tables，也就是 had to help him。

9 **could scarcely** ['skeəslɪ] **walk** 几乎无法走路

10 **it was a hard job getting him down the steep track to Wasdale** 沿陡峭的山径把他搀扶下来，到 Wasdale Head。it 是虚词，getting him down ... 是 it 的同位语。

11 **Katherine** ['kæθərɪn] **Bridges** ['brɪdʒɪz] 凯瑟琳·布里吉斯，人名

12 **Chips's** 读 ['tʃɪpsɪz]

13 **freckled cheeks** 生雀斑的面颊

14 **straw-colored hair** 稻草色的头发

15 **farm** = farmhouse

16 **on holiday** ['hɒlədɪ] 因放假而在外面游玩或旅行；度假

17 **accident** 意外，这里指 Chips 失足伤脚的事情。

18 **serious-looking** 看上去严肃的

19 **lay resting** 躺着休息。lay 是 lie 的过去式。

alone in a farmhouse sitting room, wondered vaguely[1] what the world was coming to[2]. His sprain[3] put him at her mercy[4], and it[5] was soon revealed to him how much he might need that mercy. She was a governess[6] out of a job[7], with a little money saved up[8]; she read and admired Ibsen; she believed that women ought to be admitted to the universities[9]; she even thought they ought to have a vote[10]. In politics she was a radical[11], with leanings[12] towards the views of people like Bernard Shaw and William Morris[13]. All her ideas and opinions she poured out to Chips[14] during those summer afternoons at Wasdale Head; and he, because he was not very articulate[15], did not at first think it worth while to contradict them[16]. Her friend went away, but she stayed; what *could* you do with such a person? Chips thought[17]. He used to hobble with sticks along a footpath leading to[18] the tiny church; there was a stone slab on the wall[19], and it was comfortable to sit down, facing the sunlight and the green-brown majesty of the Gable[20] and listening to the chatter of— well, yes, Chips had to admit it — a very beautiful girl[21].

1 **wondered vaguely** 模糊地怀疑。vaguely 是说没有具体的内容。在 wondered 和主语 he 之间插入了 because 引起的原因状语从句。

2 **what the world was coming to** 这世界在变成什么样子。

3 **sprain** [spreɪn]（因蹩伤而引起的）肿痛

4 **put him at her mercy** 使他由她安排。这里 put 是过去式。 **at her mercy** 在她的支配下。

5 **it** 是虚词；how much he might need that mercy 是 it 的同位语。

6 **governess** ['gʌvənɪs] 家庭女教师

7 **out of a job** 失业的

8 **saved up** 积蓄起来的

9 **admitted to the universities** 准予进大学

10 **have a vote** 有选举权

11 **In politics** ['pɒlɪtɪks] **she was a radical** [rædɪkəl] 她在政治上是激进派。

12 **leanings** 倾向

13 **William** ['wɪljəm] **Morris** ['mɒrɪs] 威廉·莫里斯（1834—1896），英国诗人、艺术家、社会主义者

14 **All her ideas and opinions she poured out to Chips** = She poured out all her ideas and opinions to Chips. ideas 是一般的想法，不一定出于理性；opinions 是意见，通常出于理性。 **poured out** 倾吐；畅谈。

15 **articulate** [ɑː'tɪkjʊlɪt] 能把要讲的话讲清楚的

16 **think it worth** [wɜːθ] **while to contradict** ['kɒntrə'dɪkt] **them** 认为值得批驳它们（ideas and opinions）。it 是虚词，to contradict them 是 it 的同位语。**worth while** 值得的；是习语。

17 **what *could* you do with such a person? Chips thought** Chips 想，对这么一个人你能怎么样呢（对这种女人真没办法）。 could 斜体表示重读。you 是泛指，等于书面语中的 one。

18 **leading to** 通往

19 **there was a stone slab on the wall** 墙（边）上有一块厚石板。

20 **green-brown majesty of the Gable** 大山墙的棕绿色的庄严（景色）；庄严的棕绿色的大山墙。

21 **listening to the chatter of — well, yes, Chips had to admit it — a very beautiful girl** well, yes, Chips had to admit it 是插入语；it 指“她是一个非常漂亮的姑娘”这一事实。 **chatter**（喋喋不休的）空谈；比较：**chat** 闲谈，谈话。

He had never met anyone like her. He had always thought that the modern type[1], this 'new woman' business[2], would repel[3] him; and here she was[4], making him positively look forward to the glimpse of her safety bicycle careering along the lakeside road[5]. And she, too, had never met anyone like *him*[6]. She had always thought that middle-aged men who read the *Times*[7] and disapproved of[8] modernity[9] were terrible bores[10]; yet here he was, claiming[11] her interest and attention far more than youths of her own age[12]. She liked him, initially[13], because he was so hard to get to know[14], because he had gentle and quiet manners, because his opinions dated from those utterly impossible seventies and eighties and even earlier —yet were, for all that, so thoroughly honest[15]; and because — because[16] his eyes were brown and he looked charming[17] when he

---

1 **the modern type** 新式的人（或物）

2 **this 'new woman' business** "新女性"这玩意儿；与 the modern type 同位。business 在这里含有轻蔑的意味。

3 **repel** [rɪ'pel] 使（人）厌恶

4 **here she was** 她（新女性）就出现在眼前

5 **making him positively look forward to the glimpse of her safety bicycle careering** [kə'rɪərɪŋ] **along the lakeside road** 使他不由得期待看到她骑着安全自行车沿湖边的道路疾驰而来。美国 Bantam Books 版中 caree*r*ing 作 caree*n*ing。career 是"疾驰"，careen [kə'riːn] 是"歪歪斜斜地前进"；这两个词在这里都讲得通。 **making** 使得；后面作宾语补足语的不定式前现在一般不用 to。 **look forward to** 盼望；to 是介词，不是不定式记号。

6 ***him*** 斜体，重读。宾格代词在一般情况下常轻读，如 me [mɪ], you [jʊ] 甚至 [jə]，him [ɪm], us [əs] 甚至 [s]，them [ðəm, ðm] 甚至 [əm, m]。这里的 *him* 不但要发正常的 [hɪm] 音，而且还要重读，以示强调。

7 **read the *Times*** 看《泰晤士报》。"read" 不一定读出声，不同于我们的"读报"；这里是过去式，读 [red]。

8 **disapproved** [dɪsə'pruːvd] **of** 不赞成

9 **modernity** [mə'dɜːnɪtɪ] 新式；现代性

10 **terrible** ['terəbl] **bores** 十分讨厌的人

11 **claiming**（有权利）要求；值得

12 **youths of her own age** 和她同年的小伙子们。 **youths** 男青年们；a youth 是一个男青年；而 youth 则是统称男女青年的集合名词。 **of her own age** 原义是"同年的"，这里是广义地指"和她年龄相仿的"。

13 **initially** [ɪ'nɪʃəlɪ] 起初

14 **because he was so hard to get to know** 因为他是很不容易认识的（而她竟认识了他）。 **get to...**（不定式）渐渐达到（某种目的或结果）。

15 **his opinions dated from those utterly impossible seventies and eighties and even earlier — yet were, for all that, so thoroughly** ['θʌrəlɪ] **honest** 虽然他的见解还是属于七八十年代或者甚至更陈旧的，然而却是彻底诚实的。**impossible** 作"难堪的"解，是口语。**seventies and eighties** 这里指 1870—1889 年。**for all that** 尽管那一切；虽然如此；for 是 in spite of 的意思。

16 **because — because** 说了一个 because，顿一顿，再说第二个 because，生动地表现了 Katherine 所以喜欢 Chips 的屈指可数的原因。

17 **he looked** [lʊkt] **charming** 他看上去很可爱。looked 是连系动词，charming 是主语补足语，或称表语。

smiled. 'Of course, *I* shall call you Chips, too[1],' she said, when she learned that that was his nickname[2] at school.

Within a week they were head over heels in love[3]; before Chips could walk without a stick, they considered themselves engaged[4]; and they were married in London a week before the beginning of the autumn term.

1 ***I* shall call you Chips, too** 我也要叫你 Chips。按 Chips 原来姓 Chipping，Chips 是他的绰号，已见前注，读下半句也自然明白。

2 **when she learned that that was his nickname** 当她知道了那（指“Chips”）是他的绰号。美国 Little, Brown 版只有一个 that，即省略作连词的第一个 that。

3 **head over heels in love** 爱得神魂颠倒；打得火热。Head over heels 是习语，也作 heels over head，但不及前者普通。

4 **they considered themselves engaged** 他们认为（自己）已经是订了婚了。

第五章

内容提要

契普斯回忆在湖区和凯瑟琳定情和结婚前夕的欢乐往事。当时凯瑟琳说：“我刚认识你的时候，还怕你是个律师、掮客、商人之类，后来才知道你是教书的，那就大不相同。教书影响人，造就人才——是多么重要。”而契普斯却说他从没有把教书想得这么重要。他还竭力贬低自己，说各方面都配不上一个胸怀宽大的姑娘。凯瑟琳听了，只是哈哈大笑。

凯瑟琳没有父母，是她姑母给她出嫁的。

5

When Chips, dreaming through the hours[1] at Mrs. Wickett's, recollected those days, he used to look down at his feet[2] and wonder which one it was that had performed so signal a service[3]. That, the trivial cause[4] of so many momentous happenings, was the one thing of which details evaded him[5]. But he resaw[6] the glorious hump of the Gable[7] (he had never visited the Lake District since[8]), and the mouse-grey depths of Wastwater under the Screes[9]; he could resmell the washed air after heavy rain[10], and refollow the ribbon of the pass across to Sty Head[11]. So clearly it lingered[12], that time of dizzy happiness[13], those evening strolls[14] by the waterside, her cool voice[15] and her gay laughter. She had been a very happy person, always.[16]

They had both been so eager, planning a future together[17]; but he had been rather serious about it, even a little awed[18]. It[19] would be all right, of course, her coming

1 **dreaming through the hours** 整个整个小时一直处于梦境之中；终日如醉如梦。

2 **look down at his feet** 俯视他的双脚。比较：**look down upon** 蔑视。

3 **which one it was that had performed so signal a service** 是哪一只脚起了如此重要的作用；是哪一只脚蹩伤而让他和 Katherine 相识并结婚的。which one = which foot.

4 **That, the trivial** ['trɪvɪəl] **cause** That 指上句蹩伤一只脚的事；the trivial cause 是 That 的同位语。

5 **the one thing of which details** ['di:teɪlz] **evaded him** 他唯一记不清细节的事情。他样样都记得，唯有蹩伤的是哪一只脚那件事的细节记不清楚。 **the one** 唯一的。

6 **resaw** 在回忆中重又看到

7 **the glorious hump of the Gable** 大山墙（指上一章的 Great Gable）的山峰

8 **since** 从此，是副词；从爬山邂逅 Katherine 的那次之后。

9 **the mouse-gray depths** [depθs] **of Wastwater** ['wɒstwɔ:tə] **under the Screes** 散石山坡下沃斯特湖的灰鼠色的深渊

10 **resmell the washed** [wɒʃt] **air after heavy rain** 回忆中重又嗅到大雨后清新的空气。 **washed** 经大雨冲洗过的。

11 **refollow the ribbon of the pass across to Sty** [staɪ] **Head** 回忆中重又循着如带的山径跨越到斯代岬。

12 **So clearly it lingered** ['lɪŋgəd] = It lingered so clearly. It 以 that time of dizzy happiness, those evening strolls by the waterside, her cool voice and her gay laughter 作它的同位语。

13 **dizzy happiness** 使人头昏目眩的（极度的）欢乐

14 **evening strolls** [strəʊlz] **by the waterside** 黄昏时分在湖边的散步

15 **cool voice** 文静的声音

16 **She had been a very happy person, always.** = She had always been a very happy person. always 放在句末，更口语化，更生动。

17 **planning a future together** 一同计划未来（的生活方式）。

18 **he had been rather serious about it, even a little awed** [ɔ:d] 他对此相当谨慎，甚至有所畏惧。 **it** 指 future。 **awed** 此处是过去分词；**had been awed** 畏惧。

19 **It** 引起后面的同位语 her coming to Brookfield。

to Brookfield; other housemasters were married[1]. And she liked boys, she told him[2], and would enjoy living among them[3]. 'Oh, Chips, I'm so glad you are what you are[4]. I was afraid you were a solicitor[5] or a stockbroker[6] or a dentist or a man with a big cotton business[7] in Manchester[8]. When I first met you[9], I mean[10]. Schoolmastering's[11] so different, so important, don't you think? To be influencing[12] those who are going to grow up and matter to the world[13] ...'

Chips said he hadn't thought of it like that — or, at least, not often[14]. He did his best; that was all anyone could do in any job[15].

'Yes, of course, Chips. I do love you for saying simple things like that.[16]'

And one morning — another memory gem-clear when he turned to it[17] — he had for some reason[18] been afflicted with an acute desire[19] to depreciate[20] himself and all his attainments[21]. He had told her of[22] his only mediocre degree[23], of his occasional difficulties

1 **were married** 是结了婚的（指状态）。比较：**marry** 结婚（指行动）。

2 **she told him** 是插入语。

3 **enjoy living among them** 注意 enjoy 后接动名词，不可接不定式。

4 **you are what you are** 你是这样一个人。

5 **solicitor** [sə'lɪsɪtə] 律师

6 **stockbroker** 股票经纪人

7 **a big cotton business** ['bɪznɪs] 一家大的棉纺厂。business 作"工商企业"解时，是可数名词。

8 **Manchester** ['mænt∫ɪstə] 曼彻斯特（英国工业城市，纺织业中心）

9 **When I first met you** 承接上句，修饰 I was afraid。

10 **I mean** 我的意思是说。I mean 拖在句末，在口语中很普通，同样类型的如下句中的 don't you think?

11 **Schoolmastering's** = Schoolmastering is. **Schoolmastering** 在学校中当教师。

12 **To be influencing** 说明上句中 Schoolmastering 的作用。

13 **are going to grow up and matter to the world** 将成长起来，对世界发挥作用。**matter** 关系重大；是不及物动词。

14 **not often** = had not often thought of it like that. **it** 指上节 Katherine 所说当教师的重要作用。

15 **that was all anyone could do in any job** 那是任何人做任何事情所能做到的一切；只是尽力而为。all 后省略关系代词 that。

16 **I do love you for saying simple things like that.** 我就喜欢你说那样简单明了的话。do love 是 love 的着重式，do 重读。for 后接动名词，表示原因。

17 **another memory gem-clear** ['dʒemklɪə] **when he turned to it** 另一段回忆，在他想到它时，清晰地活现眼前。 **gem-clear** 像宝石般晶莹明澈的，是形容词，它前面省略 that was 或 which was。 **turned to it** 想到它；it = memory。放在两个破折号内的这句话是插入语，它前面的 one morning 修饰它后面 he had for some reason been afflicted 中的谓语动词 had been afflicted。

18 **for some reason** 为某种理由

19 **had been afflicted with an acute desire** 为一个强烈的意愿所苦；急切要做到某一点的心情使自己苦恼。

20 **depreciate** [dɪ'pri:∫ɪeɪt] 贬低

21 **attainments** 学识，造诣；习惯用复数。

22 **He had told her of …** 他告诉他（某事）。注意用 of。这里 told her 后面接有四个并列的"of …"，表示他所告诉她的各项内容。

23 **his only mediocre** ['mi:dɪəʊkə] **degree** 他仅有的平凡的学位（如仅有一个学士学位）

of discipline[1], of the certainty that he would never get a promotion, and of his complete ineligibility[2] to marry a young and ambitious girl. And at the end of it all[3] she had laughed in answer[4].

She had no parents and was married from the house of an aunt in Ealing[5]. On the night before the wedding, when Chips left the house to return to his hotel, she said, with mock gravity:[6] 'This is an occasion, you know — this last farewell of ours.[7] I feel rather like a new boy beginning his first term with you. Not scared[8], mind you[9] — but just, for once, in a thoroughly respectful mood[10]. Shall I call you "sir"[11] — or would "Mr. Chips" be the right thing[12]? "Mr. Chips", I think.[13] Good-bye, then — Good-bye, Mr. Chips ...'

(A hansom[14] clop-clopping[15] in the roadway[16]; green pale gas lamps flickering on a wet pavement; newsboys shouting something about South Africa[17]; Sherlock Holmes[18] in Baker Street[19].)

'Good-bye, Mr. Chips ...'

---

1 **difficulties of discipline** 管教学生守纪律的困难

2 **complete ineligibility** [ɪn,elɪdʒə'bɪlɪtɪ] 完全没有资格；根本不配

3 **at the end of it all** 在他说完这一番话之后。it泛指上面Chips所说的一番话。

4 **laughed** [lɑ:ft] **in answer** 以哈哈大笑作为回答。

5 **was married from the house of an aunt in Ealing** ['i:liŋ] 被从伊林（地名，在伦敦之西）的姑母（或姨母等）家嫁出去。

6 **with mock gravity** ['grævɪtɪ] 装出一本正经的样子。

7 **This is an occasion** [ə'keɪʒən], **you know — this last farewell of ours.** 你知道，这是个重大的时刻——我们这回最后的告别。 **occasion** 重大时刻。**you know** 是插入语。**this last farewell of ours** 与句首的主语 This 同位。把结婚前夜的告别说成是他们之间最后的告别，因结婚后一起生活，无需再告别。

8 **Not scared** 是 I'm not scared 的简略说法。**scared** 惊慌的，是形容词。

9 **mind you** 请你注意我的话；亦作 mind，口语中常用；you 是 mind 的主语。

10 **just, for once, in a thoroughly** ['θʌrəlɪ] **respectful mood** 只是仅此一回地心情无限恭敬起来。（平时对 Chips 很随便，这一下对他毕恭毕敬起来。）**for once** 就这一次，是习语。**in a thoroughly respectful mood** 同 Not scared 并列、对比。

11 **Shall I call you "sir"** 我可否称你'先生'？ sir（不带姓名）是对陌生人或上司等的称呼。注意对英国 knight 和 baronet 两种爵士称 Sir（大写，后接姓名或名，如 Sir John Smith 或 Sir John），是另一回事。

12 **the right thing** 恰当的称呼

13 **"Mr. Chips", I think.** = I think I shall call you "Mr. Chips". Chips 实际上是 Chipping 的绰号，已见前。

14 **hansom** 一种马车（驾车人坐在车顶后面）

15 **clop-clopping** 发出得得的马蹄声

16 **roadway** 车行道（别于人行道而言）

17 **newsboys shouting something about South Africa** 报童们叫喊着关于南非的新闻。按：当时英国正在非洲南部与荷尔人的后代布尔人进行战争，历史上称为"布尔战争"（Boer War, 1899—1902）。

18 **Sherlock** ['ʃɜ:lɔk] **Holmes** [həʊmz] 福尔摩斯（英国小说家 Conan Doyle 所著一系列侦探小说中的主人公。当时第一部福尔摩斯探案 *The Adventures of Sherlock Holmes*（1901）刚出版，轰动一时。）

19 **Baker Street** 小说中福尔摩斯居住的街道。这一节括号中四个名词词组，有声有色地描绘了 Chips 和 Katherine 在结婚前夜分手时的周围情景。

第六章

内容提要

契普斯和凯瑟琳婚后的生活非常愉快。在她的新思想影响下，契普斯眼界开阔了，性格也变了。上课时候开始讲起笑话来。

有一次，凯瑟琳建议，让布鲁克菲尔德办的慈善机关所属学校的学生们来布鲁克菲尔德比赛足球，契普斯大为震惊，校方也认为把这些穷小子弄到“上等子弟”的学校里来比球，一定要出岔子，万万使不得。但她据理力争，契普斯转而支持她的建议。终于球赛举行，一切顺利。

多年后，一个曾来赛球的慈善机关学生碰到契普斯，问起他妻子，他说她在那次赛球后不到一年就去世了。

6

There had followed then a time of such happiness[1] that Chips, remembering it long afterwards, hardly believed it could ever have happened[2] before or since[3] in the world[4]. For his marriage was a triumphant success. Katherine conquered Brookfield as she had conquered[5] Chips; she was immensely popular with boys and masters alike[6]. Even the wives of the masters, tempted at first to be jealous of someone so young and lovely[7], could not long resist her charms[8].

But most remarkable of all was the change she made in Chips[9]. Till his marriage he had been a dry and rather neutral sort of person[10]; liked and thought well of by Brookfield in general[11], but not of the stuff that makes for great popularity[12] or that stirs great affection. He had been at Brookfield for over a quarter of a century, long enough to have established himself as a decent fellow[13] and a hard

1 **There had followed then a time of such happiness** 这句子里 There 是虚词，又因用了 There 而主谓倒装。

2 **hardly believed it could ever have happened** 几乎不相信这（指 a time of such happiness）可能会发生。

3 **before or since** 在这一段幸福的时光之前和之后。before 和 since 两词都是副词。

4 **in the world** 世界上，天下；是习语，用以加强语气。

5 **conquered** ['kɒŋkəd] 征服。Katherine 是“新女性”，而 Chips 和 Brookfield 都是比较守旧的，但终于都接受她、喜欢她，所以说她征服了他和它。

6 **popular with boys and masters alike** = popular both with boys and masters. **masters** 教师们。注意: popular 后惯用 with。

7 **tempted at first to be jealous** ['dʒeləs] **of someone so young and lovely** 开始时候（因受狭隘心理的影响而）倾向于妒忌 Katherine 那样一个年轻美貌的人。 **tempted** 是过去分词，修饰 the wives of the master。**jealous** 后惯接 of。**somene** 美国 Little, Brown 版作 one。**so young and lovely** 是后置修饰语，修饰 someone。

8 **could not long resist her charms** 不能长期抵御她的魅力；不久就不由得喜爱她的妩媚可亲。 **charms** 妩媚；可爱之处；用复数。

9 **most remarkable of all was the change she made in Chips** = the change (that 或 which) she made in Chips was most remarkable of all. 倒装句加强语气；又，最高级形容词作表语时常不加冠词 the。

10 **a dry and rather neutral sort of person** 冷漠的、思想感情属于中性的人；既没有强烈的感情，也不坚持某种思想的人。

11 **liked and thought well of by Brookfield in general** 被大部分的 Brookfield 师生所喜爱和认可。liked 和 thought 都是过去分词，修饰 a dry and neutral sort of person。 **think well of** 认为好；**think ill of** 认为不好；都是习语。

12 **not of the stuff that makes for great popularity** 不是属于能够赢得众人十分爱戴的性格的。这个否定的介词短语，与上面 liked 和 thought 组成的分词短语并列，也是修饰 a dry and neutral sort of person 的。 **makes for** 有助于，导致；是习语。

13 **established himself as a decent** ['di:snt] **fellow** 使自己被公认为正派的人。**established himself** 受到承认，立足；是习语。

worker; but just too long for anyone to believe him capable of ever being much more[1]. He had, in fact, already begun to sink into that creeping dry rot of pedagogy[2] that is the worst and ultimate pitfall of the profession[3]; giving the same lessons year after year[4] had formed a groove[5] into which the other affairs of his life adjusted themselves with insidious ease[6]. He worked well; he was conscientious; he was a fixture[7] that gave service, satisfaction, confidence, everything except inspiration[8].

And then came this astonishing girl-wife[9] whom nobody had expected[10]—least of all Chips himself[11]. She made him, to all appearances, a new man[12]; though most of the newness was really a warming to life of things that were old, imprisoned, and unguessed[13]. His eyes gained sparkle; his mind, which was adequately if not brilliantly equipped[14], began to move more adventurously[15]. The one thing he had always had, a sense of humour[16], blossomed into a sudden richness[17] to which his years lent

1 **too long for anyone to believe him capable of ever being much more**（Chips 在 Brookfield 的时间）太久，所以任何人都不会相信他可能有一天有更大的突出成就（如升职等）。**capable of ...** 是 believe 的宾词补足语。

2 **sink into that creeping dry rot of pedagogy** ['pedəgɒgɪ] 陷入教学工作（所特有）的那种逐渐干枯腐朽的状态；教学年头长了，渐渐变得迂腐。 **dry rot** 原义“（树木的）枯朽”，转义“（社会、道德等的）败坏”。

3 **that is the worst and ultimate pitfall of the profession** 这是教学职业最糟糕的最终陷阱（易犯的毛病）。美国 Little, Brown 版上 that 作 which。这个定语从句修饰 that creeping dry rot of pedagogy。

4 **giving the same lessons year after year** 年年（教来教去）教同样的那些课。**giving** 动名词，作 had formed 的主语。 **year after year** 年复一年；是习语。

5 **formed a groove** 形成一条槽；[转义] 成为老一套。

6 **into which (= groove) the other affairs of his life adjusted themselves with insidious** [ɪn'sɪdɪəs] **ease** 他生活中的其他事情不知不觉地自然纳入这老一套。**adjusted themselves** 使自己适应。

7 **fixture** 久居其位的人

8 **everything except inspiration** [ˌɪnspə'reɪʃən] 承接 gave。 **gave everything except inspiration** 给人以一切，就是不给人以灵感；独不善于启发。

9 **astonishing girl-wife** 惊人的年轻妻子

10 **nobody had expected** 任何人都没有料想到。expected 是“料想”，不是“期望”。

11 **least of all Chips himself** 后面省略 had expected；Chips 自己最没有料想到。

12 **She made him, to all appearances, a new man** 她使他显然成了一个崭新的人。 **to all appearances** 从各方面看来，显然；是习语。美国多用 to all appearances，英国多用 to all appearance。

13 **a warming to life of things that were old, imprisoned, and unguessed** 旧有的、被约束着的和想不到的种种（思想、感情、生活习惯等）（重新）活跃起来。 **warming to life** 活跃起来。

14 **adequately** ['ædɪkwɪtlɪ] **if not brilliantly equipped**（智力上）虽没有出色的准备，但也有适当的准备。 **if not brilliantly** 倘不能说是出色的话；实际上就有“虽不出色”的意义，因而 if 有“虽然”的意思。

15 **move** [muːv] **more adventurously** 更大胆地活动

16 **The one thing he had always had, a sense of humour** 他唯一的向来就有的幽默感。 **a sense of humour** 幽默感；是主语 The one thing 的同位语。

17 **blossomed into a sudden richness** 突然百花盛开；突然焕发。

maturity[1]. He began to feel a greater strength[2]; his discipline improved to a point[3] at which it could become, in a sense[4], less rigid; he became more popular. When he had first come to Brookfield he had aimed to be loved[5], honoured and obeyed — but obeyed, at any rate[6]. Obedience he had secured[7], and honour had been granted him[8]; but only now came love[9], the sudden love of boys for a man who[10] was kind without being soft[11], who understood them well enough, but not too much[12], and whose private happiness linked him with their own[13]. He began to make little jokes, the sort[14] that schoolboys like — mnemonics and puns[15] that raised laughs[16] and at the same time imprinted something in the mind[17]. There was one[18] that never failed to please[19], though it was only a sample[20] of many others. Whenever his Roman History forms[21] came to deal with[22]

---

1 **to which (= richness) his years lent maturity** [mə'tjʊərɪtɪ] 他的年龄给繁盛带来成熟（使他的幽默感不但丰富而且圆熟）。

2 **feel a greater strength** 觉得有更大的力量。美国 Little, Brown 版上 strength 作 sureness。**sureness** 把握；有“不惑”的意思。

3 **improved to a point** 改善到某一程度。

4 **in a sense** 在某种意义上；是习语。

5 **had aimed to be loved** 原来想要人家喜爱他。aim 后接不定式是美国用法；

英国用法是 aim 后接 at + 动名词。

6 **obeyed** [ə'beɪd], **at any rate** 无论如何要让人服从自己。要是其他做不到，这一点一定要做到。

7 **Obedience** [ə'biːdjəns] **he had secured** = He had secured obedience. 宾语放句首，突出宾语，这里还与下面 honour 对照。

8 **honour had been granted him** 荣誉已经给他。grant 可以有双宾语，这里 him 是它的保留间接宾语。

9 **only now came love** = love came only now 爱现在刚来；现在刚得到人们的喜爱。

10 **the sudden love of boys for a man who ...** 学生们对一个……的人的突然喜爱；这个名词词组是前面 love 的同位语。

11 **kind without being soft** 和蔼而不是软心肠的

12 **not too much** 承接 understood them，说"并不了解得太多"，意即并不苛求学生们样样要被先生知道。

13 **whose private happiness linked him with their own** 他私下的快乐使他和学生们自己的快乐连成一气；美国 Little, Brown 版上 him 作 them，实际上意思相同。

14 **the sort** = the sort of jokes，是前面 jokes 的同位语，说明他讲的是哪一类笑话。

15 **mnemonics** [ni(ː)'mɒnɪks] **and puns** 记忆术和双关语，这两词又是 the sort (of jokes) 的同位语，进一步具体说明是怎样的笑话。 **mnemonics** 这里指帮助记忆的笑话。

16 **raised laughs** 引起哈哈大笑。注意：laugh 是可数名词，而 laughter 在现代英语中是不可数名词。

17 **imprinted something in the mind** 在学生头脑中留下印记；使学生牢记不忘。

18 **one** 一个笑话

19 **failed to please** 不使人欢喜；不引人发笑

20 **sample** 例子

21 **Roman** ['rəʊmən] **History forms** 罗马（帝国）史班

22 **came to deal with** 讲到。came 后接不定式，表示"开始"、"终于"的意思。**deal with** 论述，涉及。

the Lex Canuleia[1], the law that permitted patricians[2] to marry plebeians[3], Chips used to add[4]: 'So that[5], you see[6], if Miss Plebs wanted Mr. Patrician to marry her[7], and he said he couldn't[8], she probably replied: "Oh, yes, you can[9], you liar[10]!"' Roars of laughter.

And Kathie broadened his views and opinions[11], also[12], giving him an outlook far beyond the roofs and turrets of Brookfield[13], so that he saw his country as something deep and gracious[14] to which Brookfield was but one of many feeding streams[15]. She had a cleverer brain than his, and he could not confute[16] her ideas even if and when he disagreed with them[17]; he remained, for instance, a Conservative in politics, despite all her radical-socialist talk[18]. But even where he did not accept, he absorbed[19]; her young idealism worked upon his maturity[20] to produce an amalgam very gentle and wise[21].

---

1 **Lex Canuleia**（拉丁词）古罗马由人民选出的保民官（tribune）Gaius Canuleius 提出的使贵族和平民间婚姻合法化的法律。

2 **patricians** [pəˈtrɪʃənz]（古罗马的）贵族

3 **plebeians** [plɪˈbi(:)ənz]（古罗马的）平民

4 **used to add** 常补充一句。 **used to** [ju:s*t* to] 后接不定式，表示过去经常的动作。**add** 附加说（或写）。

5 **So that** 所以；这是从属连词，照理它引起从属从句，不能独立，但这里独立成句，是模拟 Chips 在讲了罗马法律允许贵族和平民结婚后，随口接下去讲的口气。

6 **you see** 你们知道；是插入语。

7 **if Miss Plebs** [plebz] **wanted Mr. Patrician to marry her** 如果 Plebs 小姐要 Patrician 先生娶她。作者把上面所说的 patricians 和 plebeians 化成两个姓氏（pleb = plebeian）编成笑话。

8 **he couldn't** = he couldn't marry her.

9 **you can** = you can marry me.

10 **you liar** ['laɪə] 你这个说谎的人（实际能娶，而说“不能”，当然是说谎。）

11 **broadened his views and opinions** 使他的看法和观点开阔起来。

12 **also** 修饰前面的 broadened，不是修饰后面的 giving。

13 **giving him an outlook far beyond the roofs and turrets** ['tʌrɪts] **of Brookfield** 使他的眼界扩大到 Brookfield 之外的广阔天地。 **far beyond the roofs and turrets of Brookfield** 远远超越 Brookfield 的屋顶和塔楼；是“远远超越 Brookfield”的形象化的写法。

14 **deep and gracious** 深邃宽厚（将国家比作大海，看下半句自明。）

15 **but one of many feeding streams** 只是许多注流入海的河流之一。

16 **confute** 驳倒。confute her ideas 和 confute her 都可以说。

17 **even if and when he disagreed with them** 即使他不同意她的意见。 **even if** 即使。when 承接 even；**even when** 即使在……的时候。

18 **he remained, for instance, a Conservative** [kən'sɜːvətɪv] **in politics, despite all her radical-socialist talk** 比如，尽管她对他讲了所有这些激进社会主义的话，他在政治上依旧是个保守党人。 **despite** 虽有……的存在；尽管；是介词。

19 **even where he did not accept, he absorbed** 即使有些地方他不接受（她那些观点），他脑子里也吸收了。

20 **her young idealism** [aɪ'dɪəlɪzəm] **worked upon his maturity** 她的青年的理想主义对他的老成发生作用。

21 **an amalgam** [ə'mælgəm] **very gentle and wise** 一种非常温和而明智的混合物。gentle 和 wise 是后置修饰词。

Sometimes she persuaded[1] him completely. Brookfield, for example, ran a mission in East London[2], to which boys and parents contributed generously with money but rarely with personal contact. It was Katherine who suggested that a team from the mission should come up to Brookfield[3] and play one of the School's elevens at soccer[4]. The idea was so revolutionary[5] that from anyone but Katherine it could not have survived its first frosty reception[6]. To introduce[7] a group of slum boys to the serene pleasances[8] of better-class youngsters[9] seemed at first a wanton stirring[10] of all kinds of things that had better be left untouched[11]. The whole staff[12] was against it[13], and the School, if its opinion could have been taken, was probably against it too[14]. Everyone was certain that the East End[15] lads would be hooligans[16], or else that they would be made to feel uncomfortable[17]; anyhow, there would be 'incidents[18]',

---

1 **persuaded** [pə'sweɪdɪd] 说服，劝服。注意：不只是“说”或“劝”，而是“说”或“劝”而使对方真的“服”了。

2 **run a mission in East London** 在伦敦东区办一个慈善机构。**East London** 指下文所说 the East End，是伦敦的贫民区。

3 **come up to Brookfield** 到 Brookfield 来。**come up** 挨近，趋近。

4 **play one of the School's elevens at soccer** ['sɒkə] 与 Brookfield 公学的一个足球队比赛足球。**play** 与……比赛。**elevens**（由十一人组成的）足球

队。 **soccer** 英式足球，由 asso*c*iation football 衍化而来。

5 **The idea was so revolutionary** 这个想法是多么革命的想法。（保守派看来如此，见下句。）

6 **from anyone but Katherine it could not have survived its first frosty reception** = if the idea had come from anyone but Katherine … 要是这个想法是 Katherine 之外的任何人提出的，它不可能经受最初的冷遇而终于被接受；这是虚拟语气，表示与过去事实相反，实际上正是 Katherine 提出的，因而虽然最初受到冷遇，但是终被接受。

7 **introduce** 引入

8 **serene** [sɪ'riːn] **pleasances** ['plezənsɪz] 幽静的大庭院（此处指 Brookfield 校园）

9 **better-class youngsters** 较上层阶级的子弟

10 **wanton** ['wɒntən] **stirring** 任意搅乱

11 **that had better be left untouched** ['ʌn'tʌtʃt] 最好让它们照原样不要碰动。**that** 指 things。 **had better** 还是……好；最好；是习语，后接没有 to 的不定式。 **untouched** 没有碰动的，原样的；是形容词，这是作 be left 的主语补足语。

12 **the whole staff** [stɑːf] 全体教职员

13 **was against it** 反对这个想法

14 **the School, if its opinion could have been taken, was probably against it too** 如果可以向学校征求意见，学校大概也是反对的。上面已讲教职员们的意见，学校本身自然不会发表意见。这里用虚拟语气，表示与事实相反，犹如“天若有情天亦老”的说法。作者在这里只是竭言全校反对。

15 **the East End** 伦敦东区（贫民区）

16 **hooligans** ['huːlɪgənz] 街头的小流氓

17 **or else that they would be made to feel uncomfortable** [ʌn'kʌmfətəbl] 承接上面的 certain; 说“他们不是小流氓的话，也一定会被弄得感到不自在。”**or else** 不然的话，否则。make 作“使得”解，用不定式作宾语补足语时，一般不用不定式记号“to”，如 make them feel；但如 make 用于被动语态时，“to”不可省略，如这里的 be made to feel。

18 **incidents** ['ɪnsɪdənts] 偶然事件；事故。这里 there would be ‘incidents’ 是“出乱子”、“出事情”的意思。

and everyone would be confused and upset[1]. Yet Katherine persisted.

'Chips,' she said, 'they're wrong, you know, and I'm right. I'm looking ahead to the future, they and you are looking back to the past. England isn't always going to be divided into officers and "other ranks"[2]. And those Poplar boys[3] are just as important — to England — as Brookfield is. You've got to have them here[4], Chips. You can't satisfy your conscience by writing a cheque for a few guineas and keeping them at arm's length.[5] Besides, they're proud of Brookfield — just as you are. Years hence, maybe, boys of that sort will be coming here[6] — a few of them[7], at any rate. Why not?[8] Why ever not?[9] Chips, dear, remember this is eighteen-*ninety*-seven[10] — not *sixty*-seven, when you were up at Cambridge[11]. You got your ideas well stuck in those days[12], and good ideas they were too[13], a lot of them[14]. But a few — just a few, Chips — want unsticking[15]...'

Rather to her surprise[16] he gave way[17] and suddenly

1 **be confused and upset** 被弄得昏头昏脑，七颠八倒。

2 **be divided into officers and "other ranks"** 分成军官和士兵；分成治人者和治于人者。 **other ranks** 普通士兵们；是惯用语。

3 **Poplar** ['pɒplə] **boys** Poplar 的孩子们。 **Poplar** 以前伦敦东部的工业区，Brookfield 所办的慈善机构当在此。

4 **You've got to have them here** 你该让他们到这里来。**'ve (have) got to** 口语，= have to。

5 **You can't satisfy your conscience** ['kɒnʃəns] **by writing a cheque** [tʃek] **for a few guineas** [gɪnɪz] **and keeping them at arm's length.** 你不能开张支票给他们几个几尼而同他们保持一定距离，就得到良心上的安宁。 **cheque** 是英国拼法，美国作 check。 **guineas** 原为英国金币，后是计账货币，等于 21 先令，即略高于 1 英镑（1 英镑原等于 20 先令，今取消先令，1 英镑等于 100 便士）；1 几尼等于 1 镑 5 便士。 **keep at arm's length** 同……保持一定距离；是习语；注意：arm 前没有 an。

6 **boys of that sort will be coming here** 那种孩子（指 Poplar boys）将要到这里（Brookfield）来（念书）。 **will be coming** = will come 口语中常用将来进行时代替一般将来时，更见生动。

7 **a few of them** = a few of them will be coming here.

8 **Why not?** = Why will boys of that sort not come here?

9 **Why ever not?** 是 Why not 的强调的说法。其他如 "what ever", "how ever" 等同样是强调的说法。

10 **eighteen-*ninety*-seven** 1897 年，*ninety* 斜体，应重读，强调是 90 年代，而不是下面紧接着说的 60 年代。

11 **were up at Cambridge** [keɪmbrɪdʒ] 在剑桥大学读书。 **up** 这里表示在高等学府。

12 **got your ideas well stuck in those days** 在当时（在剑桥大学学习时）把你的思想牢牢滞留了；你当时的思想定型了。 **stuck** 是 stick 的过去分词，作形容词，在句中是 got 的宾语补足语。

13 **good ideas they were too** = they (your ideas) were good ideas, too.

14 **a lot of them** 与 they 同位，补充说明 Chips 的许多想法。

15 **a few — just a few, Chips — want unsticking** 有一些——就只是有一些——想法需要摆脱掉，Chips。want 后接主动态动名词表示被动的意思，所以 want unsticking = want to be unstuck。

16 **Rather to her surprise** 令她颇为惊讶；多少出乎她意料。

17 **gave way** 让步；是习语。

became a keen advocate[1] of the proposal, and the *volte-face*[2] was so complete that the authorities were taken unawares[3] and found themselves consenting to[4] the dangerous experiment[5]. The boys from Poplar arrived at Brookfield one Saturday afternoon, played soccer with the School's second team[6], were honourably defeated by seven goals to five[7], and later had high tea[8] with the School team in the Dining Hall[9]. They then met the Head and were shown over the School[10], and Chips saw them off[11] at the railway station in the evening. Everything had passed without the slightest hitch of any kind[12], and it was clear that the visitors[13] were taking away with them as fine an impression as they had left behind[14].

They took back with them also the memory of a charming woman who had met them and talked to them; for once[15], years later, during the War[16], a private[17] stationed[18] at a big military camp near Brookfield called on Chips and said he had been one of that first visiting team[19]. Chips gave him tea and chatted with him, till at length[20], shaking hands, the man[21] said: 'And 'ow's the

1 **keen advocate** ['ædvəkət] 热心的拥护者

2 **volte-face** ['vɒlt'fɑːs]（意见、政策等的）大转变；原是法语，故用斜体。

3 **were taken unawares** ['ʌnə'weəz] 被弄得不知所措；被突然袭击。 **unawares** 出其不意地；是副词。

4 **found themselves consenting to** 发现自己不由自主地应允了。

5 **the dangerous experiment** [ɪks'perɪmənt] 这危险的试验（这里指球赛）

6 **the School's second team** Brookfield 的第二个足球认（就是“乙队”）

7 **were honourably defeated by seven goals** [gəʊlz] **to five** 光荣地以七比五被击败。慈善机构的球队同公学的球队比赛，能打到七比五，虽输犹荣。honourably 还可能包含一层意思，即 Poplar 球队踢球风格很好，不像保守派原先想象他们是一群小流氓会踢出事情来。

8 **high tea**（有肉食的）正式茶点

9 **Dining Hall** 餐厅。这里用大写开头，是指以此命名的餐厅。

10 **were shown over the School** 被带领去参观 Brookfield 的各个部分。

11 **saw them off** 送别他们

12 **Everything had passed without the slightest hitch** [hɪtʃ] **of any kind** 一切顺利进行，连任何细小的障碍都没有发生。故事已讲到送行，这里回顾一天的活动，所以用过去完成式。

13 **visitors** 指 Poplar boys。

14 **taking away with them as fine an impression as they had left behind** 带回去的印象同他们留下的印象一样好；在 Brookfield 留下很好的印象，同时他们带回去了对 Brookfield 的同样的好印象。

15 **for once** 这里 for 是并列连词，作“因为”解；once 是副词，作“有一次”解；与习语 for once（就只一次）无关。

16 **the War** 指第一次世界大战。

17 **private** 士兵；它的谓语动词是 called 和 said。

18 **stationed = who was stationed** 驻扎（在某处）的。是过去分词，修饰 private。

19 **one of that first visiting team** 第一次来访的那个球队中的一员

20 **at length** 最后

21 **the man** 即上文的 private。

missus, sir?[1] I remember 'er very well.'

'Do you?[2]' Chips answered eagerly. 'Do you remember her?'

'Rather.[3] I should think anyone would.[4]'

And Chips replied: 'They don't[5], you know. At least, not here.[6] Boys come and go, new faces all the time[7], memories don't last[8]. Even masters don't stay for ever. Since last year — when old Gribble[9] retired — he's — um — the School butler[10] — there hasn't been anyone here who ever saw my wife. She died, you know, less than a year after your visit. In ninety-eight.[11]'

'I'm real sorry to 'ear that[12], sir. There's two or three o' my pals[13], anyhow, who remember 'er clear as anything[14], though we did only see 'er that wunst[15]. Yes, we remember 'er all right[16].'

'I'm very glad ... That was a grand day we all had[17] — and a fine game, too[18].'

'One o' the best days aht I ever 'ad in me life.[19] Wish it

1 **And 'ow's the missus, sir?** 您太太好吗，先生？ And 用于句首，口语中很普遍，文章中也有。'ow's = how is；把 how 发成 ow 的音，表示说话人教

育不良。missus 是 missis 的讹读；the missis 太太；妻子；女主人。 sir 是对陌生人或上司的尊称。

2 **Do you?** = Do you remember her?

3 **Rather** 当然；的确；英国口语中用以回答问题，读作 ['rɑːðə]。

4 **I should think anyone would.** I should think 比 I think 婉转。anyone would = anyone would remember her.

5 **They don't** = They don't remember her.

6 **At least, not here.** = They do not remember her here, at least. 至少这里（在 Brookfield）他们不记得她。

7 **new faces all the time = there are new faces all the time** 时时有新面孔（出现）

8 **memories don't last** 人的记忆力不能持久。

9 **Gribble** ['grɪbl] 格里布尔，姓氏

10 **he's — um — the School butler** 他（Gribble）是 Brookfield 的总管事；这是插入语。

11 **In ninety-eight** 承接上文，= She died in ninety-eight（1898）.

12 **I'm real sorry to 'ear that** 我听到这个消息，非常难过。real 作副词，= really；是口语。'ear 是 hear 的讹读。

13 **pals** 同伴；好朋友；是口语；这里指上文所说到 Brookfield 来比球的 Poplar boys。

14 **remember 'er clear as anything** 十分清楚地记得她。'er 是 her 的讹读。**clear** 这里是副词。 **as anything** 非常；是习语。

15 **did only see 'er that wunst** 只见过她那一次。**did only see** = only saw. **wunst** 是 once 的讹读。

16 **all right** 确实地

17 **That was a grand day we all had** 那是我们一起过的不平常的一天（指比球的那天）。

18 **and a fine game, too** 而且也是一场精彩的比赛。

19 **One o' the best days aht I ever 'ad in me life.** = That is one of the best days that I ever had in my life. 作者用 o' (of), aht (that), 'ad (had), me (my), 都表示说话人教育不良。

was then and not nah[1], straight, I do[2]. I'm off to Frawnce[3] to-morrer[4].'

A month or so later Chips heard that he had been killed at Passchendaele[5].

1 **Wish it was then and not nah** = I wish it was then and not now. 但愿此刻是当时而不是现在。当时到 Brookfield 比球，多快活；而现在就要前往法国去打仗（见下句）。

2 **straight, I do** 真的，我是这样希望。 **straight** 老实地，率直地；是副词。I do = I wish it was then and not now.

3 **Frawnce** 是 France 的讹读，即把 [frɑːns] 念成 [frɔːns]。

4 **to-morrer** [tə'mɒrə] 是 tomorrow [tə'mɒrəʊ] 的讹读，但美国人在口语中常把 tomorrow 读作 [tə'mɒrə]，而英国人说 tomorrow morning 等语时，也常把 tomorrow 读作 [tə'mɒrə]。

5 **Passchendaele** ['pɑːsəndɑːlə] 比利时西北部的一个村庄，第一次世界大战时曾在此发生激战。

第七章

内容提要

凯瑟琳生前的形象和当时的情景经常浮现在契普斯眼前。

在契普斯要严厉处罚学生的时候，她常认为有些情况不能全怪学生，劝他宽恕。反之，有时候契普斯准备宽恕某一学生，她却认为那样自以为是的学生，既然他自讨惩罚，那就应予惩罚。

凯瑟琳的劝告，契普斯十有八九都听。偶尔不听，过后也多半懊悔。

契普斯回忆中有许多有趣的小事，可是现在谁都忘了，只存留在契普斯的脑海里。他一直要写一本书，把这些都记录下来。

7

And so it stood, a warm and vivid patch in his life, casting a radiance that glowed in a thousand recollections.[1] Twilight[2] at Mrs. Wickett's, when the School bell clanged for call-over, brought them back to him in a cloud[3] — Katherine scampering along the stone corridors[4], laughing beside him at some 'howler' in an essay he was marking[5], taking the cello part in a Mozart trio[6] for the School concert — her creamy arm sweeping over the brown sheen of the instrument[7]. She had been a good player[8] and a fine musician. And Katherine furred and muffed for the December house matches[9], Katherine at the Garden Party that followed Speech Day Prize-giving[10], Katherine ten-

---

1 **And so it stood, a warm and vivid patch in his life, casting a radiance that glowed in a thousand recollections.** 他生活中一个温暖、生动的片断就这样存在着，发出光来，照亮上千的回忆。用 And 引起句子，已见前；这里

甚至章节开始也用 And。**so it stood** = it stood so 这样地存在着。**a warm and vivid patch** 是 it 的同位语。 **patch** 原是“补丁”，这里是“一片”的意思，也就是“以见一斑”的“斑”。

2 **Twilight** ['twaɪlaɪt] 黄昏时或黎明时的光线；这里指黄昏，它的谓语动词是 brought。

3 **brought them back to him in a cloud**（黄昏）把它们（上千个回忆）在一片云雾般的朦胧中带回给他；“带回给他”就是使他重新回忆起。

4 **Katherine scampering along the stone corridors** ['kɒrɪdɔːz] Katherine 沿着石头走廊快跑。这是回忆中的情景之一，下面还有 laughing，taking the cello part，这三个用分词构成的短语是并列的，都修饰 Katherine，描绘她的一个个形象。

5 **laughing beside him at some “howler”** ['haʊlə] **in an essay he was marking** 在他身旁，对他在评分的一篇作文中某个闹笑话的大错哈哈大笑。 **howler** 闹笑话的大错；是口语，所以加了引号。 **marking** 给（试卷）批分数；**he was marking** 前省略 which 或 that，是定语从句，修饰 essay。

6 **taking the cello** ['tʃeləʊ] **part in a Mozart** ['məʊtsɑːt] **trio** [tri(ː)əʊ] 在莫扎特三重奏中拉大提琴。 **Mozart** Wolfgang Amadeus Mozart，莫扎特，奥地利作曲家（1756—1791）。

7 **her creamy arm sweeping over the brown sheen of the instrument** ['ɪnstrʊmənt] 她那肤色如脂的手臂在乐器的棕色光泽中迅速移动；这是独立结构，描写她拉大提琴的风姿。

8 **player** ['pleɪə] 演奏者

9 **Katherine furred** [fɜːd] **and muffed** [mʌft] **for the December house matches** 穿着皮大衣，戴着皮手筒来观看 12 月举行的各宿舍之间的体育比赛的 Katherine。英国公学中的 house 相当于美国的 dormitory。这里 Katherine furred and muffed 和 Katherine at the Garden Party，Katherine tendering her advice 三个名词词组并列，furred 和 muffed 是过去分词，at the Garden Party 是介词短语，tendering 是现在分词，分别修饰三个“Katherine”，描绘 Katherine 的三个形象。

10 **Speech Day Prize-giving**（英国学校一年一度有来宾演说的）授奖典礼日的授奖仪式。因有所专指，故用大写。

dering her advice[1] in any little problem that arose. Good advice[2], too — which[3] he did not always take, but which[4] always influenced him.

'Chips, dear, I'd let them off if I were you[5]. After all, it's nothing very serious[6].'

'I know. I'd like to let them off, but if I do[7] I'm afraid they'll do it again[8].'

'Try telling them that, frankly[9], and give them the chance[10].'

'I might[11].'

And there were other things, occasionally[12], that *were* serious[13].

'You know, Chips, having all these hundreds of boys cooped up here[14] is really an unnatural arrangement[15], when you come to think about it[16]. So that[17] when anything does occur that oughtn't to[18], don't you think it's a bit

---

1 **tendering her advice** 提出劝告。注意:advice 作"劝告"解,是不可数名词;一个劝告,应作"a piece of advice"。advices 是古英语里"消息"的意思。

2 **Good advice** 承接上句,= Her advice was good advice。

3 **which** = and her good advice,是非限制性用法。

4 **but which** 这个 which 同前一 which 并列,也是非限制性用法。

5 **I'd let them off if I were you** 假如我是你，我就饶恕他们。这是虚拟语气，所以主句中用 I'd（= I would），从句中用 I were。 **let off** 放掉；轻轻放过。 **them** 这里没有先行词，但 Katherine 当时说这话，自然是在一定场合，或者另有上文，指的是犯规的学生们。

6 **nothing very serious** 没有什么大不了的事。

7 **if I do** = if I let them off.

8 **they'll do it again** 他们会再犯。这个 do 同上半句的 do 不同。又，do it 的 it 并无所专指，是一种含糊用法。

9 **Try telling them that, frankly** 把那个话（指上文说"饶了他们，怕他们再犯"的话）坦率地告诉他们试试看。try 后接不定式或动名词都可以；接动名词表示尝试做某事。这里对学生有两种办法，一是罚，一是坦率对他们讲；Katherine 劝 Chips 试试看后一办法。 **frankly** 修饰 telling。

10 **give them the chance** 给他改正错误的机会。

11 **might = I might try** 我可以试试看；省去"假如你要我这样做"等含意的条件从句。

12 **occasionally** [ə'keɪʒnəlɪ] 偶然。这是个插入的副词，把它前面的 things 和它后面的定语从句 that *were* serious 隔开了。

13 *were* 斜体，重读，表示强调。 ***were* serious** 确实是严重的。

14 **having all these hundreds of boys cooped** [ku:pt] **up here** 把这几百个孩子一起禁闭在这里。**have ...** 后接过去分词，表示"使……被……"。 **coop** 原是名词，是关家禽的笼子；作动词，是"把（家禽等）关进笼子"，引申为"禁闭"； **coop up** 禁闭起来。

15 **unnatural arrangement** [ə'reɪdʒmənt] 不自然的办法。孩子们好动，现在把几百个好动的孩子关在学校里，成了"笼中鸟"，那是"不自然"的。

16 **when you come to think about it** 假如你往这方面想想的话。这并不是说"当想的时候，这办法是不自然的。""不自然"是客观的，只是"假如你想一想，就会觉得这是不自然的。"

17 **So that** 所以；这是从属连词，照理它所引起的从句是从属从句，不能独立，但这里承接上文，独立成句。

18 **anything does occur** [ə'kɜː] **that oughtn't to** 不应该发生的事情竟然发生。does occur 是 occurs 的强调式，does 要重读。oughtn't to = ought not to occur.

unfair[1] to come down on[2] them as if it were their own fault for being here[3]?'

'Don't know about that[4], Kathie[5], but I do know that, for everybody's sake, we have to be pretty[6] strict about this sort of thing[7]. One black sheep[8] can contaminate others.'

'After he himself has been contaminated to begin with.[9] After all, that's what probably *did* happen, isn't it[10]?'

'Maybe.[11] We can't help it[12]. Anyhow, I believe Brookfield is better than a lot of[13] other schools. All the more reason to keep it so.[14]'

'But this boy, Chips ... you're going to sack him?[15]'

'The Head probably will, when I tell him.'

'And you're going to tell the Head?'

'It's a duty, I'm afraid.'

'Couldn't you think about it a bit[16] ... talk to the boy again ... find out[17] how it began ... after all — apart from this business[18] — isn't he rather a nice boy[19]?'

'Oh, he's all right[20].'

---

1 **a bit unfair** 有些不公平。 **a bit** 有些儿；作状语。

2 **come down on** 惩罚；也作 come down upon。

3 **as if it were their own fault for being here** 仿佛他们在这里是他们自己的过

错。 **as if** 仿佛；它引起的从句用虚拟语气，所以 it 后用 were。

4 **Don't know about that** = I don't know about that.

5 **Kathie** ['kæθɪ] 凯茜，Katherine 的昵称

6 **pretty** 十分；很；是副词，口语中常用。

7 **this sort of thing** 这一类事。既成为一类，当有许多，但 this（或 a, the）sort of 后面的名词多用单数。

8 **black sheep** 犹言"害群之马"。**One black sheep can contaminate** [kən'tæmɪneɪt] **others** 意即一个坏学生会带坏其他学生。

9 **After he himself has been contaminated to begin with.** 他自己先被带坏之后（才会带坏其他同学）。这是承上面的话说的，否则 After 引起的从句不能独立。这种不完全的句子口语中很多。**to begin with** 首先；是习语。

10 **that's what probably *did* happen, isn't it?** 大概实际情况就是那样，是不是？反义疑问句（tag question）中的动词用前面动词的否定式。

11 **Maybe** 承接上面 isn't it，= Maybe it is.

12 **can't help it** 没有办法；无可奈何；是习语。

13 **a lot of** 许多，也作 lots of，后面可数、不可数名词都可以接。比较：a number of 后只接可数名词。a great（或 good）deal of 后只接不可数名词。

14 **All the more reason to keep it so.** = We have all the more reason ...（正因为 Brookfield 比许多其他学校好，）我们更有理由要把它保持下去（保持比人家好）。

15 **But this boy, Chips ... you're going to sack him?** 可是 Chips，你准备把这个学生开除掉吗？先说了"这个学生"，再说"他"，出现重复的宾语，这种现象在中外口语中都常有。

16 **think about it a bit** 想一想此事。 **a bit** 稍微；是状语短语。

17 **find out** 弄明白

18 **apart from this business** 撇开这件事。**apart from** 除掉；撇开；是习语。**this business** 指这一回犯规的事；business 在这里不是"生意"、"业务"，而作"事情"解，且带有贬义。

19 **rather a nice boy** 也可以说 a rather nice boy，前者在口语中较常见。

20 **all right** 很不错的

'Then, Chips dear, don't you think there *ought* to be some other way[1] ...'

And so on.[2] About once in ten times[3] he was adamant[4] and wouldn't be persuaded[5]. In about half of these exceptional cases[6] he afterwards[7] rather wished he had taken her advice[8]. And years later[9], whenever he had trouble with a boy[10], he was always at the mercy of a softening wave of reminiscence[11]; the boy would stand there, waiting to be told his punishment, and would see, if he were observant[12], the brown eyes twinkle into a shine[13] that told him all was well[14]. But he did not guess[15] that at such a moment Chips was remembering something that had happened long before he was born[16], that Chips was thinking[17]: Young ruffian, I'm hanged if *I* can think of any reason to let him off[18], but I'll bet *she* would have done[19]!

But she had not always pleaded for leniency[20]. On

---

1 **there *ought* to be some other way** 应该有什么另外的办法（来处理这个犯规的学生）。

2 **And so on.** 诸如此类；等等。单独用 And so on 作为一个句子，且用在一节的前头，这是一种随笔式的写法。

3 **once in ten times** 十次中有一次

4 **adamant** ['ædəmənt] 坚定不移的

5 **wouldn't be persuaded** 不肯被说服；不肯听从劝说；不是“不要别人劝”的意思。

6 **In about half of these exceptional cases** 在这些例外情况的大约一半中。上面说他十次中只有一次听从劝说，这里说“一半”，是二十来次中才有一次。

7 **afterwards** ['ɑːftəwədz] 事后；后来

8 **wished he had taken her advice** 但愿他是听了她的劝告；懊悔当时没有听她的劝告。

9 **years later** 若干年后。years 修饰 later。

10 **had trouble with a boy** 跟学生有纠葛；即碰到要处理学生犯规的情况。

11 **at the mercy of a softening wave of reminiscence** [ˌremɪ'nɪsns] 在一阵使人心软的回忆的支配下。（回忆起 Katherine 劝他宽恕学生的往事，他心肠就软下来了。）**a wave of reminiscence** 回忆的浪潮；像浪潮般涌起的回忆。

12 **if he were observant** [əb'zɜːvənt] 假如他注意观察的话。这是虚拟语气，所以 he 后用 were。这个条件从句插在主句的谓语动词 would see 和它的复合宾语 the brown eyes twinkle 中间，把它们隔开了。

13 **twinkle into a shine** 闪烁而发亮起来

14 **all was well** 万事大吉

15 **did not guess** 没有想到（不是“没有猜想”）

16 **long before he was born** 远在他出生之前。he 指学生。

17 **that Chips was thinking** 这个 that- 从句和前面一个 that- 从句并列，是 guess 的宾语。

18 **I'm hanged** [hæŋd] **if *I* can think of any reason to let him off** 我是死也想不出饶恕他的理由。**I'm hanged if...** 是习语，意思是“决不”。***I*** 重读，与下面 *She*（也重读）强调对比。 **think of** 想到。

19 **but I'll bet *she* would have done** 但是我可以断定她会饶恕他。 **bet** 打赌；这里转义为“可以断定”。**would have done** = would have let him off，这是虚拟语气，表示与过去事实相反，因为 Katherine 早已不在人世，不可能再要饶恕谁。

20 **pleaded for leniency** ['liːnjənsɪ] 请求宽恕

rather rare occasions[1] she urged severity[2] where Chips was inclined to be forgiving[3]. 'I don't like his type[4], Chips. He's too cocksure of himself[5]. If he's looking for trouble I should certainly let him have it.[6]'

What a host of little incidents[7], all deep-buried in the past[8] — problems[9] that had once been urgent, arguments that had once been keen, anecdotes that were funny only because one remembered the fun[10]. Did any emotion really matter when the last trace of it had vanished from human memory[11]; and if that were so[12], what a crowd of emotions clung to him as to their last home before annihilation[13]! He must be kind to them, must treasure them in his mind before their long sleep[14]. That affair of Archer's resignation[15], for instance — a queer business, that was[16]. And that affair about the rat[17] that Dunster[18] put in the organ loft[19] while old Ogilvie[20] was taking choir practice[21]. Ogilvie

---

1 **On rather rare occasions** 在非常难得的情况下。注意：occasion 前用 on；比较：同义的 case 前用 in。

2 **urged severity** [sɪ'verɪtɪ] 竭力主张要严厉。

3 **where Chips was inclined to be forgiving** 在 Chips 倾向于要饶恕的情况下。 **where** 在……情况下。

4 **his type** 他那种类型（的人）

5 **cocksure** ['kɒk'ʃʊə] **of himself** 自以为是；骄横。注意用介词 of。

6 **If he's looking for trouble I should certainly let him have it.** 既然他要找麻烦，那我自然应该给他麻烦（即惩罚）。**If** 这里是“既然”的意思。**have it** 吃苦头；**let him have it** 给他吃苦头；是美国俚语。

7 **What a host** [həʊst] **of little incidents** 好多的小事情啊。用 What 表示感叹，常用一个名词词组独立成句，没有谓语。

8 **all deep-buried in the past** 全都是深埋在过去中的。修饰 incidents。

9 **problems** 和下面 arguments 和 anecdotes ['ænɪkdəʊt] 并列，都是 incidents 的同位语，进一步说明是什么 incidents。

10 **anecdotes that were funny only because one remembered the fun** 只有记得个中妙趣的人才觉得有趣的轶事。

11 **Did any emotion really matter when the last trace of it had vanished from human memory** 任何感情，在它已经从人的记忆中消失干净之后，还有什么真正的意思呢？这是个修辞学上的反问，用疑问的形式表示强调的陈述。意思就是：任何感情，既经忘却，便无意义。

12 **if that were so** 假如是（上面所说）那样的话。这是虚拟语气，所以 that 后用 were。

13 **what a crowd of emotions clung to him as to their last home before annihilation** [ˌənaɪə'leɪʃən] 有一大堆的感情都依附着他，好像是在它们消失之前依附着它们最后的家。这些感情现在只有 Chips 记得，在他之后，将不再有人记得。

14 **treasure** ['treʒə] **them in his mind before their long sleep** 在它们（这些感情）消亡之前，把它们珍藏在他心里。

15 **That affair of Archer's** ['ɑːtʃəz] **resignation** Archer 辞职的事。**Archer** 亚契，姓氏。作者随便举例提到这一件事，并不详细交代经过情况。这种写法现代文艺作品中常见。

16 **a queer business, that was** = that was a queer business 那是件怪事。that 可以说是与 That affair of Archer's resignation 同位的。

17 **And that affair about the rat** 还有关于老鼠的那件事。这是个名词句。

18 **Dunster** ['dʌnstə] 邓斯特，姓氏

19 **organ loft** ['ɔːgn lɒft] 放置管风琴的楼厢

20 **Ogilvie** ['əʊglvɪ] 奥吉尔维，姓氏

21 **taking choir** ['kwaɪə] **practice** 排练合唱

was dead and Dunster drowned at Jutland[1]; of others who had witnessed or heard of the incident, probably most had forgotten[2]. And it had been like that, with other incidents, for centuries[3]. He had a sudden vision of thousands and thousands of boys, from the age of Elizabeth[4] onwards; dynasty upon dynasty of masters[5]; long epochs[6] of Brookfield history that had left not even a ghostly record[7]. Who knew why the old fifth-form room[8] was called 'the Pit[9]'? There was probably a reason, to begin with; but it had since been lost[10] — lost like the lost books of Livy[11]. And what happened at Brookfield when Cromwell fought at Naseby[12], near by[13]? How did Brookfield react to the great scare of the 'Forty-Five[14]'? Was there a whole holiday when news came of Waterloo[15]? And so on, up to the earliest time that he himself could remember — 1870[16], and Wetherby[17] saying, by way of small talk[18] after their first and only interview: 'Looks as if[19] we shall have to settle with the Prus-

---

1 **Dunster drowned at Jutland** ['dʒʌtlənd] = Dunster was drowned at Jutland。这里省掉 was，借用上半句 Ogilvie was dead 中的 was。**Jutland** 日德兰半岛。

2 **of others who had witnessed or heard of the incident, probably most had for-**

gotten 在其他目睹或听到（Dunster 溺毙）这件事情的人们中，也许大多数人都已经忘记了。如把 most 移放在 of others 前面，就更容易理解。

3 **it had been like that, with other incidents, for centuries** 几百年来，其他的事情也是那样。（事情过去，就被遗忘了。）**it** 这里无所专指，可理解为“情况”。 **with** 对于……来说；关于。

4 **the age of Elizabeth** 英国女王伊丽莎白一世时代（1558—1603）

5 **dynasty** ['dɪnəstɪ] **upon dynasty of masters** 一个朝代又一个朝代的教师们

6 **long epochs** ['i:pɒks] 悠长的一个个时代

7 **had left not even a ghostly** ['gəʊstlɪ] **record** 连个纪录的影子也没有留下。**ghostly** 幽灵般的；渺茫的。

8 **fifth-form room** 五年级教室

9 **'the Pit'** “地狱”。pit 有“坑”、“地窖”、“深渊”等解释；“地狱”称 the pit。

10 **it had since been lost** 它（为什么把五年级教室称为“地狱”的理由）在那个时候之后就一直没有人知道了。 **since** = since then，这里是副词。

11 **the lost books of Livy** ['lɪvɪ] 已经湮没的李维的著作。 **Livy** Titus Livius，罗马历史家（公元前 59—公元 17）。

12 **Cromwell** ['krɒmwəl] **fought at Naseby** ['neɪzbɪ] 克伦威尔（Oliver Cromwell, 1599—1658）在纳西比作战。1645 年克伦威尔在纳西比与保皇党决战，大胜。

13 **near by** 附近；指在 Brookfield 附近。

14 **the great scare of the 'Forty-Five'** “1745 年之乱”的大恐慌。 **the 'Forty-Five'** 指英国詹姆士二世党徒在 1745 年的政变。

15 **Waterloo** [ˌwɔ:tə'lu:] 滑铁卢，比利时城镇，1815 年英国威灵顿（Wellington）大败拿破仑于此地。

16 **up to the earliest time that he himself could remember—1870**（从伊丽莎白一世时代起）一直到他自己所能记忆的最早的年代——1870 年（Chips 是 1870 年来到 Brookfield 的，见第一章。）

17 **Wetherby** 韦瑟比，Chips 刚到 Brookfield 时的该校校长

18 **by way of small talk** 作为闲谈

19 **Looks as if = It looks as if** 看来似乎

sians ourselves[1] one of these fine days[2], eh?'

When Chips remembered things like this he often felt that he would write them down[3] and make a book of them[4]; and during his years at Mrs. Wickett's[5] he sometimes went even so far as to make desultory notes[6] in an exercise book. But he was soon brought up against difficulties[7] — the chief one being that writing tired him[8], both mentally and physically. Somehow, too, his recollections lost much of their flavour[9] when they were written down; that story about Rushton and the sack of potatoes, for instance — it would seem quite tame in print[10], but, Lord[11], how funny it had been, at the time[12]! It was funny, too, to remember it; though, perhaps, if you didn't remember Rushton[13] ... and who would, anyway, after all those years? ... it was such a long time ago ... Mrs. Wickett, did you ever know a fellow named Rushton? Before your time[14], I dare say[15] ... went to Burma in some government job[16] ... or was it Borneo[17] ... very funny fellow, Rushton[18]...

And there he was, dreaming again before the fire[19],

---

1 **we shall have to settle with the Prussians ourselves** 我们自己还得和普鲁士

人较量一下。Wetherby 说这话时是 1870 年，正当普法战争的时候。 **settle with** 跟……解决问题；跟……清算。

2 **one of these fine days** 总有一天；这是习语。

3 **write them down** 把它们（这些事情）写下来。

4 **make a book of them** 把它们（这些事情）写成一本书。

5 **at Mrs. Wickett's** 在 Wickett 夫人的家（Chips 退休后寄寓她家，见第一章。）

6 **went even so far as to make desultory** ['desəltərɪ] **notes** 甚至记起零星的笔记来。 **went so far as**（后接不定式）做到……地步。

7 **was soon brought up against difficulties** 不久遇到了困难。

8 **the chief one being that writing tired him** 主要的困难是写作使他疲劳。这是个独立结构。one = difficulty.

9 **his recollections** [ˌrekə'lekʃənz] **lost much of their flavour** 他的回忆失去了好多（原有的）味儿（即大为减色）。

10 **that story about Rushton** ['rʌʃtən] **and the sack of potatoes, for instance — it would seem quite tame in print** 例如 Rushton 和那袋土豆的故事——（写成文字）印出来就会变得平淡无味。it 和 that story 可认为是同位语，否则这个 it 是多余的。

11 **Lord** 上帝；天哪；这里有感叹词的作用，没有具体意义。

12 **at the time** 在当时

13 **if you didn't remember Rushton ...** 假如你不记得 Rushton 的话（那也就没有什么有趣了）；后半句不写出来，是含蓄的写法；而且这样使下面一句 who would（remember him）接得更紧凑。

14 **Before your time** 在你（Mrs. Wickett）到 Brookfield 学校工作之前。承接上文 it was such a long time ago. = It was before your time.

15 **I dare say** 我看；大概；这是习语，并不真存在敢说不敢说的问题。dare say 也作 daresay。

16 **went to Burma in some government job** 为了干政府的某个差事而到缅甸去；作为公职人员去缅甸。went 前省略 he。

17 **Borneo** ['bɔːnɪəʊ] 婆罗洲（加里曼丹的旧称）

18 **very funny fellow, Rushton** = Rushton was a very funny fellow.

19 **dreaming again before the fire** 又在火炉前梦想着。

dreaming of times[1] and incidents in which he alone could take secret interest[2]. Funny and sad, comic and tragic[3], they[4] all mixed up in his mind, and some day[5], however hard it proved[6], he *would* sort them out and make a book of them[7]...

1 **times** 时期；时代

2 **he alone could take secret interest** 只有他能暗自感到其中妙趣。（别人都不知道。）

3 **Funny and sad, comic and tragic** 修饰后面的 they。

4 **they** 指 times 和 incidents。

5 **some day** 总有一天

6 **however hard it proved** 无论它被证实如何困难。it 所指的是下面"sort them out and make a book of it"这件事。

7 **he *would* sort them out and make a book of them** 他一定要把它们（times 和 incidents）整理出来，写成一本书。（这只是 Chips 的一个想法。）

第八章

内容提要

1898 年 4 月 1 日，凯瑟琳和初生的婴儿在同一天死去。

契普斯悲痛欲绝，神思恍惚。

学生向他请假，说要去车站接他家里的人。契普斯糊里糊涂，尽是“好，好”，只差没有说：“你见鬼去也好。”

他照样上课。讲台上有一叠给他的信，拆开来看，全是白纸。他也莫名其妙。过了几天，他才明白，原来那天是愚人节，——同学们还在跟他开玩笑。

8

And there was always in his mind that spring day in ninety-eight[1] when he had paced through Brookfield village as in some horrifying nightmare[2], half struggling to escape into an outside world[3] where the sun still shone[4] and where everything had happened differently. Young Faulkner[5] had met him there[6] in the lane outside the School. 'Please, sir, may I have the afternoon off?[7] My people are coming up.[8]'

'Eh?[9] What's that?[10] Oh, yes, yes…'

'Can I miss Chapel[11], too, sir?'

'Yes ... yes ...'

'And can I go to the station to meet[12] them?'

He nearly answered: 'You can go to blazes for all I care[13]. My wife is dead and my child is dead, and I wish I were dead myself[14].'

1 **ninety-eight** 1898 年

2 **he had paced through Brookfield village as in some horrifying nightmare** 他像在什么可怕的梦魇里那样，一步步走遍了整个 Brookfield 村。

3 **half struggling to escape into an outside world** 多少挣扎着想逃往一个外在的世界（挣脱梦魇）。 **half** 相当地；有几分；是副词，修饰 struggling。

4 **where the sun still shone** 那儿（外在世界）太阳依旧照耀着。（Chips 丧妻丧子，如在痛苦的梦魇中，而周围世界依旧像在 Katherine 在世时一样欢乐。）

5 **Faulkner** ['fɔːknə] 福克纳，姓氏

6 **there** 指在 Chips 独步其间的 Brookfield 村里。

7 **Please, sir, may I have the afternoon off?** 请问，先生，我（今天）下午可以请假吗？这里的 Please 是招呼语。

8 **My people are coming up.** 我家里的人要来。**people** 亲人（尤指父母）；是口语。 **are coming up** 将到来；现在进行时表示将来。

9 **Eh** [eɪ]**?** 嗯？表示疑问等。

10 **What's that?** 是怎么回事？

11 **Can I miss Chapel** ['tʃæpəl] 赶不上做礼拜行吗？ can 在这里不表示有无能力，而表示可否这样做，等于 may，在征求意见或提出请求时常用。 **Chapel** 原指（学校等的）教堂，这里指在学校的教堂里做礼拜，等于是一堂课。

12 **meet** 迎接

13 **You can go to blazes for all I care** 你要到地狱去也可以，反正不关我的事；随便你要怎样就怎样。（Chips 伤心至极，所以说话如此。blaze 原是“火焰”的意思；blazes 指地狱，因为《圣经》上说地狱里有硫磺火。）

14 **I wish I were dead myself** 但愿我自己死了。（这是 Chips 的伤心话。）

Actually he nodded[1] and stumbled on[2]. He did not want to talk to anybody or to receive condolences[3]; he wanted to get used to things, if he could, before facing the kind words of others[4]. He took his fourth form[5] as usual[6] after call-over, setting them grammar to learn by heart[7] while he himself stayed at his desk in a cold, continuing trance[8]. Suddenly someone said: 'Please, sir, there are a lot of letters for you.[9]'

So there were[10]; he had been leaning his elbows on them[11]; they were all addressed to him by name[12]. He tore them open one after the other[13], but each contained nothing but a blank sheet of paper. He thought in a distant way[14] that it[15] was rather peculiar, but he made no comment[16]; the incident gave hardly an impact upon his vastly greater preoccupations[17]. Not till days afterwards did he realize[18] that it had been a piece of April foolery[19].

They had died on the same day, the mother and the child just born[20]; on April 1st, 1898.

---

1 **Actually he nodded** 他竟然点点头。

2 **stumbled on** 蹒跚前行（描写他神志恍惚）

3 **receive condolences** [kən'dəʊlənsɪz] 接受吊慰。这里必须用复数式 condo-

lences。

4 **he wanted to get used to things, if he could, before facing the kind words of others** 如果他能够的话，他要在习惯了（突然丧妻丧子的）情况之后，才去接受别人的安慰话。 **get used to** 渐渐习惯于……，开始适应。**if he could** = if he could get used to things before facing the kind words of others，是插入的条件从句。

5 **took his fourth form** 主持他的四年级（的预备课，即第一章所讲的 prep）。

6 **as usual** 照常；是习语。

7 **setting them grammar to learn by heart** 规定他们（学生们）要记牢的语法。**learn by heart** 记牢。

8 **in a cold, continuing trance** [trɑːns] 在冷漠的、持续的出神状态中。

9 **Please, sir, there are a lot of letters for you.** 请看，先生，这里有许多给你的信。Please 是招呼语。

10 **So there were** = There were a lot of letters for him.

11 **leaning his elbows** ['elbəʊz] **on them** 把臂肘搁在这些信上面。

12 **addressed to him by name** 指名写给他。

13 **one after the other = one after another** 一封接一封地

14 **thought in a distant way** 漠然想道

15 **it** 这件事（指收到空白纸的信）

16 **made no comment** ['kɒmənt] 不加评论；不说什么

17 **the incident gave hardly an impact upon his vastly greater preoccupations** 这件小事（指收到空白纸的信）对于萦绕在他心头的大得多的事几乎没有影响。

18 **Not till days afterwards did he realize** = He did not realize till days afterwards 几天之后他才了解。 **Not till** 不……直到……；直到……才……。这个句子句首用否定的状语短语，故主谓语倒装。

19 **a piece of April foolery** 愚人节开的一个玩笑。（西方风俗，4 月 1 日为愚人节——April Fools' Day，或称 All Fools' Day，在这一天可以任意愚弄他人。）

20 **They had died on the same day, the mother and the child just born** 母亲和刚生下来的孩子在同一天死去。the mother and the child 是 They 的同位语；just born 修饰 child。

第九章

内容提要

契普斯变了，变老了。但是他说：“霍尔斯伯里八十二岁当财务大臣，活到了九十九岁。我只五十岁，还是个娃娃呢。”

他在学校里的威望渐高。他有些逐步定型的近于怪诞的生活习惯和癖性，学校里也能容忍。甚至首相劳埃·乔治来校，他也倚老卖老地对他说：“我记得你年轻时候是怎样的，现在可进步了。”校长在旁，愕然不知所措，但首相只是哈哈大笑，丝毫不以为意。

他每天晚饭后点名。学生在操场上排成长队，契普斯站在木凳上，呼唤一个个名字，连缀起来，像在唱歌，又像在朗诵诗句。同学们最喜欢学他点名时的这副腔调。

9

Chips changed his more commodious apartments in School House for his old original bachelor quarters[1]. He thought at first he would give up his housemastership[2], but the Head persuaded him otherwise[3]; and later he was glad. The work gave him something to do, filled up an emptiness in his mind and heart[4]. He was different[5]; everyone noticed it. Just as marriage had added something, so did bereavement[6]; after the first stupor of grief[7] he became suddenly the kind of man whom boys, at any rate, unhesitatingly classed as 'old'[8]. It was not that he was less active[9] — he could still knock up a half century on the cricket field[10]; nor was it that[11] he had lost any interest or keenness[12] in his work. Actually, too, his hair had been greying for years[13]; yet now, for the first time[14], people seemed to notice it[15]. He was fifty. Once, after some energetic fives[16],

1 **changed his more commodious** [kə'məʊdjəs] **apartments in School House for his old original bachelor quarters** 从他在学校（的主要）大楼里较宽敞舒适的公寓，搬到他原先的旧独身宿舍里。 **changed ... for ...** 用……掉换……；这里掉换房子，即搬家。 **apartments** 在英国 apartment 指一间房间，apartments（复数）指一套公寓，即一个 flat；在美国 apartment（单数）就指一套公寓。

2 **give up his housemastership** 辞去他舍监的职务。

3 **persuaded him otherwise** 劝服他改变想法，即终于不再请辞舍监职务。

4 **filled up an emptiness in his mind and heart** 填补他心灵上的空虚。mind 偏重理性，heart 偏重感情。

5 **He was different** 他变了样了。

6 **Just as marriage had added something, so did bereavement** [bɪ'ri:vmənt] 正像以前结婚（给他）增添了些什么，现在丧偶也是这样（也给他增添了些什么）；见下文自明。 as ..., so ... 是"正像……，……"的意思，如：As she likes popular fiction, so he likes poetry. 是"他喜欢诗，正像她喜欢通俗小说一样"的意思，不是讲因果关系。

7 **after the first stupor** ['stju:pə] **of grief** 经过因忧伤而产生的开始一段时间的麻木之后。

8 **unhesitatingly classed as 'old'** 毫不犹豫地列为"老"的一类。 **classed** 这里是及物动词，= classified，它的宾语是 whom。

9 **It was not that he was less active** 并不是说他没有过去那样活跃。 **It was not that ...** 是一种惯用句型，表示"这并不是说"、"并非"。

10 **knock up a half century on the cricket field** 在板球场上打上五十分。板球戏计分，a century = a hundred runs。 **knock up**（板球）得（分）。

11 **nor was it that ...** = it was not either that ... 也并非……

12 **keenness** ['ki:nnɪs] 热心

13 **his hair had been greying for years** 几年来他的头发已愈发灰白。

14 **for the first time** 第一次，刚才

15 **notice it** 注意到这一点。这里 it 不是具体指 hair，而是指"头发灰白了"这一现象。

16 **after some energetic** [ˌenə'dʒetɪk] **fives** [faɪvz] 打一阵手球以后。 **fives** 英国手球的一种。

during which he had played as well as many a fellow half his age[1], he overheard[2] a boy saying: 'Not half bad for an old chap like him.[3]'

Chips, when he was over eighty, used to recount[4] that incident with many chuckles. 'Old at fifty, eh?[5] Umph — it was Naylor who said that[6], and Naylor can't be far short of fifty[7] himself by now[8]! I wonder if he still thinks that fifty's such an age?[9] Last I heard of him[10] he was lawyering[11], and lawyers live long — look at Halsbury[12] — umph — Chancellor at eighty-two[13], and died at ninety-nine. There's an — umph — age for you![14] Too old at fifty — why, fellows like that are too *young* at fifty[15] ... I was myself ... a mere infant[16]...'

And there was a sense in which it was true.[17] For with the new century[18] there settled upon Chips a mellowness[19]

---

1 **played as well as a fellow half his age**（打球）打得同比他年纪小一半的人一样好。这里 as well as 照字面作“同……一样好”解；与习语 as well as（作“除……之外”解）不同，比较：He is interested in literature as well as linguistics。他既喜爱语言学，又喜爱文学。**a fellow half his age** = a fellow of half his age 这个 of 常省去。

2 **overheard** 无意中听到

3 **Not half bad for an old chap like him.** = It is not half bad .... **not half bad** 一点也不差；not half原是“不到一半”的意思，引申出去，作“一点也不”解。**for**

对……来说，就……而论。 **chap** 家伙；是口语。

4 **recount** [rɪ'kaʊnt] 详细叙述

5 **Old at fifty, eh?** = Is it old at fifty? 五十岁算老吗?

6 **it was Naylor** ['neɪlə] **who said that** 这是 Naylor said that 的强调式，强调是 Naylor 说的。 **that** 指上文 Chips 听见有人说 "Not half bad for an old chap like him."

7 **can't be far short of fifty** 不可能离五十岁很远。can't 不是 "不能够"，而是 "不可能"，"决不" 的意思。 **short of** 不足；不到。

8 **by now** 到现在（为止）

9 **I wonder if he still thinks that fifty's such an age?** 我不知道他现在还以为五十岁是那样的年龄（指上述的 "老年"）吗? 有 "现在他大概不以为五十岁是老年了吧" 的含意。**if** = whether. **fifty's** = fifty is. 全句原是陈述句，但因有疑问口气，所以句末用疑问号。

10 **Last I heard of him** = Last time I heard of him，也就是 When I last I heard of him 的意思。**hear of** 是 "听到关于……的话"，与 hear（听见）不同。

11 **lawyering** ['lɔːjərɪŋ] 当律师（lawyer）

12 **Halsbury** ['hɔːlzbərɪ] 霍尔斯伯里，指 1st Earl of Halsbury。即 Hardinge Stanley Giffard ['dʒɪfəd]（1823—1921），英国政治家兼法学家。

13 **Chancellor** ['tʃɑːnsələ] **at eighty-two** = was Chancellor at eighty-two 八十二岁任大法官。

14 **There's an — umph — age for you!** 你还有得活哩!

15 **Too old at fifty — why, fellows like that are too *young* at fifty**（说什么）五十岁太老——嗨，像他（Halsbury）那些人五十岁还太年轻呢! **like that** 像上面所说的那样（的），是习语，既可作定语，也可作状语；这里作定语。

16 **I was myself ... a mere infant.** 我当时（五十岁的时候）还只是个婴儿呢。

17 **And there was a sense in which it was true.** = In a sense it was true. 从某种意义上说，（Chips 说的）这话也是真的。

18 **with the new century** 随着新世纪（这里指 20 世纪）的到来。

19 **there settled upon Chips a mellowness** = A mellowness settled upon Chips 一种成熟在 Chips 身上稳定下来；Chips 有了某种成熟。主语 mellowness 因后接较长的定语从句，需移置在谓语后面，于是要求在句首用虚词 there。

that gathered all his developing mannerisms and his oft-repeated jokes into a single harmony[1]. No longer did he have[2] those slight and occasional disciplinary troubles[3], or feel diffident about[4] his own work and worth. He found that his pride in Brookfield reflected back[5], giving him cause for[6] pride in himself and his position. It was a service that gave him freedom to be supremely and completely himself.[7] He had won, by seniority and ripeness[8], an uncharted no-man's-land of privilege[9]; he had acquired the right to those gentle eccentricities that so often attack schoolmasters and parsons[10]. He wore his gown[11] till it was almost too tattered to hold together[12]; and when he stood on the wooden bench by Big Hall steps[13] to take call-over[14], it was with an air of mystic abandonment to ritual[15]. He held the School List[16], a long sheet curling over a board[17]; and each boy, as he passed, spoke his own name[18] for Chips to verify[19] and then tick off on the list[20]. That verify-

---

1 **gathered all his developing mannerisms and his oft-repeated jokes into a single harmony** 把所有他正在形成的种种癖性和他经常重复讲述的笑话融合成单一的和谐（即浑然一体，所以说是“成熟”）。

2 **No longer did he have** = He no longer had. 为突出否定状语短语 No longer，所以把它放在句首，于是要求主谓倒装。

3 **disciplinary** ['dɪsɪplɪnərɪ] **troubles** 维持课堂纪律的困难

4 **feel diffident** ['dɪfɪdənt] **about** 对于……觉得缺乏自信

5 **his pride in Brookfield reflected back** 他对 Brookfield 感到的骄傲反射回来；即 Brookfield 也反过来对他感到骄傲。注意 pride 后接 in。

6 **giving him cause for** 给他……的原因（或理由）。注意 cause 前没有 a。

7 **It was a service that gave him freedom to be supremely and completely himself.** 在此任职使他可以极度地、完全地自由自在。**be oneself** 处于正常状态；真诚自然；是习语。注意 freedom 后接不定式。

8 **by seniority** [ˌsiːnɪ'ɒrɪtɪ] **and ripeness** 凭着年老和成熟；是插入的状语从句，修饰 had won。

9 **an uncharted no-man's-land of privilege** ['prɪvɪlɪdʒ] 不受限制的特权。**no-man's-land** 原义为荒地；无主土地；真空地带。**uncharted no-man's-land** 没有测绘过或作出过任何标志的无人之境，这里用以喻特权的不受限制。privilege 在这里是不可数名词。

10 **had acquired the right to those gentle eccentricities** [ˌeksen'trɪsɪtɪz] **that so often attack schoolmasters and parsons** 已经有权可以有那些教师和牧师常患的文雅的怪癖。注意：right（权利）后接介词 to。

11 **gown** [gaʊn]（教师穿的）长外衣

12 **too tattered to hold together** 破烂不堪到不能连成一体（成为一件衣裳）的地步；衣衫褴褛。

13 **by Big Hall steps** 在大礼堂的台阶旁边

14 **take call-over** 点名

15 **with an air of mystic abandonment to ritual** ['rɪtjʊəl] 带着一种神往于仪式的神秘色彩。

16 **School List** 全校的学生名单

17 **a long sheet curling over a board** 在一块板的上面卷过去的长长的一张纸（与 School List 同位）

18 **as he passed, spoke his own name** 每个学生在（依次）经过（Chips 面前）时，报出自己的名字。he 和 his 都指 boy。

19 **verify** ['verɪfaɪ] 核实

20 **tick off on the list** 在名单上用记号勾出。

ing glance[1] was an easy and favourite subject of mimicry[2] throughout the School — steel-rimmed spectacles slipping down the nose[3], eyebrows lifted[4], one a little higher than the other[5], a gaze half rapt, half quizzical[6]. And on windy days with gown and white hair and School List[7] fluttering in uproarious confusion[8], the whole thing became a comic turn sandwiched between afternoon games and the return to classes[9].

Some of those names, in little snatches of a chorus[10], recurred to him ever afterwards[11] without any effort of memory. '… Ainsworth, Attwood, Avonmore, Babcock, Baggs, Barnard, Bassenthwaite, Battersby, Beccles, Bedford-Marshall, Bentley, Best[12]…'

Another one[13]:

'… Unsley, Vailes, Wadham, Wagstaff, Wallington, Waters Primus, Waters Secundus, Watling, Waveney, Webb[14]...'

And yet another[15] that comprised, as he used to tell his fourth-form Latinists, an excellent example of a hex-

1 **verifying glance** 进行核实的一瞥

2 **an easy and favourite subject of mimicry** ['mɪmɪkrɪ] 一个容易模仿且备受欢迎的事物（指这一动作）

3 **steel-rimmed spectacles slipping down the nose** 钢丝边眼镜滑落在鼻梁上。这是独立结构。

4 **eyebrows lifted** = eyebrows being lifted 眉毛竖起。

5 **one a little higher than the other** = one eyebrow being lifted a little higher than the other eyebrow 一条眉毛比另一条眉毛抬得高一些。

6 **a gaze half rapt** [ræpt], **half quizzical** ['kwɪzɪkəl] 注视的目光半似得意，半似疑惑。疑惑的当是有没有名字搅错或人非其名。

7 **with gown and white hair and School List** gown 和 School List 是可数名词，照理单数的可数名词前面应有冠词或其他指定词，但在两个以上的单数名词并列时，冠词可省略。

8 **fluttering in uproarious** [ʌp'rɔːrɪəs] **confusion** [kən'fjuːʒən] 胡乱地飘舞。

9 **the whole thing became a comic turn sandwiched between afternoon games and the return to classes** 整件事（指点名）成为插在下午游戏和回到教室上课之间的喜剧性的节目。 **sandwich** 原是名词，动词作“夹”解。

10 **in little snatches of a chorus** ['kɔːrəs] 像断断续续的合唱的小片段。

11 **ever afterwards**（自从点名那时起）以后一直……

12 **Ainsworth** ['aɪnzwɜːθ], **Attwood** ['ætwʊd], **Avonmore** ['eɪvənmɔː], **Babcock** ['bæbkɒk], **Baggs** [bægz], **Barnard** ['bɑːnəd], **Bassenthwaite** ['bæsənθweɪt], **Battersby** ['bætəzbɪ], **Beccles** ['beklz], **Bedford-Marshall** ['bedfəd'mɑːʃəl], **Bentley** ['bentlɪ], **Best** [best] 都是被点到名的学生的姓。

13 **Another one** = Another snatch of a chorus 被点到名的另一连串学生的姓。

14 **Unsley** ['ʌnzlɪ], **Vailes** [veɪlz], **Wadham** ['wɒdəm], **Wagstaff** ['wægstɑːf], **Wallington** ['wɒlɪŋtən], **Waters** ['wɔːtəz] **Primus** ['praɪməs], **Waters Secundus** [sɪ'kʌndəs], **Watling** ['wɒtlɪŋ], **Waveney** ['weɪvnɪ], **Webb** [web] 学生的姓。**Primus**（男校中）同姓学生年龄最大或在校时间最长的；**Secundus** 年龄或在校时间次于 Primus 的，第二。

15 **And yet another** 再有另一连串学生的姓。

ameter[1]:

'... Lancaster, Latton, Lemare, Lytton-Bosworth, MacGonigall, Mansfield[2]...'

Where had they all gone to[3], he often pondered; those threads he had once held together, how far had they scattered, some to break, others to weave into unknown patterns[4]? The strange randomness of the world beguiled him[5], that randomness which never would, so long as the world lasted, give meaning to those choruses again[6].

And behind Brookfield[7], as one may glimpse a mountain behind another mountain when the mist clears, he saw the world of change and conflict; and he saw it, more than he realized, with the remembered eyes of Kathie[8]. She had not been able to bequeath him all her mind[9], still less the brilliance of it[10]; but she had left him with a calmness[11] and a poise[12] that accorded well with his own inward

---

1 **comprised, as he used to tell his fourth-form Latinists, an excellent example of a hexameter** [hek'sæmɪtə] 有如他常对四年级拉丁语学生们说的，构成一个极好的六音步诗行的例子。 **hexameter** 由六个（扬抑抑格的）音步组成的诗行。Latinists 原是"拉丁语学家"，这里指拉丁语学生，是幽默的说法。

2 **Lancaster** ['læŋkəstə], **Latton** ['lætən], **Lemare** [lə'meə], **Lytton-Bosworth**

['lɪtn'bɒzwə(:)θ], **MacGonigall** [mak'gɒnɪgɔ:l], **Mansfield** ['mænsfi:ld] 都是学生的姓。

3 **Where had they all gone to** = Where had they all gone to? 是接后面 pondered 的宾语从句。照理，作为间接引语应作 Where they had all gone to。

4 **those threads** [θredz] **he had once held together, how far had they scattered, some to break, others to weave into unknown patterns** 这一段也是 pondered 的内容；how far had they scattered 是 pondered 的宾语从句，those threads (that) he had once held together 是 they 的同位语；some 和 others = some threads 和 other threads，分别是表示结果的不定式 to break 和不定式短语 to weave into unknown patterns 的逻辑上的主语。全段的意思是：他曾经握在一起的那一根根的线（比喻学生），都四散得多么远，有的断掉，有的织成不知什么图案。

5 **The strange randomness of the world beguiled him** 世事的奇异的偶然性使他觉得有趣。

6 **that randomness which never would, so long as the world lasted, give meaning to those choruses again** 将永世不再赋予那些合唱（指点名时呼叫一连串一连串的名字）以意义的那种偶然性；因世事无常，这些名字永世不再有什么意义。 **so long as the world lasted** 只要世界存在，永远……；是插入的状语从句。

7 **behind Brookfield** 修饰 he saw 的 saw，被 as 引起的也是修饰 saw 的状语从句隔开了。

8 **he saw it, more than he realized, with the remembered eyes of Kathie** 他是用记忆中的 Katherine 眼睛来看这个（在变化和冲突的世界）的，这一点他并没有充分意识到。

9 **bequeath him all her mind** 把她所有的思想传给他。

10 **still less the brilliance of it = still less had she been able to bequeath him the brilliance of her mind. still less ...** 更不能说……；更谈不上……

11 **left him with a calmness** ['kɑ:mnɪs] 传给他一种宁静。注意：这里 left 和上面的 bequeath 同义，但 bequeath 后接双宾语，而 left 后接宾语（继承者）往往再用 with 接介词宾语（遗下的东西）。

12 **poise** [pɔɪz] 平衡；沉着；有“不偏不倚、无过无不及”的意思。

emotions[1]. It was typical of him that he did not share the general jingo bitterness against the Boers.[2] Not that he was a pro-Boer[3] — he was far too traditional for that[4], and he disliked the kind of people who *were* pro-Boers; but still, it did cross his mind at times that[5] the Boers were engaged in a struggle that had a curious similarity to those of certain English history-book heroes[6] — Hereward the Wake[7], for instance, or Caractacus[8]. He once tried to shock his fifth form by suggesting this[9], but they only thought it was one of his little jokes[10].

However heretical he might be[11] about the Boers, he was orthodox[12] about Mr. Lloyd George[13] and the famous Budget[14]. He did not care for either of them[15]. And when, years later, L. G.[16] came as the guest of honour[17] to a Brookfield Speech Day, Chips said, on being presented to him[18]: 'Mr. Lloyd George, I am nearly old enough — umph — to remember you as a young man[19], and — umph — I

---

1 **accorded well with his own inward emotions** 同他自己内在的情感很协调。

2 **It was typical** [ˈtɪpɪkəl] **of him that he did not share the general jingo bitterness against the Boers.** 他对布尔人没有一般人的狂热好战的狠毒，这是他的特点。注意：typical 后接 of，与 It's very kind *of* you. 同例。布尔战争见第 63 页注释 17。

3 **pro-Boar** 亲布尔分子

4 **he was far too traditional for that** 他的传统思想很深，因而不可能那样（即不可能是亲布尔分子）。

5 **it did cross his mind at times that ...** 有时确实想到……。 **cross his mind** 在他脑海里闪过。

6 **were engaged in a struggle that had a curious similarity** [ˌsɪmɪˈlærɪtɪ] **to those of certain English history-book heroes** 进行着同某些英国历史书中英雄们的斗争有奇妙的相似之处的斗争。similarity 后介词用 to，与 similar 后用 to 同。those = the struggles.

7 **Hereward** [ˈherɪwəd] **the Wake** 英国历史上的传奇人物，曾于 1070 年在 Ely [ˈiːlɪ] 岛率众起义，反抗征服英国的诺曼底公爵威廉一世。

8 **Caractacus** [kəˈræktəkəs] 古代不列颠西部 Silures [ˈsɪljʊriːz] 部落的王，抗击罗马入侵，于公元 51 年被罗马人所俘。

9 **suggesting this** 提出这个说法（说布尔人的斗争与英国历史英雄的斗争有相似之处）。

10 **they only thought it was one of his little jokes** = they thought it was only one of his little jokes.

11 **However heretical** [hɪˈretɪkəl] **he might be** 无论他怎样持有异端的立场。

12 **orthodox** [ˈɔːθədɒks] 正统的

13 **Lloyd** [lɔɪd] **George** [dʒɔːdʒ] 劳埃 · 乔治（David Lloyd George, 1863—1945，英国自由党领袖，1916—1922任首相）

14 **the famous Budget** [ˈbʌdʒɪt] 著名的预算案，指劳埃 · 乔治任英国财政大臣时提出的1909年预算案，其中包括按土地价值征税、矿山专利权税和所得税特别附加税，曾引起激烈争论。

15 **did not care for either of them** 对 Lloyd George 和 the famous Budget 两者都不感兴趣。

16 **L. G.** = Lloyd George

17 **guest of honour** 主宾

18 **on being presented** [prɪˈzentɪd] **to him** 在（Chips）被介绍给他（Lloyd George）时。

19 **old enough — umph — to remember you as a young man** 老得足以记得你还是小伙子时候的情况。（这话和下面一句话显然 Chips 是倚老卖老，尽管是对首相说话也无所讳忌。）

confess that you seem to me — umph — to have improved — umph — a great deal[1].' The Head, standing with them, was rather aghast[2]; but L. G. laughed heartily[3] and talked to Chips more than to anyone else[4] during the ceremonial that followed[5].

'Just like Chips[6],' was commented[7] afterwards. 'He gets away with it[8]. I suppose at that age anything you say to anybody is all right.[9]...'

1 **I confess that you seem to me — umph — to have improved — umph — a great deal** 我承认，在我看来你似乎已经大大进步了。 **a great deal** 状语短语，修饰 to have improved。

2 **aghast** [ə'gɑːst] 吓呆的；常作表语。

3 **laughed heartily** 畅怀大笑

4 **talked to Chips more than to anyone else** = talked to Chips more than he talked to anyone else. **more** 这里是副词，修饰 talked。

5 **ceremonial** [ˌserɪ'məʊnjəl] **that followed** 随后举行的仪式（这里指那天 Speech Day 授奖仪式）。

6 **Just like Chips** = That's just like Chips. Chips 就是那个样子。

7 **commented** 议论。comment 无论作动词还是名词用均读作 ['kɒment]。

8 **gets away with it** 做坏事（或错事）而不受处分，这是习语，这里指 Chips 对首相倚老卖老全无问题。

9 **I suppose at that age anything you say to anybody is all right.** 我看，到（Chips）那年纪，你对任何人说任何话都没问题。**you** 泛指"任何人"。

第十章

内容提要

1900年，老校长梅尔德伦去世，契普斯一度代理校长，后罗尔斯顿被正式聘任为校长。罗尔斯顿年轻、能干，但盛气凌人，契普斯不喜欢这样的人。

1910年，英王爱德华七世逝世。爱德华王朝的十年间，英国社会动荡。布鲁克菲尔德附近铁路工人罢工。布鲁克菲尔德的学生在铁路沿线巡逻。契普斯同罢工工人谈起话来，且似甚欢洽，一时在学校里传为新闻。契普斯想，倘凯瑟琳活着，她一定会赞成他这样做的。他对英国还有信心，不过他看到英国的安逸日子已经过去了。

1912年“泰坦尼克号”邮轮沉没。契普斯为他学生格雷森的父亲幸免于难而为格雷森庆幸。不料后来他反而得向格雷森的父亲吊唁格雷森的阵亡。

10

In 1900[1] old Meldrum[2], who had succeeded Wetherby as Head[3] and had held office[4] for three decades[5], died suddenly from pneumonia[6]; and in the interval before the appointment of a successor[7], Chips became Acting Head[8] of Brookfield. There was just the faintest chance[9] that the Governors might make the appointment a permanent one[10]; but Chips was not really disappointed when they brought in a mere youngster of thirty-seven[11], glittering with Firsts and Blues[12] and with the kind of personality[13] that could reduce Big Hall to silence by the mere lifting of an eyebrow[14]. Chips was not in the running with that kind of person[15]; he never had been and never would be[16], and he knew it[17]. He was an altogether milder and less ferocious animal[18].

Those years before his retirement in 1913 were stud-

1 **1900** 读作 nineteen hundred。

2 **Meldrum** ['meldrəm] 梅尔德伦，姓氏

3 **succeeded Wetherby as Head** 接替 Wetherby 任校长。

4 **held office** 任职；在任

5 **decades** ['dekədz] 几个十年；几十年

6 **died suddenly from pneumonia** [nju(ː)'məʊnjə] 因患肺炎突然去世。“因（某病）而死”也用 die of。

7 **in the interval** ['ɪntəvəl] **before the appointment of a successor**（在 Meldrum 死后）任命接任校长之前的一段间隔时间里。

8 **Acting Head** 代理校长

9 **just the faintest chance** 仅只是最微小的可能性

10 **the Governors might make the appointment a permanent one** Brookfield 校董们可能把这（代理校长的）任命变成永久的任命。

11 **brought in a youngster of thirty-seven** 请来一个三十七岁的青年（任新校长，即后面所讲的 Ralston）。

12 **glittering with Firsts and Blues** 带着光耀夺目的比赛第一名和牛津（或剑桥）大学代表的标志。

13 **personality** [ˌpɜːsə'nælɪtɪ] 个性

14 **could reduce Big Hall to silence by the mere lifting of an eyebrow** 只要竖起一条眉毛就能使整个大礼堂寂然无声。

15 **was not in the running with that kind of person** 不是那种人的对手。 **in the running** 是习语，原是“参加比赛”或“比赛中有取胜希望”的意思，这里是用的转义。

16 **he never had been and never would be** = he never had been in the running with that kind of person and never would be in the running with that kind of person.

17 **he knew it** 他知道这一点。 **it** 指上文 Chips 过去、现在、将来都不是那种人的对手这一点。

18 **He was an altogether milder** ['maɪldə] **and less ferocious** [fə'rəʊʃəs] **animal** 他（Chips）全然是个比 Ralston 温和、不像 Ralston 那么凶狠的人。 **animal**（有野性的）人。

ded with sharply remembered pictures[1].

A May morning; the clang of the School bell at an unaccustomed time[2]; everyone summoned to assemble in Big Hall[3]. Ralston[4], the new Head, very pontifical and aware of himself[5], fixing the multitude with a cold presaging severity[6]. 'You will all be deeply grieved to hear that His Majesty King Edward the Seventh[7] died this morning. ... There will be no school this afternoon[8], but a service will be held[9] in the Chapel[10] at four-thirty.'

A summer morning on the railway line[11] near Brookfield. The railwaymen were on strike[12], soldiers were driving the engines[13], stones had been thrown at trains. Brookfield boys were patrolling the line[14], thinking the whole business great fun[15]. Chips, who was in charge[16], stood a little way off[17], talking to a man at the gate of a cottage[18]. Young Cricklade[19] approached. 'Please, sir, what shall we do if we meet any strikers?[20]'

'Would you like to meet one[21]?'

'I — I don't know, sir.'

1 **were studded with sharply remembered pictures** 满是记得清清楚楚的景象。 **stud** 原是名词,指装饰在大门或皮件上的饰钉,用作动词,由"装饰钉"转义为 "点缀"、"散布"。

2 **at an unaccustomed time** 在不是平常(敲钟)的时间

3 **everyone summoned to assemble in Big Hall** 每个人都被召集到大礼堂集合。这是名词句,同上面 A May morning 和 the clang of the School bell 一样;summoned 是过去分词,修饰 everyone。

4 **Ralston** ['rɔːlstən] 罗尔斯顿,姓氏,即第一段所讲的 "37 岁的青年"。

5 **very pontifical** [pɒn'tɪfikəl] **and aware of himself** 非常傲慢,深知自己(处于校长)的地位。

6 **fixing the multitude with a cold, presaging** ['presɪdʒɪŋ] **severity** [sɪ'verɪtɪ] 用冷冷的、预示了什么的严肃神态凝视全场的人。

7 **His Majesty** ['mædʒɪstɪ] **King Edward** ['edwəd] **the Seventh** 英王爱德华七世陛下(1901—1910 在位)

8 **There will be no school this afternoon** 今天下午不上课。

9 **a service will be held** 将举行礼拜仪式。

10 **Chapel** ['tʃæpəl](学校等附属的)小教堂

11 **on the railway line** 在铁路线上

12 **on strike** 在罢工。在美国,也说 on a strike。

13 **driving the engines** ['en*d*ʒɪnz] 驾驶机车

14 **patrolling** [pə'trəulɪŋ] **the line** 在这条铁路线上巡逻。

15 **thinking the whole business great fun** 认为整件事(罢工和巡逻)十分有趣。business 这里作 "事情" 解。

16 **was in charge** 主管

17 **stood a little way off** 站在不远的地方。

18 **at the gate of a cottage** 在村舍的大门口。gate 当是指村舍的篱笆或围墙的大门,而不是指村舍本身的门。

19 **Cricklade** ['krɪkleɪd] 克里克雷德,一个学生的姓

20 **Please, sir, what shall we do if we meet any strikers?** 请问,先生,假如我们碰到罢工工人怎么办? **Please** 在这里是招呼语。

21 **one** = a striker

God bless the boy[1] — he talked of them as if they were queer animals out of a zoo[2]! 'Well, here you are[3] then — umph — you can meet Mr. Jones[4] — he's a striker. When he's on duty[5] he has charge of the signal box at the station[6]. You've put your life in his hands many a time.[7]'

Afterwards the story went round the School[8]: There was Chips, talking to a striker.[9] Talking to a striker.[10] Might have been quite friendly, the way they were talking together.[11]

Chips, thinking it over[12] a good many times[13], always added to himself[14] that Kathie would have approved, and would also have been amused[15].

Because always[16], whatever happened and however the avenues of politics twisted and curved, he had faith in England, in English flesh and blood, and in Brookfield[17] as a place whose ultimate worth depended on whether she

---

1 **God bless the boy** 愿上帝保佑这孩子；实际上并不一定是认真的祝福，只是一种口头禅，有"可怜这孩子"、"啊呀"等感叹的意思。bless 是虚拟语气。

2 **talked of them as if they were queer animals out of a zoo** 讲到他们（罢工工人）的时候，仿佛他们是动物园里逃出来的什么怪兽。

3 **Well, here you are** 嗯，这里就有（一个罢工工人）。Well 是语气助词，口

语中常用。

4 **you can meet Mr. Jones** [dʒəʊnz] 你得见见 Jones 先生。 **can** 在这里同 may 一样，并没有能不能够的意思。

5 **on duty** 值勤；在班上

6 **has charge of the signal box at the station** 管理车站上的信号所；也可解释作：在车站上管理信号所；因为，这里 at the station 作为定语短语修饰 signal box 和作为状语短语修饰 has charge 都讲得通。

7 **You've put your life in his hands many a time.** 你曾多次把生命交在他手中。他管铁路信号，为旅客安危所系，所以说生命在他手中。**many a** 许多；被它修饰的名词用单数。

8 **the story went round the School** 这件事传遍全校。 **story** 不单指"故事"，这里是指 Chips 和罢工工人交谈的"新闻"。

9 **There was Chips, talking to a striker.** = Chips was talking to a striker. 用了虚词 There 引起的 There was Chips, ... 的句型，有"有 Chips 这样的人，在跟罢工工人交谈"的意味。

10 **Talking to a striker.** 重复上句的这几个词，表现出人们的惊奇。

11 **Might have been quite friendly, the way they were talking together.** 从他们谈话的情况看，很可能他们十分友好呢。"情态动词 might + 完成不定式"表示对过去的猜测。

12 **thinking it over** 思量（上面所讲的）此事；考虑此事。

13 **a good many times** 许多次

14 **added to himself**（思量后）接着自忖。比较：say to oneself 是"自忖"、"想"的意思。

15 **Kathie would have approved, and would also have been amused** 这是虚拟语气，省去"if she had been living"之类的条件从句。意思是：（假如 Kathie 还活着，）她会赞成（Chips 同罢工工人交谈）的，而且还会感到有趣。

16 **Because always** 接后面 he had faith，中间被 whatever 和 however 引起的两个状语从句隔开。

17 **in English flesh and blood, and in Brookfield** 这两个 in 引起的介词短语与上面 in England 并列，都修饰 had faith，意思是对英国、对英国人、对 Brookfield 都抱有信心。

fitted herself into the English scene with dignity and without disproportion[1]. He had been left a vision[2] that grew clearer with each year[3] — of an England for whom days of ease were nearly over[4], of a nation steering into channels where a hair's breadth of error might be catastrophic[5]. He remembered the Diamond Jubilee[6]; there had been a whole holiday[7] at Brookfield, and he had taken Kathie to London[8] to see the procession[9]. That old and legendary lady[10], sitting in her carriage like some crumbling wooden doll[11], had symbolized impressively so many things that, like herself, were nearing an end[12]. Was it only the century, or was it an epoch?[13]

And then that frenzied Edwardian decade[14], like an electric lamp that goes brighter and whiter just before it

---

1 **as a place whose ultimate** [ʌltɪmɪt] **worth depended on whether she fitted herself into the English scene with dignity and without disproportion**（Chips 对 Brookfield 抱有信心，是把 Brookfield）作为这样一个地方，它的最终价值取决于它是否有尊严地、协调地适应英国这个国家的背景（即国情），成为英国浑然一体的一部分。**depended on** 也作 depended upon，意为“依靠”、“取决于”，这里作后者解。whether 引起的名词性从句，是 depended on 的宾语。 **she** 代替 Brookfield；英语中常用 she 代替国家、船只、小动物等，这里代替 Brookfield，表示亲切。 **disproportion** 不协调；**without disproportion** 没有不协调地，即协调地。

2 **He had been left a vision** ['vɪʒən] 他被留下一个印象；有个印象留存在他脑海里。vision 在这里是保留宾语，被后面一个 that- 从句和两个用 of 引起的介词短语所修饰。

3 **grew clearer with each year** 随着一年年（时光的流逝）而越来越清晰。

4 **for whom days of ease were nearly over** 对它（英国）来说，安逸的日子差不多已经过去了。美国 Little, Brown 版 whom 作 which。

5 **steering into channels where a hair's breadth of error** ['erə] **might be catastrophic** [ˌkætə'strɒfɪk] 驶入稍有错误就将造成大祸的航道。用这个分词短语修饰 nation，是将国家比作船只，说这时候的英国已不能不步步谨慎。hair's breadth 也可写作 **hair(s)breadth** 一发之间；**a hair's breadth of error** 毫厘之差。

6 **the Diamond** ['daɪəmənd] **Jubilee** ['dʒuːbɪliː] 英国维多利亚女王在位六十周年纪念（1897 年）。维多利亚女王生于 1819 年，1837 年即位，至 1901 年去世。**diamond jubilee** 六十周年纪念；有时也指七十五周年纪念。

7 **a whole holiday** 全天放假

8 **taken Kathie to London** 带 Kathie 到伦敦去。

9 **procession** 庆祝行列

10 **That old and legendary** ['ledʒəndərɪ] **lady** 那个年老的传奇式的贵妇人（指维多利亚女王）

11 **crumbling wooden doll** 摇摇欲坠的木偶

12 **symbolized** ['sɪmbəlaɪzd] **impressively so many things that, like herself, were nearing an end** 给人深刻印象地象征了那么多的东西，正像她自己一样，将近末日。

13 **Was it only the century, or was it an epoch** ['iːpɒk]**?** = Was it only the century that was nearing an end, or was it an epoch that was nearing an end? 将近末日的只是这个世纪（即 19 世纪），还是一个时代？；只是本世纪将近末日，还是一个（兴盛的）时代将近末日？

14 **And then that frenzied Edwardian** [ed'wɔːdjən] **decade** 然后是爱德华（七世）时代的狂乱的十年（指 1901—1910）。这个名词词组承接上节 He remembered。Chips 回想到 the Diamond Jubilee，然后又回想到 that frenzied Edwardian decade。

burns itself out[1].

Strikes and lock-outs[2], champagne suppers and unemployed marchers[3], Chinese labour[4], tariff reform[5], H. M. S. *Dreadnought*[6], Marconi[7], Home Rule for Ireland[8], Doctor Crippen[9], suffragettes[10], the lines of Chatalja[11]...

An April evening, windy and rainy; the fourth form construing Virgil[12], not very intelligently[13], for there was exciting news in the papers[14]; young Grayson[15], in particular[16], was careless and preoccupied[17]. A quiet, nervous boy[18].

'Grayson, stay behind — umph — after the rest[19].'

Then[20]:

'Grayson, I don't want to be — umph — severe, because you are generally pretty good — umph — in your work[21], but today — you don't seem — umph — to have

---

1 **goes brighter and whiter just before it burns itself out**（电灯）在正要熄灭之前发出更亮、更白的光。 **burn itself out** 烧尽；熄灭；是习语。

2 **Strikes and lock-outs** 罢工和闭厂（闭厂或停业是资本家威胁工人接受其条件的一种手段）。这一节里用一系列名词词组列举上节所称爱德华时代狂乱的十年间发生的种种。

3 **champagne** [ʃæm'peɪn] **suppers and unemployed marchers** 香槟晚宴和失业工人的游行行列。两者对照，写出一片"朱门酒肉臭，路有冻死骨"的景象。

4 **Chinese labor** 华工（这里指第一次世界大战期间被当时的中国政府派出支援协约国的中国劳工）。

5 **tariff reform** 关税改革；指当时英国反对自由贸易（free trade），要求增加进口税。美国历史上的 tariff reform 正相反，是要求削减进口税，反对保护贸易（protectionism）。

6 **H. M. S.** ***Dreadnought*** ['drednɔːt]（1906 年建成的）英国战舰"无畏号"。**H. M. S. = His**（女王在位时用 **Her**）**Majesty's Ship** 英国船。注意 H. M. S. 中的 H 是代表 His 或 Her，所以前面不可用 the。

7 **Marconi** [mɑː'kəunɪ] Marchese Guglielmo Marconi，马可尼（1874—1937），意大利电机学家，发明无线电报术，获得 1909 年诺贝尔物理学奖。

8 **Home Rule for Ireland** ['aɪələnd]（英国 1870 年左右开始争论的）爱尔兰自治（问题）

9 **Doctor Crippen** ['krɪpən] Hawley Harvey Crippen（1862—1910），克里平，在英国定居的美国医生，谋杀其妻，偕化装成男孩的情妇潜逃，在横渡大西洋途中被捕，于 1910 年在伦敦被处死，轰动一时。

10 **suffragettes** [ˌsʌfrə'dʒets]（英国 20 世纪初）争取妇女参政的女性

11 **the lines of Chatalja** 查特吉的诗行。 **Chatalja** 指印度小说家 Bankim Chandra Chatterji（1838—1894）。所著《阿难陀寺院》（*Anandamāth*）中有一首诗《膜拜母亲》（*Hail to the Mother*），其中有些诗句后来成为印度争取独立的口号。

12 **construing** [kən'struːɪŋ] **Virgil** ['vɜːdʒɪl] 对维吉尔的作品做语法分析和翻译解释。 **Virgil** 也作 Vergil，罗马诗人（公元前 70 — 前 19）。

13 **not very intelligently** [ɪn'telɪdʒəntlɪ] 不大理解地。not very 是委婉的说法。

14 **in the papers** 在报纸上

15 **Grayson** ['greɪsn] 格雷森，一个学生的姓

16 **in particular** [pə'tɪkjʊlə] 尤其

17 **preoccupied** [pri(ː)'ɒkjʊpaɪd] 心事重重的

18 **A quiet and nervous boy**（Grayson 是）文静而胆怯的孩子

19 **stay behind — umph — after the rest** 在其他同学放课后留下来。

20 **Then** 然后；这里当指 Grayson 被留下来后，Chips 跟他谈话。

21 **generally pretty good — umph — in your work** 平时功课总是很好。 **generally** 总的说来；在一般情况下。 **pretty good** 是口语，= very good.

been trying at all[1]. Is anything the matter?[2]'

'N—no[3], sir.'

'Well — umph — we'll say no more about it[4] — but — umph — I shall expect better things next time[5].'

Next morning it was noised around the School that Grayson's father had sailed on the *Titanic*[6], and that no news had yet come through as to his fate[7].

Grayson was excused from lessons[8]; for a whole day the School centred emotionally upon his anxieties[9]. Then came news that[10] his father had been among those rescued[11].

Chips shook hands with[12] the boy. 'Well, umph — I'm delighted, Grayson. A happy ending[13]. You must be feeling pretty pleased with life[14].'

'Y—yes, sir.'

A quiet, nervous boy. And it was Grayson Senior, not Junior, with whom Chips was destined later to condole[15].

---

1 **don't seem — umph — to have been trying at all**（刚才上课时候）似乎根本不在努力（想要做好功课）。**Have been trying** = have been trying to be good.

2 **Is anything the matter?** 有什么事出了毛病了吗？ **the matter** 是习语，有形容词的性质，与 wrong 同义。

3 **N—no** 是说“No”的时候，打了个顿。

4 **say no more about it** 对（这次上课不用心）这件事不再多谈了。

5 **expect better things next time** 希望下回情况好些（即上课时好好用心）。**things** 作“情况”解，用复数式。

6 **it was noised around the School that Grayson's father had sailed on the *Titanic*** [taɪ'tænɪk] Grayson 的父亲在泰坦尼克号船上的消息哄传全校。it 引起两个 that- 从句，除这里一个之外，下面还有一个。**sailed** 乘船旅行。***Titanic*** 泰坦尼克号，英国大客轮，1912 年 4 月首次航行，触冰山沉没，乘客 2200 人，死 1500 余人。

7 **no news had yet come through as to his fate** 还没有关于他（Grayson 的父亲）生死安危的消息传来。**as to** 这里作“关于”解，= about；不作“至于”解。

8 **was excused lessons** 免予上课。lessons 是保留宾语。

9 **centred emotionally upon his anxieties** [æŋ'zaɪətɪz] 情绪激动地关注在他（Grayson）所焦虑的事情上。anxiety 作“焦虑”解时是不可数名词，作“焦虑的事情”解时是可数名词。

10 **Then came news that...** came 和 news 主谓倒装。that ... 是同位语从句。came news that ... 和 news came that ... 中的 news 前不用 the 比用 the 普遍。

11 **among those rescued** 在获救者之列

12 **shook hands with** 同（某人）握手

13 **happy ending** 欢乐的结局；“大团圆”的结尾

14 **feeling pretty pleased with life** 对生活感到非常满意。

15 **it was Grayson Senior** ['siːnjə], **not Junior** ['dʒuːnjə], **with whom Chips was destined later to condole** Chips 后来注定要慰唁的倒是老 Grayson，而不是小 Grayson。老 Grayson 乘泰坦尼克号遇险而获救，小 Grayson 倒死了，所以 Chips 要向老 Grayson 慰唁。全书前后多次讲到 Chips 的同事和学生死于第一次世界大战，小 Grayson 也成了炮灰。英美人往往父子同名，在名姓后分别加 Senior 和 Junior，以示区别；学校等集体有长幼同姓的，也常在姓后加 Senior 和 Junior。**condole** 吊唁；慰问；注意这是不及物动词，在表示被慰唁者的词前面需用介词 with，在表示所以慰唁的事件的词前面用介词（up）on，如 Chips condoled *with* old Grayson *on* the death of his son.

第十一章

内容提要

1908年，校长罗尔斯顿要契普斯退休，嫌他不修边幅，拉丁读音老式。契普斯总是穿件破长袍，学校里的确有人取笑他，但他素不介意。至于拉丁读音，他说他在前任校长在任时就是这样读的，而前任再前任的校长自己就是这样读的。罗尔斯顿说他总是不听指示，若是在年轻教师，这就叫不服从上级。契普斯听了，大发雷霆。而罗尔斯顿还是坚持要他辞职。

全校都支持契普斯，校董会也支持。校董会主席原先是契普斯的学生，他来到学校，对契普斯说："罗尔斯顿得罪了你，我们很遗憾。罗尔斯顿虽然聪明能干，但像这样的人需要随时提防。你尽管留下，我们希望你留到一百岁。"

11

And then the row[1] with Ralston. Funny thing, Chips had never liked him[2]; he was efficient, ruthless, ambitious, but not, somehow, very likeable[3]. He had, admittedly[4], raised the status of Brookfield as a school[5], and for the first time in memory there was a longish waiting list.[6] Ralston was a live wire[7]; a fine power transmitter[8], but you had to beware of him[9].

Chips had never bothered to beware of him[10]; he was not attracted by the man[11], but he served him willingly enough and quite loyally. Or rather, he served Brookfield.[12] He knew that Ralston did not like him, either[13]; but that didn't seem to matter[14]. He felt himself sufficiently protected by age and seniority from the fate of other masters whom Ralston had failed to like.[15]

Then suddenly, in 1908, when he had just turned

1 **row** [raʊ] 吵嘴；是口语。注意：作“划船”和“排、行”解的 row 是另外两个词，读 [rəʊ]。

2 **Funny thing, Chips had never liked him** = It was a funny thing that Chips had never liked him.

3 **he was efficient** [ɪ'fɪʃənt], **ruthless** ['ruːθlɪs], **ambitious** [æm'bɪʃəs], **but not, somehow, very likeable** 他（Ralston）能力强，不留情，有雄心壮志，可是不知怎的，不大讨人喜欢。

4 **admittedly** 被公认地

5 **raised the status** ['steɪtəs] **of Brookfield as a school** 提高了 Brookfield 作为一所学校的地位。

6 **a longish** ['lɒŋɪʃ] **waiting list** 较长的等待批准入学的申请人名单。long 加了后缀 -ish 是“略长”的意思。

7 **live** [laɪv] **wire** 本义是“通电的电线”，转义为“活力充沛的人”，“非常活跃的人”。

8 **power transmitter** [trænz'mɪtə] 本义是“‘输电器”，转义为“很有魄力的人”。

9 **you had to beware** [bi'weə] **of him** 你必须提防他。 **you** 泛指任何人。

10 **had never bothered to beware of him** 从来不屑去为防他而操心。

11 **was not attracted by the man** 不被这个人吸引；不爱其人。the man 这里有 Ralston the man 或 Ralston as a man，即“Ralston 其人”的意思。

12 **Or, rather, he served Brookfield.** 或者与其说他是为 Ralston 服务，不如说是为 Brookfield 服务。**Or** 或者说。

13 **did not like him, either** 也不喜欢他。

14 **didn't seem to matter** 似乎无关紧要。

15 **He felt himself sufficiently protected by age and seniority** [ˌsiːnɪ'ɒrɪtɪ] **from the fate of other masters whom Ralston had failed to like.** 他觉得自己因年长和资深，足以避免遭受其他 Ralston 所不喜欢的教师的那种命运。 **protected** 过去分词，作宾语补足语。 **fate** 注定的命运；这里当指被 Ralston 训斥、处分或解职等。**had failed to like** = had not liked; fail 后接不定式，不一定是“没有做成（什么事）”的意思，而往往就作“不”解。

sixty[1], came Ralston's urbane ultimatum[2]. 'Mr. Chipping[3], have you ever thought you would like to retire?'

Chips stared about him[4] in that book-lined study[5], startled[6] by the question, wondering why Ralston should have asked it[7]. He said, at length[8]: 'No — umph — I can't say that — umph — I have thought much about it — umph — yet[9].'

'Well, Mr. Chipping, the suggestion is there for you to consider. The Governors would, of course, agree to your being adequately pensioned[10].'

Abruptly Chips flamed up[11]. 'But — umph — I don't want — to retire. I don't — umph — need to consider it.'

'Nevertheless, I suggest that you do.[12]'

'But — umph — I don't see — why — I should[13]!'

'In that case, things are going to be a little difficult'[14].

'Difficult? Why — difficult?'

And then they set to[15], Ralston getting cooler and

---

1 **had just turned sixty** 刚过 60 岁。**turned** 超过；是及物动词。

2 **urbane** [ɜːˈbeɪn] **ultimatum** [ˌʌltɪˈmeɪtəm] 温文有礼的最后通牒，即婉转地要他退休。

3 **Chipping** 契宾，是 Chips 的正式姓氏，已见前。

4 **stare about him** 向他周围看看。

5 **book-lined study** 四周是书的书房。

6 **startled** 这是过去分词，修饰 Chips。

7 **wondering why Ralston should have asked it** 不知 Ralston 怎么竟然问了这个问题。 **wondering** 疑惑不解，不知；现在分词，可理解为表示 startled 的伴随动作或原因。**should** 这里是情态动词；should + 不带 to 的完成不定式表示过去竟然发生的动作。

8 **at length** 最后；终于

9 **I can't say that — umph — I have thought much about it — umph — yet** 我不能说我已经对这个问题很好地考虑过；是"I have not thought much about it yet"的婉转说法。这里的 that 不是代词，是 that- 从句的连词；由于 umph 哼了一声打了个顿，才把它和 I have thought ... 拆开了。

10 **agree to your being adequately** ['ædɪkwɪtlɪ] **pensioned** 同意你被充分地给予养老金；同意给你充分的养老金。 **agree to** 同意，后接表示建议、措施等的词。比较：agree with，后接表示人或意见等的词。**being pensioned** 是动名词；它具有名词的性质，所以前面可以用限定词 your；同时也保留其动词的性质，所以用副词 adequately 修饰它。

11 **Abruptly** [ə'brʌptlɪ] **Chips flamed up**. Chips 勃然大怒。英语中副词在句子里的位置常可移动，如这一句也可说成 Chips abruptly flamed up 或 Chips flamed up abruptly。这里放在句首，是为加强语势。flame up 的主语可以是人，也可以是 face，anger。

12 **Nevertheless** [ˌnevəðə'les]**, I suggest that you do.**（尽管你说无需考虑）然而我仍然建议你考虑。**you do** = you consider it. 在 suggest 的宾语从句中，动词用虚拟语气；这里是 you do，看不出是虚拟语气；倘是 he do，就明显了。又，you do 也可作 you should do。

13 **I should** = I should consider it. should 是情态动词，作"应该"解。

14 **In that case, things are going to be a little difficult.** 那么，事情就有些难办了。**In that case** 在那个情况下；那么。 **a little** 有一点儿；这里故意用语气较轻的 a little，是一种 understatement。

15 **set to** 吵起来；是习语；也可作"打起来"、"认真做起来"解。这个 to 是副词。

harder, Chips getting warmer and more passionate[1], till at last Ralston said, icily[2]: 'Since you force me to use plain words[3], Mr. Chipping, you shall have them[4]. For some time past[5], you haven't been pulling your weight here[6]. Your methods of teaching are slack and old-fashioned; your personal habits are slovenly[7]; and you ignore my instructions[8] in a way[9] which, in a younger man, I should regard as rank insubordination[10]. It won't do[11], Mr. Chipping, and you must ascribe it to my forbearance that I have put up with it so long[12].'

'But ...' Chips began, in sheer bewilderment[13]; and then he took up isolated words out of that extraordinary indictment[14]. '*Slovenly* — umph — you said?[15]'

'Yes, look at the gown you're wearing. I happen to know[16] that that gown of yours[17] is a subject of continual

---

1 **Ralston getting cooler and harder, Chips getting warmer and more passionate** Ralston 越来越冷静、强硬，Chips 越来越慷慨激昂。这是两个并列的独立结构，修饰 set to，描述他们两个争吵时不同的架势，cooler 有“看来不动声色，实际寸步不让”的含意。

2 **till at last Ralston said, icily** ['aɪsɪlɪ] 直到最后 Ralston 冷冰冰地说。这个状语从句修饰 set to。

3 **force me to use plain words** 逼我说出直白的话；一定要我直言不讳。

4 **you shall have them** 你就听我直说。 **them** = plain words. **shall** 用于第二人称，表示说话人的意向、命令等。

5 **For some time past** 过去一段时间

6 **pulling your weight here** 在这儿（Brookfield）努力发挥你的作用。 **pull one's weight** 原是指"共同划船时有效地使出自己的力气"，这里用它的转义"在集体工作中使出自己该出的力"。

7 **your personal habits are slovenly** ['slʌvnlɪ] 你的个人习惯不修边幅。

8 **ignore** [ɪg'nɔː] **my instructions** 不听我的指示。instruction（单数，不可数名词）是"教导"的意思；复数形式 instructions 作"指示"、"命令"解。

9 **in a way** 以某种方式。这里不作习语；way 指具体的方式，是后面 which 的先行词。in a way 作习语时，作"在某种程度上"、"有些儿"解。

10 **which, in a younger man, I should regard as rank insubordination** ['ɪnsəˌbɔːdɪ'neɪʃən] 这种不听我指示的方式，如果发生在一个年纪较轻的人身上，我就要认为是不服从上级。 **which** 代替 way，是 should regard as 的宾语。全句是虚拟语气。 **in a younger man** = if it were in (the case of) a younger man.

11 **It won't do** 这是不行的。It 指不听指示。

12 **you must ascribe** [əs'kraɪb] **it to my forbearance** [fɔː'beərəns] **that I have put up with it so long** 你应该把我那么长期地容忍你的不听从指示归因于我的克制；因为我克制，所以才能长期容忍。第一个 it 是虚词，引起 that- 从句；第二个 it 是指不听从指示。 **put up with** 容忍；是习语。

13 **in sheer bewilderment** [bɪ'wɪldəmənt] 全然愣住了；茫然不知所措。

14 **took up isolated words out of that extraordinary indictment** [ɪndaɪtmənt] 从（Ralston 的）那不寻常的指责中抓住几个孤立的词。indictment 原是"控告"、"起诉"的意思，这里用以说明 Ralston 指责的口气很严重。

15 ***Slovenly* — umph — you said?** 你说"不修边幅"吗？ ***Slovenly*** 斜体，要重读。这就是上面所说 Chips 抓住的几个孤立的词之一。

16 **I happen to know** 我正好知道。happen 后接不定式，表示"正好"、"碰巧"。

17 **that gown of yours** 你的那件长袍；强调"那件"。

amusement[1] throughout the School.'

Chips knew it, too[2], but it had never seemed to him a very regrettable matter.

He went on[3]: 'And — you also said — umph — something about *insubordination*?'

'No, I didn't[4]. I said that in a younger man I should have regarded it as that[5]. In your case[6] it's probably a mixture of slackness and obstinacy[7]. This question of Latin pronunciation, for instance — I think I told you years ago that I wanted the new style used throughout the School[8]. The other masters obeyed me; you prefer to stick to your old methods[9], and the result is simply chaos and inefficiency[10].'

At last Chips had something tangible that he could tackle[11]. 'Oh, *that*?[12]' he answered scornfully. 'Well, I — umph — I admit that I don't agree with the new pronunciation. I never did.[13] Umph — a lot of nonsense, in my opinion.[14] Making boys say "Kickero" at school when — umph — for the rest of their lives they'll say "Cicero" — if they ever — umph — say it at all.[15] And instead of "vicissim"

1 **a subject of continual amusement** 一直被人取笑的话题

2 **Chips knew it, too** Chips 也知道这事（指他的长袍是一直被人取笑的话题。后面还有个 it，所指同。）

3 **went on** 继续（说）下去

4 **I didn't** = I didn't say that.

5 **regarded it as that** 把不听从我的指示认为是不服从上级。it 泛指上文再三提到的"不听从 Ralston 的指示"；that 代替 insubordination。

6 **In you case** 就你的情况来说，至于你

7 **it's probably a mixture of slackness and obstinacy** ['ɒbstɪnəsɪ] 那也许是散漫和固执的混合（一半是散漫，一半是固执）。it 指不听从 Ralston 的指示。

8 **I wanted the new style used throughout** [θruː'aʊt] **the School** 我要让新式发音法在全校范围内采用。 **used** 过去分词，作 wanted 的宾语补足语。

9 **you prefer** [prɪ'fɜː] **to stick to your old methods** 你（不服从我采用新式发音法的指示，而）偏要坚持你的老式发音。

10 **the result is simply chaos** ['keɪɒs] **and inefficiency** 其结果只能是（教学上的）混乱和低效。 **simply** 简直；是口语。

11 **had something tangible** ['tændʒəbl] **that he could tackle** 有可以对付的具体目标了。

12 **Oh, *that*?** 噢，原来是那个（新老式发音法的问题）吗?

13 **I never did.** = I never agreed with the new pronunciation.

14 **Umph — a lot of nonsense** ['nɒnsəns], **in my opinion.** = In my opinion — umph — that's a lot of nonsense. 在我看来，新式发音法是一派胡闹。

15 **Making boys say 'Kickero'** ['kɪkərəʊ] **at school when — umph — for the rest of their lives they'll say 'Cicero'** ['sɪsərəʊ] **— if they ever — umph — say it at all.** 这个句子是用动名词词组 Making ... 构成的单部句（one-element sentence）。没有 to 的不定式 say 是 Making 的宾语补足语；when 引起的状语从句修饰 Making；when 在这里 = while，作"虽然（实际上是）"解。**for the rest of their lives** 在他们一生的其余时间里（即离开学校后）。 **Cicero** 西塞罗，罗马政治家、演说家、作家，生于公元前 106 年，卒于公元前 43 年。**if they ever — umph — say it at all** 这个条件从句修饰 when 引起的从句中的 say；意思是：他们可能一生也不会再说到这个罗马名字；假如说到的话，他们也仍是读老式发音，读成 Cicero，而不会读成 Kickero 的。（新式发音法 c 发 k 音。）

— God bless my soul — you'd make them say — "We kiss 'im"![1] Umph — umph!' And he chuckled momentarily[2], forgetting that he was in Ralston's study and not in his own friendly form room[3].

'Well, there you are[4], Mr. Chipping — that's just an example of what I complain of[5]. You hold one opinion and I hold another[6], and since you decline to give way[7], there can't very well be any alternative[8]. I aim to make Brookfield a thoroughly up-to-date school.[9] I'm a science man[10] myself, but for all that[11], I have no objection to the classics[12] — provided that[13] they are taught efficiently. Because they are dead languages is no reason why they should be dealt with in a dead educational technique.[14] I understand, Mr. Chipping, that your Latin and Greek lessons are exactly the same as they were when I began here[15] ten years ago?'

Chips answered, slowly and with pride: 'For that matter[16] — umph — they are the same as when your predeces-

---

1 **And instead of 'vicissim' ['vɪsɪsɪm] — God bless my soul — you'd make them say — 'We kiss 'im'!** 还有——啊，天哪——你不教他们读 'vicissim'，而教他们读成了 'We kiss 'im'! 因新发音 c 发 k 音，所以把 vicissim 读成 [vɪ'kɪsɪm]，听来像 We kiss 'im 了。**vicissim** 拉丁词，作"交替"解。

2 **chuckled momentarily** ['məʊməntərɪlɪ]（美国人读 [ˌməʊmən'terɪlɪ]）轻声笑了一下。 **momentarily** 瞬息之间；短暂地。

3 **in his own friendly form room** 在他自己的气氛友好的教室里（那里可以随随便便）。

4 **Well, there you are** 喏，你就是这样。

5 **what I complain of** 我所抱怨（不以为然）的事情。注意 complain 是不及物动词，后接 of。

6 **You hold one opinion and I hold another** 你持有一种意见，而我持有另一种意见。one 与 another 对照；another = another opinion.

7 **decline to give way** 不肯让步。decline 与 refuse 同义，但语气较轻。 **give way** 让步；屈服；是习语。

8 **there can't very well be any alternative** [ɔ:l'tɜ:nətɪv] 不太可能有任何其他合适的选择（只有请 Chips 退休）。 **not very** 不太；是委婉的说法。

9 **I aim to make Brookfield a thoroughly** ['θʌrəlɪ] **up-to-date school.** 我要把 Brookfield 办成一所全新的学校。英国人原用 aim at doing，美国人用 aim to ...（不定式），但现在英国人也常用 aim to ...。

10 **science man** 研究科学的人

11 **for all that** 尽管如此；虽然我是研究科学的人。

12 **have no objection to the classics** 不反对古代希腊、罗马古典著作（指在学校设这方面的课）。

13 **provided that** 以……为条件；假使；是连词，也作 provided；也有人用 providing that 或 providing。

14 **Because they are dead languages is no reason why they should be dealt with in a dead educational technique** [tek'ni:k]. 它们（古希腊、罗马文学的语言）是死语言，不能成为它们应该被用死教学方法去对待的理由；不能因为它们是死语言而用死教学方法去教它们。Because 引起名词性从句，作 is no reason 的主语，这种用法英美人常有，但不合逻辑，也不算正当，最好改用 That。 **dead language** 已死亡的语言，如古希腊语、拉丁语。 **deal with** 对付；处理；是习语。

15 **when I began here** 我开始来这里的时候；我刚进这学校时

16 **For that matter** 至于那个；即讲到拉丁语、希腊语课程。

sor[1] — Mr. Meldrum — came here, and that — umph — was thirty-eight years ago. We began here, Mr. Meldrum and I, in — umph — in 1870[2]. And it was — um — Mr. Meldrum's predecessor, Mr. Wetherby, who first approved my syllabus[3]. "You'll take the Cicero for the fourth[4]," he said to me. Cicero, too — not Kickero![5]'

'Very interesting, Mr. Chipping, but once again it proves my point[6] — you live too much in the past, and not enough in the present and future[7]. Times are changing[8], whether you realize it or not[9]. Modern parents are beginning to demand something more for their three years' school fees than a few scraps of languages that nobody speaks[10]. Besides, your boys don't learn even what they're supposed to learn[11]. None of them last year got through the Lower Certificate[12].'

And suddenly, in a torrent of thoughts too pressing to be put into words[13], Chips made answer to himself[14]. These examinations and certificates and so on[15] — what did they matter[16]? And all this efficiency and up-to-date-

1 **predecessor** ['pri:dɪsesə] 前任

2 **in — umph — in 1870** 两个 in 重复，因中间哼了一声，打了个顿。

3 **who first approved** [ə'pruːvd] **my syllabus** ['sɪləbəs] 他（Mr. Wetherby）第一个赞成我的教学大纲。

4 **take the Cicero for the fourth** 教四年级的西塞罗课。**the fourth** = the fourth form. **Cicero** 西塞罗的著作；Cicero 前用 the，因为指的是四年级的西塞罗著作课。

5 **Cicero, too — not Kickero!**（他说的）也是 Cicero，不是 Kickero！

6 **once again it proves my point** 这又一次证明了我的看法（是对的）。

7 **— you live too much in the past, and not enough in the present and future** ——你过多地活在过去，在当下和未来却活得不够。破折号后这一段话就是 Ralston 所说"my point"的内容，所以这个破折号等于一个连词 that。

8 **Times are changing** 时代在变化。

9 **whether you realize it or not** 不管你意识到这一点与否。it 指时代在变化。这个 whether 引起的状语从句，修饰 are changing。

10 **demand something more for their three years' school fees than a few scraps of languages that nobody speaks.** 付了三年学费，要求（学到）一些比一鳞半爪没有人说的语言更多的东西。（即不只是为了学几句希腊语、拉丁语。）**scrap** 原义为"碎片"。

11 **your boys don't learn even what they're supposed to learn** 你（教）的学生连应该学好的也没有学好。这里 learn 作"学会"、"学好"解。**are supposed to ...**（不定式）被认为应该……。

12 **got through the Lower Certificate** [sə'tɪfɪkɪt] 初级考试及格（而获得证书）。

13 **a torrent** ['tɒrənt] **of thoughts too pressing to be put into words** 一连串想法汹涌而来，来不及用语言表达出来。 **too pressing to ...**（不定式）太急迫，因而不能……；紧迫得不能……。 **put into words** 把……形成文字。

14 **made answer to himself** 自己（心里）回答。注意：make answer 中 answer 前面不用冠词。

15 **and so on** 以及诸如此类；等等；是习语。

16 **what did they matter?** 它们有什么要紧？ they 和 These examinations and certificates and so on 同位；为了突出 examinations 等，所以把它们列在句首。

ness[1] — what did *that* matter, either[2]? Ralston was trying to run Brookfield like a factory[3] — a factory for turning out a snob culture based on money and machines[4]. The old gentlemanly traditions of family and broad acres[5] were changing, as doubtless they were bound to[6]; but instead of widening them to form a genuine inclusive democracy of duke and dustman[7], Ralston was narrowing them upon the single issue of a fat banking account[8]. There never had been so many rich men's sons at Brookfield. The Speech Day Garden Party[9] was like Ascot[10]. Ralston met these wealthy fellows in London clubs and persuaded them that Brookfield was *the* coming school[11], and since they couldn't buy their way into Eton or Harrow[12], they greedily swallowed the bait[13]. Awful fellows, some of them[14] — though others were decent enough[15]. Financiers, company

---

1 **all this efficiency and up-to-dateness** 所有这种效率和时新。这里把 efficiency 和 up-to-dateness 作为一个合一的概念，所以前面限定词用单数 this，又因此下面的同位语也用单数 *that*。

2 **what did *that* matter, either** 那又有什么要紧

3 **run Brookfield like a factory** 像办工厂一样办 Brookfield 这所学校。

4 **a factory for turning out a snob culture based on money and machines** [məˈʃiːnz] 生产出以金钱和机器为基础的势利文化的工厂。

5 **The old gentlemanly traditions** [trəˈdɪʃənz] **of family and broad acres** [ˈeɪkəz]

以家族（即门第）和广大田地为基础的各种古老的绅士传统。注意：family 作“门第”解是不可数名词。

6 **as doubtless they were bound to** 因为它们（指各种古老的绅士传统）必定要变化。were bound to = were bound to change. **be bound to ...**（不定式）必定，必须；是习语。

7 **instead of widening them to form a genuine** ['dʒenjʊɪn] **inclusive democracy** ['dɪ'mɒkrəsɪ] **of duke and dustman** ['dʌs*t*mən] 不是扩大它们（各种古老的绅士传统）以形成一种把公爵和清洁工都包括在内的真正的民主（而是……）。duke 和 dustman 都是可数名词，因两者并列，所以虽是单数但可以不用冠词。这里用 duke 和 dustman 指贵族和平民，是因为 duke 和 dustman 两个词的开首音都是 [d]，有头韵（alliteration）之妙。

8 **narrowing** ['nærəʊɪŋ] **them upon the single issue** ['ɪsjuː, 'ɪʃuː] **of a fat banking account** 把它们（各种古老的绅士传统）缩小到单纯是一个巨额存款的银行账户的问题。

9 **Speech Day Garden Party** 授奖典礼日的游园会

10 **Ascot** ['æskət] 在英国阿斯科特赛马场举行的（盛大）赛马会

11 ***the* coming school** 最理想的、前途有望的学校。 ***the*** 斜体，读作 [ðiː]，要重读，表示“唯一的”、“最理想的”、“最典型的”等。（the 不印斜体，作一般冠词时，在元音开始的词前面读 [ðɪ]，在辅音开始的词前面读 [ðə]，甚至只发 [ð] 音。

12 **buy their way into Eton** ['iːtn] **or Harrow** ['hærəʊ] 靠花钱疏通进入伊顿公学或哈罗公学。 **buy** 可作“行贿收买”解，这里当指通过对学校巨额捐赠等方式，换取子弟入学。伊顿和哈罗都是英国著名的培养上层精英的公学。

13 **greedily swallowed** ['swɒləʊd] **the bait** 争相上钩。 **swallow the bait** 原义是“（鱼）吞饵”，转义为“上钩”、“入圈套”；既攀不上伊顿、哈罗，听见 Brookfield 是“*the* coming school”，就拼命把子弟往 Brookfield 送。

14 **Awful fellows, some of them** = Some of them（指 these wealthy fellows) were awful fellows. Awful 的含义很广，这里是“极坏的”、“糟透的”之意，是口语。

15 **decent** ['diːsnt] **enough** 还不错的。decent 是“正派的”、“体面的”之意。enough 在这里作“尚还”解，不是“足够”的意思。

promoters, pill manufacturers[1]. One of them gave his son five pounds a week pocket money[2]. Vulgar ... ostentatious ... all the hectic rotten-ripeness of the age …[3] And once, Chips had got into trouble because of some joke he had made about the name and ancestry of a boy named Isaacstein[4]. The boy wrote home about it[5], and Isaacstein *père*[6] sent an angry letter to Ralston. Touchy, no sense of humour, no sense of proportion[7] — that was the matter with them, these new fellows[8]... No sense of proportion. And it was a sense of proportion, above all things[9], that Brookfield ought to teach — not so much Latin or Greek or Chemistry or Mechanics[10]. And you couldn't expect to test that sense of proportion by setting papers and granting certificates[11]...

All this flashed through his mind in an instant of protest and indignation[12], but he did not say a word of it. He merely gathered his tattered gown together[13] and with

---

1 **Financiers** [faɪ'nænsɪəz, fɪ'nænsɪəz], **company promoters, pill manufacturers** 金融家、公司创办人、丸药制造商。承接上文，列举三种人，可理解为 They are financiers, company promoters, pill manufacturers. 说明他们都是这

么一些人物。

2 **gave his son five pounds a week pocket-money** 给他儿子每星期 5 镑的零用钱。这里说“5 镑”是 20 世纪初的 5 镑，就购买力而论，相当于现在好几十镑。 **five pounds a week** 状语短语，修饰 gave。

3 **Vulgar ... ostentatious** [ˌɒstenˈteɪʃəs] **... all the hectic rotten-ripeness of the age ...** 庸俗……浮华……这个时代忙乱而烂熟的一切…… 这个句子支离破碎，反映 Chips 头脑中对这些有钱人的零乱的概念，大致可以这样连缀成完整的句子：They are vulgar, ostentious ..., representing all the rotten-ripeness of the age.

4 **Isaacstein** [ˈaɪzəkstaɪn] 艾萨克斯坦，姓氏

5 **wrote home about it** 写信到家中讲述此事（指 Chips 拿 Isaacstein 这个学生的姓和他的家世讲笑话的事）。

6 **Isaacstein *père*** [peə] 老 Isaacstein；学生 Isaacstein 的父亲。***père*** 父亲；是法语。美国 Little, Brown 版作 his father。

7 **Touchy** [ˈtʌtʃɪ], **no sense of humour, no sense of proportion** 容易为小事情而生气，没有幽默感，没有分寸感。列举这些新一代人的三点毛病；这三个词（组）在语法上不一致：Touchy 是形容词，后两个是名词词组。严格地说，这里两个 no 应改为 without，或者把 Touchy 改为 Touchiness；但改了反见不自然。 **sense of proportion** 分寸感，就是并不感情用事而善于辨别事物轻重缓急的能力。

8 **that was the matter with them, these new fellows** 那就是他们这些新一代人的毛病。And once ... these fellows 一段，英国 Coronet Books 版中无。

9 **above all things** 比一切都更重要；首先。这里是插入的状语短语。

10 **not so much Latin or Greek or Chemistry or Mechanics** [mɪˈkænɪks] = ought not to teach so much Latin ... .

11 **you couldn't expect to test that sense of proportion by setting papers and granting certificates** 你不能期望用出考题和发证书的办法来测验那分寸感。

12 **in an instant of protest** [ˈprəʊtest] **and indignation** 在反对和气愤的一瞬间。 **protest** 抗议；反对；这里是不可数名词，作动词时读 [prəˈtest]。

13 **gathered his tattered gown together** 拉好他破碎的长袍。

an 'umph — umph' walked a few paces away[1]. He had had enough of the argument[2]. At the door he turned and said: 'I don't — umph — intend to resign — and you can — umph — do what you like about it[3]!'

Looking back upon that scene in the calm perspective of a quarter of a century[4], Chips could find it in his heart to feel a little sorry for Ralston[5]. Particularly when[6], as it happened[7], Ralston had been in such complete ignorance of the forces he was dealing with[8]. So, for that matter, had Chips himself.[9] Neither had correctly estimated the toughness of Brookfield tradition, and its readiness to defend itself and its defenders.[10] For it had so chanced that[11] a small boy, waiting to see Ralston that morning, had been listening outside the door during the whole of the interview[12]; he had been thrilled by it, naturally, and had told his friends. Some of these, in a surprisingly short time[13], had told their parents; so that very soon it was common knowledge[14] that Ralston had insulted Chips and had demanded his resignation. The amazing result was a spontaneous outburst of sympathy and partisanship such as Chips, in his wildest dreams, had never envisaged.[15] He

1 **walked a few paces away** 走开几步。away 修饰 walked；a few paces 又修饰 away。

2 **had had enough of the argument** 已经争论得够了（不愿再争论下去）。

3 **you can — umph — do what you like about it** 你对这个问题（Chips 的退休问题）要怎么办就怎么办。（有“看你怎么办”的意思。）

4 **Looking back upon that scene in the calm perspective of a quarter of a century** 二十五年后冷静地回顾当时的争吵。

5 **could find it in his heart to feel a little sorry for Ralston** 居然会觉得心里有点可怜 Ralston。 it 是虚词，引起不定式短语 to feel a little sorry for Ralston。

6 **Particularly when** 特别是在……的情况下；特别是考虑到……

7 **as it happened** 当时的实际情况是这样。这是插入语。 it 泛指情况。

8 **had been in such complete ignorance** [ˈɪgnərəns] **of the forces he was dealing with** 当时那样全然不知道他在对付着的（是什么）势力。

9 **So, for that matter, had Chips himself.** = Chips had been so himself in that matter. Chips 在那一点上自己也是那样（不知道这种势力）。**So** = in such complete ignorance of the forces.

10 **Neither had correctly estimated the toughness** [ˈtʌfnɪs] **of Brookfield tradition, and its readiness to defend itself and its defenders.**（Ralston 和 Chips）两个人都没有正确估计到 Brookfield 传统的顽强性，以及这种传统对于保卫自己和保卫其保卫者的时刻准备。

11 **it had so chanced that ...** 事情是这样偶然发生的；恰巧。it 引起 that- 从句。在这句型中，有时不用“so”，意义相同。

12 **interview** [ˈɪntəvjuː] 会谈，即 Chips 和 Ralston 的争吵。

13 **in a surprisingly short time** 在短得惊人的时间内；在极短时间内。

14 **common knowledge** 人尽皆知的事。注意不是指“常识”；也注意前面没有 a 或 the。

15 **The amazing result was a spontaneous** [spɒnˈteɪnjəs] **outburst** [ˈaʊtbɜːst] **of sympathy and partisanship** [ˌpɑːtɪˈzænʃɪp] **such as Chips, in his wildest dreams, had never envisaged** [ɪnˈvɪzɪdʒd]. 其惊人的结果是，Chips 即使在最荒诞的梦中也没有梦见过的同情和偏袒的自然爆发。 **such as** 像……那样的。

found, rather to his astonishment[1], that Ralston was thoroughly unpopular; he was feared[2] and respected, but not liked; and in this issue of Chips[3] the dislike rose to a point where it conquered fear and demolished even respect[4]. There was talk of[5] having some kind of public riot[6] in the School if Ralston succeeded in banishing Chips[7]. The masters, many of them young men[8] who agreed that Chips was hopelessly old-fashioned[9], rallied round him nevertheless[10] because they hated Ralston's slave driving[11] and saw in the old veteran a likely champion[12]. And one day the Chairman of the Governors, Sir John Rivers[13], visited Brookfield, ignored Ralston[14], and went direct to Chips[15]. 'A fine fellow, Rivers[16]', Chips would say, telling the story to Mrs. Wickett for the dozenth time[17]. 'Not — umph — a very brilliant boy in class[18] — I remember he could never — umph — master his verbs[19]. And now — umph — I see in the papers — they've made him — umph — a baronet[20]. It just shows you — umph — it just shows you.[21]'

Sir John had said, on that morning in 1908, tak-

1 **rather to his astonishment** 令他格外惊异地。这是插入的状语短语。

2 **he was feared** 他令人畏惧。he 指 Ralston。

3 **in this issue of Chips** 在 Chips 这个问题上

4 **the dislike rose to a point where it conquered fear and demolished** [dɪ'mɒlɪʃt] **even respect** 憎恶上升到战胜畏惧，甚至破除尊敬的程度。

5 **There was talk of** 有……的传说。注意：talk 泛指“谈话”或“传说”时，是不可数名词；作“一次谈话或演说”解时，为可数名词。

6 **public riot** ['raɪət] 公开闹事

7 **succeeded in banishing** ['bænɪʃɪŋ] **Chips** 成功赶走 Chips；做到赶走 Chips。 **succeed in doing** 做成（某事）；“做成”不一定是有意的，“某事”也不一定是好事，如 He somehow succeeded in giving her a very bad impression。 **banishing** 原义“放逐”、“流放”，这里用来表示叫 Chips 退休，等于把他从 Brookfield“放逐”出去。

8 **many of them young men** = many of them being young men.

9 **hopelessly old-fashioned** 老派得无可救药

10 **rallied round him nevertheless** 并不因此（指他老派得无可救药）而不团结在他的周围；Chips 虽然老派得无可救药，（教师们）还是护卫他。nevertheless（虽然如此）还是。rallied 的主语是 The masters。

11 **slave driving** 驱使奴隶；像监督奴隶一样严厉监督。

12 **saw in the old vetevan** ['vetərən] **a likely champion** ['tʃæmpjən] 在这个老前辈身上看到一个比较可靠的支持者；认为 Chips 可以支持他们。注意：这里的介词用 in。

13 **Chairman of the Governors, Sir John Rivers** ['rɪvəz] 校董会主席约翰·里弗斯爵士

14 **ignored Ralston** 不理会 Ralston

15 **went direct to Chips** 直接去看了 Chips。注意：用 direct，不用 directly。

16 **A fine fellow, Rivers** = Rivers is a fine fellow.

17 **for the dozenth** ['dʌznθ] **time** 第十二次地；重复到第十二次地。“十二”，言其多。

18 **Not — umph — a very brilliant boy in class** 前面省去 He was。

19 **master his verbs** 掌握他（所学到）的（拉丁语）动词。

20 **they've made him — umph — a baronet** ['bærənɪt] 他们（泛指英国统治者们）已封他为从男爵。这句话前面省去连词 that，是 see 的宾语从句。

21 **It just shows you** 这就给你看了（读书不大聪明的人却封了从男爵）。

ing Chips by the arm[1] as they walked round the deserted cricket pitches[2]: 'Chips, old boy, I hear you've been having the deuce of a row[3] with Ralston. Sorry to hear about it[4], for your sake[5] — but I want you to know that the Govenors are with you to a man[6]. We don't like the fellow a great deal.[7] Very clever and all that[8], but a bit *too* clever, if you ask me[9]. Claims[10] to have doubled the School's endowment funds by some monkeying on the Stock Exchange[11]. Dare say he has[12], but a chap like that wants watching[13]. So if he starts chucking his weight about with you[14], tell him very politely he can go to the devil[15]. The Governors don't want you to resign. Brookfield wouldn't be the same without you[16], and they know it. We all know it. You can stay here till you're a hundred if you feel like it[17] — indeed it's our hope that you will[18].'

And at that — both then and often when he recounted it afterwards — Chips broke down.[19]

---

1 **taking Chips by the arm** 挽着 Chips 的手臂。注意：不说 taking Chips's arm 或 taking Chips by his arm。

2 **deserted** [dɪ'zɜːtɪd] **cricket pitches** 当时没有人在的板球场两个三门柱之间的中心部分；空着的球场。

3 **the deuce** [djuːs] **of a row** 一场大吵。 **deuce** 在口语中，用于诅咒和加强

语气，等于 devil。

4 **Sorry to hear about it** = I was (或 am) sorry to hear about it.

5 **for your sake** 为了你（为 Chips 抱憾，而不是为 Ralston）。

6 **are with you to a man** 全体都站在你这一边。 **to a man** 包括每一个人（没有一个例外）。

7 **We don't like the fellow a great deal.** 我们不大喜欢这个家伙（指 **Ralston**）。“不大喜欢”是“不喜欢”的委婉说法。**the fellow** 这个家伙，是对人的蔑称。

8 **Very clever and all that = He is very clever and all that.** and all that 表示“以及诸如此类”。这里说他“聪明”之外还有“能干”等长处。

9 **if you ask me** 假如你问我的话（我就这么说）。连同它的主句，并不是“假如你问，他就聪明，（不问就不聪明）”的意思。

10 **Claims = He claims** 他自称……；他以……居功

11 **doubled the School's endowment** [ɪn'daʊmənt] **funds by some monkeying** ['mʌŋkɪɪŋ] **on the Stock Exchange** 在交易所里耍些花样而使捐赠给学校的基金翻了倍。

12 **Dare say he has = I dare say (that) he has doubled the School's endowment funds.** I dare say 也作 I daresay，我可以说；我想；大概。

13 **wants watching** 需要留心。want 和 need 等词后面用主动式动名词，表示被动的意思。

14 **chucking his weight about with you** 向你耀武扬威。 **chuck one's weight about** 一般用 throw one's weight about（弄权；耀武扬威）。

15 **tell him very politely he can go to the devil** 很客气地对他说，他好去见鬼了。既说“客气”，又说“见鬼”，这是幽默说法。意思是：客客气气地对他说，使他明白大可不必来这一套。 **go to the devil** 见鬼去；滚开；是习语，也作“堕落”、“毁灭”解。

16 **wouldn't be the same without you** 要是没有你，就会不一样。

17 **stay here till you're a hundred if you feel like it** 如果你高兴的话，就在这里待到一百岁。 **feel like** 想要；是口语，后面接名词或动名词，或者像这里泛指某事的 it。

18 **you will** = you will stay here till you're a hundred.

19 **And at that — both then and often when he recounted it afterwards — Chips broke down.** 当时听到这一番话时，以及后来每每提及时，他都情不自禁地哭泣起来。

第十二章

内容提要

1911年，校长罗尔斯顿辞职。新任校长查特里斯很尊重契普斯，契普斯也喜欢他。

1913年，契普斯患支气管炎休息半年后，决定辞职，时年六十五岁。7月，在学年终结宴会上，契普斯接受了退休赠礼，并发表演说。演说中历述往事，妙语连珠，满堂笑声不绝。

8月，契普斯去德国威斯巴登疗养，住在德国老师施特弗尔家。9月归来，迁居学校对面的维克特太太家。他虽然退休，和学校仍保持密切联系。所有新来学生，他都要叫来喝茶；并且每星期总要和教师共餐一次。他担任了布鲁克菲尔德校友会主席，间或为布鲁克菲尔德杂志写些文章。

12

So he stayed on[1] at Brookfield, having as little to do with Ralston as possible[2]. And in 1911 Ralston left, 'to better himself[3]'; he was offered the headship of[4] one of the greater public schools. His successor was a man named Chatteris[5], whom Chips liked; he was even younger than Ralston had been — thirty-four[6]. He was supposed to be very brilliant[7]; at any rate, he was modern (Natural Sciences Tripos[8]), friendly, and sympathetic. Recognizing in Chips a Brookfield institution[9], he courteously and wisely accepted the situation[10].

In 1913 Chips had bronchitis[11] and was off duty for nearly the whole of the winter term[12]. It was that which made him decide to resign that summer[13], when he was sixty-five[14]. After all, it was a good, ripe age[15]; and Ralston's straight words[16] had, in some ways[17], had an effect[18]. He

1 **stayed on** 继续呆下去；on 表示"继续"的意思。

2 **having as little to do with Ralston as possible** 尽可能少同 Ralston 发生关系。**have to do with** 与……有关，同……往来（或打交道）；是习语。**as ... as possible** 尽可能……。

3 **better himself** 提高自己的地位（或改善自己的经济状况）。比较：**improve oneself** 增进自己的学识。

4 **was offered the headship of** 被授予（某学校）校长的职位。headship 是 offered 的保留宾语。

5 **Chatteris** ['tʃætərɪs] 查特里斯，姓氏

6 **even younger than Ralston had been — thirty-four** 他只 34 岁，比 Ralston（来当校长时）年纪还轻。

7 **was supposed to be very brilliant** 被大家认为很聪明

8 **Natural Sciences Tripos** ['traɪpɒs] 英国剑桥大学自然科学荣誉学位考试（的及格生）

9 **Recognizing** ['rekəgnaɪzɪŋ] **in Chips a Brookfield institution** 在 Chips 身上认出（即知道 Chips 是）Brookfield 传统的化身。**institution** 在口语中作"（在某处）恪守惯例一成不变的人"解。

10 **accepted the situation** 接受这情况（由 Chips 去按 Brookfield 的传统办事）。

11 **had bronchitis** [brɒŋ'kaɪtɪs] 患支气管炎

12 **was off duty for nearly the whole of the winter term** 几乎整个冬季学期都没有上班。**off duty** 不上班；不在班上。

13 **It was that which made him decide to resign that summer** 是那个情况（指因患支气管炎而几乎整个冬季学期没有上班）使他在那年夏天决定辞职。It was that which made him decide 是 That made him decide 的着重式，强调 that。

14 **when he was sixty-five** 当时他六十五岁。这里的 when = and at that time。这是非限制性状语从句，不作"当他在六十五岁的时候"解。

15 **ripe age** 高龄。ripe 原是"成熟"的意思，形容 age 作"年迈时"解。

16 **Ralston's straignt words** Ralston 的率直的一番话，指上一章所写的 Ralston 要 Chips 退休时所说的那些话。

17 **in some ways** 在某些方面；有些

18 **had an effect** 有影响

felt that it would not be fair to hang on[1] if he could not decently do his job[2]. Besides[3], he would not sever himself completely[4]. He would take rooms across the road[5], with the excellent Mrs. Wickett who had once been linen-room maid[6]; he could visit the School whenever he wanted, and could still, in a sense, remain a part of it[7].

At that final end-of-term dinner[8], in July, 1913, Chips received his farewell presentations[9] and made a speech[10]. It was not a very long speech, but it had a good many[11] jokes in it, and was made twice as long, perhaps, by the laughter that impeded its progress[12]. There were several Latin quotations[13] in it, as well as[14] a reference to the Captain of the School[15], who, Chips said, had been guilty of exaggeration[16] in speaking of his (Chips's) services to Brookfield[17]. 'But then[18] — umph — he comes of an — umph — exaggerating family[19]. I — um — remember — once — having to thrash his father[20] for it[21]. (Laughter.) I gave him one mark[22] — umph — for a Latin translation, and he — umph

1 **it would not be fair to hang on** 坚持不走（或赖着不走）是不合理的。 **hang on** 是习语；on 是副词。

2 **decently do his job** 像样地工作；工作得不错

3 **Besides** 这里有 on the other hand（在另一方面）的意味。

4 **sever** ['sevə] **himself completely** 完全使自己脱离（Brookfield）。

5 **take rooms across the road** 在学校对马路租借住所。

6 **linen-room maid** 洗衣间女仆

7 **could still, in a sense, remain a part of it** 在一定意义上还可以依旧是它（学校）的一部分（即保持联系）。

8 **that final end-of-term dinner** 那最后一次的期终宴会。因为 Chips 要辞职了，所以那次期终宴会是临别的"最后一次"。

9 **his farewell presentations** 送给他的临别赠礼

10 **made a speech** 发表演说

11 **a good many** 好多的，许多的

12 **was made twice as long, perhaps, by the laughter that impeded its progress**（他的演说）也许是被打断演说的笑声拖长了一倍。as long 有 as long as it should have been 的意思。

13 **Latin quotations** 拉丁文引语

14 **as well as ...** 除了……之外还有，不但……；以后者为基础突出前者，如 He knows Latin as well as English.（他不但懂英语，还懂拉丁语。）现在的倾向，as well as 有时几乎等于 and。

15 **a reference to the Captain of the School** 说及学校的首领；"首领"是指校长；不说 Headmaster 或 Head，而说 Captain，是滑稽语。

16 **guilty** ['gɪltɪ] **of exaggeration** [ɪgˌzædʒə'reɪʃən] 犯夸大的毛病

17 **his (Chips's) services to Brookfield** 他（Chips）对 Brookfield 所做的工作。注意：services 用复数。

18 **But then** 然而

19 **comes of an — umph — exaggerating family** 出身于（惯于）夸大的家庭

20 **remember — once — having to thrash his father** 记得有一次不得不鞭打他的父亲。注意：remember 后接动名词是"记得（曾经发生的事）"，remember 后接不定式是"记住（未来应做的事）"，也就是"不要忘记"的意思，如 Remember to tell him of my arrival.（别忘了告诉他我到了。）

21 **for it** 为了（他父亲）夸大

22 **one mark** 一分

— exaggerated the one into a seven[1]! Umph — umph!' Roars of laughter and tumultuous cheers[2]! A typical Chips remark, everyone thought.[3]

And then he mentioned that he had been at Brookfield for forty-two years, and that he had been very happy there. 'It has been my life,' he said simply. '*O mihi praeteritos referat si Jupiter annos*[4] ... Umph — I need not — of course — translate ...' (Much laughter.) 'I remember lots of changes at Brookfield. I remember the — um — the first bicycle. I remember when there was no gas or electric light[5] and we used to have a member of the domestic staff called a lamp-boy[6] — he did nothing else but[7] clean and trim and light lamps[8] throughout the School. I remember when there was a hard frost that lasted for seven weeks in the winter term[9] — there were no games[10], and the whole School learned to skate on the fens[11]. Eighteen-eighty-something, that was.[12] I remember when two thirds of the School went down with German measles[13] and Big Hall was turned into a hospital ward[14]. I remember the great bonfire we had on Mafeking night[15]. It was lit too near the pavilion, and we had to send for the fire brigade to put it

1 **exaggerated the one into a seven** 把这个 1 分夸大为 7 分。（可能是把 1 改成了 7，所以要挨鞭打了。）

2 **tumultuous** [tju(:)'mʌltjʊəs] **cheers** 喧哗的喝彩

3 **A typical Chips remark, everyone thought.** = Everyone thought (that) it was a typical Chips remark. 每个人都认为这是一句典型的 Chips 的话。Chips 在这里作定语；**Chips remark** Chips 风格的话。

4 ***O mihi praeteritos referat si Jupiter annos*** 拉丁语，意思是：哦，要是（罗马主神）朱庇特能还给我那已逝的年华（该多好！）

5 **I remember when there was no gas or electric light** 我记得没有煤气或电灯的那个时候。这里的 when 是连接副词，不是连词；当然不可能作"当没有煤气和电灯的时候，我记得"解。there was no gas or electric light 中的 or 也可用 nor，但现在用 or 较普遍。

6 **used to have a member of the domestic staff called a lamp-boy** 过去一直有一个叫做灯夫的杂务工。

7 **did nothing else but** 除了……不做其他任何事；只做。but = except.

8 **clean and trim and light lamps** 擦灯、修灯芯和点灯

9 **a hard frost that lasted for seven weeks in the winter term** 在冬季开学的学期里持续七个星期的严寒

10 **games** 体育比赛

11 **the whole School learned to skate on the fens** 整个学校（的师生）都在（因严寒而冰冻的）沼泽地上学溜冰。

12 **Eighteen-eighty-something, that was.** = **That was eighteen-eighty-something.** 那是一八八几年。something 表示大约的概念。

13 **two thirds of the School went down with German measles** ['miːzlz] 全校三分之二（的人）因患风疹而病倒。 **measles** 麻疹；复数形式，用作单数或复数都有。 **German measles** 风疹。

14 **was turned into a hospital ward** 变成了医院的病房

15 **the great bonfire** ['bɒnˌfaɪə] **we had on Mafeking** ['mæfɪkɪŋ] **night** 庆祝马弗京城解围的狂欢之夜我们所烧起的大营火。马弗京在南非，是当时英国殖民地贝专纳的行政厅所在地，1899 年被布尔（Boer）军包围，1900 年 5 月 17 日解围。

out[1]. And the firemen[2] were having their own celebrations[3] and most of them were — um — in a regrettable condition[4]. (Laughter.) I remember Mrs. Brool[5], whose photograph is still in the tuckshop[6]; she served there until an uncle in Australia left her a lot of money[7]. In fact, I remember so much that I often think I ought to write a book. Now, what should I call it? "Memories of Rod and Lines"[8] — eh? (Cheers and laughter. That was a good one[9], people thought — one of Chips's best.) Well, well, perhaps I shall write it, some day. But I'd rather tell you about it, really[10]. I remember ... I remember ... but chiefly I remember all your faces. I never forget them. I have thousands of faces in my mind — the faces of boys. If you come and see[11] me again in years to come[12] — as I hope you all will[13] — I shall try to remember those older faces of yours[14], but it's just possible I shan't be able to[15] — and then[16] some day you'll see me somewhere and I shan't recognize you and you'll say to yourself[17] — "The old boy doesn't remember me." (Laughter.) But I *do* remember you — as you are *now*[18]. That's the point.[19] In my mind you never grow up at all. Never. Sometimes, for instance, when people talk to me about our

1 **send for the fire brigade to put it out** 派人去叫消防队来扑灭它（营火）。

2 **firemen** 消防队员。此词也作“火夫”（即烧火工人或司炉工）解，可以说与“消防队员”的解释正相反。

3 **celebrations** 庆祝活动

4 **in a regrettable condition** 处于令人遗憾的状态，指在狂欢中喝醉了酒等；这里是婉转的说法。

5 **Brool** [bru:l] 布鲁尔，姓氏

6 **tuckshop**（英国学校里的）小卖部；食品店

7 **left her a lot of money** 遗赠给她一大笔钱。这句也可解释为“留一大笔钱在她那里，叫她保管”，但这里不是。

8 **'Memories of Rod and Lines'**《罚打罚抄回忆录》。Rod 既是责打学生用的棍棒，又是钓鱼用的钓竿；Lines 既是罚学生抄书的行数，又是钓鱼线。Chips 拟了这样一个幽默的书名，当然又是哄堂大笑，喝彩不已。

9 **a good one** 一个极妙的笑话。比较：美国俚语有 a hot one，也是类似的意思，都是 one 的特殊用法。

10 **But I'd rather tell you about it, really.**（虽然写不写不一定）但是我要把这个想法告诉你们，我告诉你们的是真的（真是想写这么一本书）。

11 **come and see** = come to see，口语中常这样说。

12 **in years to come** 在今后几年里。 **to come** 将来的，修饰 years。

13 **you all will** = you all will come and see me again in years to come.

14 **I shall try to remember those older faces of yours** 我今后要努力记住你们年龄大一些时候的面貌（因为 Chips 所记得的都是学生小时候的面貌）。

15 **it's just possible I shan't be able to** 可能我将记不住你们年龄大一些时候的面貌。be able to 后面省去 remember those older faces of yours。

16 **and then** 于是

17 **you'll say to yourself** 你会想

18 **I *do* remember you — as you are *now*** 我的确记得你们现在的样子。

19 **That's the point** 这是问题所在；这是要点

respected Chairman of the Governors, I think to myself, "Ah, yes, a jolly little chap[1] with hair that sticks up on top[2] — and absolutely no idea whatever about the difference between a Gerund and a Gerundive[3]." (Loud laughter.) Well, well, I mustn't go on — umph — all night[4]. Think of me sometimes as I shall certainly think of you. "*Haec olim meminisse juvabit*[5]"...again I need not translate...' (Much laughter and shouting and prolonged cheers[6].)

August, 1913. Chips went for a cure to Wiesbaden[7], where he lodged at the home of the German master at Brookfield[8], Herr Staefel[9], with whom he had become friendly. Staefel was thirty years his junior[10], but the two men got on excellently[11]. In September, when term began[12], Chips returned and took up residence[13] at Mrs. Wickett's. He felt a great deal stronger and fitter[14] after his holiday[15], and almost wished he had not retired. Nevertheless, he found plenty to do[16]. He had all the new boys to tea[17]. He watched all the important matches on the Brookfield ground[18]. Once a term[19] he dined with the Head, and

---

1 **a jolly little chap** 有趣的小家伙

2 **hair that sticks up on top** 直竖在头顶的头发

3 **absolutely no idea whatever about the difference between a Gerund** ['dʒerənd] **and a Gerundive** [dʒɪ'rʌndɪv] 对（拉丁语中）动名词和动形词之间有何区别，绝对没有任何概念。这里在语法上可以认为 absolutely no idea 同上面 hair 并列，都是 with 的介词宾语，也可以认为 absolutely 前省去 having 或 he had。

4 **go on — umph — all night** 整夜地继续（讲）下去

5 ***Haec olim meminisse juvabit*** 拉丁语，意思是：这将帮助记忆往事。

6 **prolonged cheers** 持续的欢呼

7 **went for a cure to Wiesbaden** ['viːsˌbɑːdn] 到德国威斯巴登去疗养。

8 **lodged at the home of the German master at Brookfield** 住宿在 Brookfield 的德语老师的家里。 **German master** 作“德语老师”解，读 ['dʒɜːmənˌmɑːstə]；作“德国老师”解，读 ['dʒɜːmən'mɑːstə]。这里也可作“德国老师”解，因为看下文，他是德国人。 **the German master at Brookfield** 说某所学校的什么老师，在校名前用 at 或 in，不用 of; German master 前用定冠词 the，表示该校只有这个德语老师。

9 **Herr** [her] **Staefel** ['ʃtefəl] 施特弗尔先生；Herr 是德语，相当于英语中的 Mr.。

10 **was thirty years his junior** 比他小三十岁

11 **got on excellently** ['eksələntlɪ] 相处极好

12 **when term began** 当学期开始时。注意：term 前面可以不用 the。

13 **took up residence** ['rezɪdəns] 定居

14 **fitter** 更健康

15 **after his holiday** 在他休养之后（指去威斯巴登休养回来）。Chips 已经辞职退休，无所谓“假日”，所以这里 holiday 不作“假日”解，而是“休息”的意思。

16 **found plenty to do** 有许多事情要做。

17 **had all the new boys to tea** 叫所有的新同学来吃茶点。 **tea** 茶点；是名词。

18 **watched all the important matches on the Brookfield ground** 观看所有在 Brookfield 球场上举行的重要比赛。注意：英语 watch matches 这样的搭配，又如 watch TV（看电视）。

19 **Once a term** 每学期一次

once[1] also with the masters. He took on[2] the preparation and editing of a new Brookfeldian Directory[3]. He accepted presidency of the Old Boys' Club[4] and went to dinners in London. He wrote occasional articles, full of[5] jokes and Latin quotations, for the Brookfield terminal magazine[6]. He read his *Times* every morning — very thoroughly; and he also began to read detective stories — he had been keen on them[7] ever since the first thrills of Sherlock[8]. Yes, he was quite busy, and quite happy, too.

A year later, in 1914, he again attended the end-of-term dinner. There was a lot of war talk[9] — civil war in Ulster[10], and trouble between Austria and Serbia[11]. Herr Staefel, who was leaving for Germany the next day[12], told Chips he thought the Balkan business[13] wouldn't come to anything[14].

1 **once** 后面省去 a term。

2 **took on** 担任

3 **the preparation and editing of a new Brookfeldian Directory** 新版 Brookfield 人名录的资料工作和编辑工作。

4 **presidency** ['prezɪdənsɪ] **of the Old Boys' Club** 校友会主席的职位

5 **full of** 充满……的；修饰 articles。

6 **terminal magazine** 每学期末出版的杂志

7 **keen on them** 热衷于读它们（侦探小说）

8 **the first thrills of Sherlock** ['ʃɜːlɒk] 福尔摩斯初期的惊心动魄的侦探小说

9 **war talk** 关于战争的谈话

10 **civil war in Ulster** ['ʌlstə] 在第一次世界大战期间，英国军队与要求独立的爱尔兰人之间在阿尔斯特进行的内战。 **Ulster** 阿尔斯特，原是北爱尔一地区，现在口语中用以称北爱尔兰。

11 **trouble between Austria** ['ɔːstrɪə] **and Serbia** ['sɜːbjə] 第一次世界大战前夕，奥地利和塞尔维亚之间的纠纷。1914 年 6 月 28 日发生奥匈帝国皇储被塞尔维亚一个民族主义分子刺杀的事件。各帝国主义国家以此为借口，发动战争，终于发展成为第一次世界大战。

12 **was leaving for Germany the next day** 将在翌日动身到德国去。 **was leaving** 是用过去进行时表示过去将来的动作，= would leave。

13 **Balkan** ['bɔːlkən] **business** 巴尔干半岛问题。巴尔干半岛是第一次世界大战前帝国主义各国矛盾集中的地区之一。

14 **wouldn't come to anything** 不会发展成什么。 **come to** 到……状态；得到……结果；是习语。

第十三章

内容提要

第一次世界大战爆发。布鲁克菲尔德师生纷纷入伍。每个星期天晚上，在学校的礼拜堂做好夜礼拜后，校长查特里斯宣读阵亡校友的名单。这些名字在查特里斯只是名字而已，而对契普斯却是一张张活现在眼前的脸。

1916年7月，查特里斯对契普斯诉说他因患糖尿病不能入伍，别人不谅解；而且学校陷于混乱，他虽日以继夜地工作，还是应付不了，实在支撑不下去了。他要求契普斯回到学校去，随便做些什么，只要属于这个学校。他相信契普斯最孚众望，只有他能使学校免于瓦解。契普斯答应了。

13

The War years.[1]

The first shock, and then the first optimism.[2] The Battle of the Marne[3], the Russian steam-roller[4], Kitchener.[5]

'Do you think it will last long[6], sir?'

Chips, questioned[7] as he watched the first trial game[8] of the season, gave quite a[9] cheery answer. He was, like thousands of others, hopelessly wrong[10]; but, unlike thousands of others, he did not afterwards conceal the fact[11]. 'We ought to have — um — finished it — um — by Christmas[12]. The Germans are already beaten. But why?[13] Are you thinking of — um — joining up[14], Forrester[15]?'

Joke[16] — because Forrester was the smallest new boy Brookfield had ever had — about four feet high above his muddy football boots[17]. (But not so much a joke[18], when

1 **The War years.** 战争年代，指第一次世界大战期间。

2 **The first shock, and then the first optimism.** 最初的震惊，随后是最初的乐观。战争爆发，当然震惊；随后以为很快可以战胜敌人结束战争，所以产生最初的乐观。

3 **The Battle of the Marne** [mɑːn] 马恩河战役。马恩河在法国东北部；因是河名，所以前面加 the。1914 年 8 月德军打到马恩河，威胁巴黎，英法军合力反击，会战于马恩河上。1918 年又发生一次马恩河大战役。

4 **the Russian steam-roller** steam-roller 原是蒸气压路机，这里是指第一次世界大战初期俄军长驱直入德国的东普鲁士，所向披靡，像“蒸气压路机”。

5 **Kitchener** ['kɪtʃɪnə] Horatio Herbert Kitchener (1850—1916)，基钦纳，英国元帅，第一次世界大战开始任陆军大臣。

6 **it will last long** 它（战争）会长久地延续下去。

7 **questioned** 被提问；是过去分词，修饰 gave。

8 **trial** ['traɪəl] **game** 预选比赛

9 **quite a …** 也可说 a quite …；口语中多用 quite a …；rather a … 也是这样。

10 **hopelessly wrong** 绝对错误的；错尽错绝的

11 **did not afterwards conceal the fact** 事后并不掩盖（曾经错误估计的）这个事实。

12 **ought to have — um — finished it — um — by Christmas** ['krɪsməs] 应该在圣诞节之前就把战争结束了的。

13 **But why?** 可是，怎么？表示惊奇，惊奇下句所说的（年纪最小的）Forrester 也想入伍。

14 **joining up** 入伍；参军

15 **Forrester** ['fɒrɪstə] 福里斯特，姓氏

16 **Joke = It was a joke** Chips 问 Forrester 是否想入伍，是在跟他说笑话。

17 **about four feet high above his muddy football boots** 穿了沾泥的足球鞋大约 4 英尺高。英尺 foot 的复数用 foot 和 feet 都可以；1 英尺 = 30.48 公分，那么这个孩子还只有 1 公尺 22 公分高，怎么入伍呢？ above his boots 不是高出靴子多少，而是“连同靴子”，即“穿上了靴子”多高，说身材高一般用 tall，但有具体尺寸时，也用 high。

18 **not so much a joke** = It was not so much a joke 并不完全是笑话（其中实有不是笑话的成分）。

you came to think of it afterwards[1]; for he was killed in 1918 — shot down in flames over Cambrai[2].) But one didn't guess what lay ahead[3]. It seemed tragically sensational[4] when the first Old Brookfeldian was killed in action[5] — in September. Chips thought, when that news came: a hundred years ago boys from this school were fighting *against* the French. Strange[6], in a way[7], that the sacrifices of one generation should so cancel out those of another[8]. He tried to express this to Blades[9], the Head of School House[10]; but Blades, eighteen years old and already in training for a cadetship[11], only laughed. What had all that history stuff to do with it, anyhow?[12] Just old Chips with one of his queer ideas[13], that's all.

1915. Armies clenched in deadlock from the sea to Switzerland.[14] The Dardanelles.[15] Gallipoli.[16] Military camps springing up[17] quite near Brookfield; soldiers using the playing fields for sports and training[18]; swift develop-

---

1 **when you came to think of it afterwards** 你事后想起这个笑话来的时候（会觉得）。

2 **shot down in flames over Cambrai**（飞行）在康布雷上空时被击落烧死。shot是过去分词。康布雷是法国北部城市，1917年、1918年曾在此发生大战。

3 **one didn't guess what lay ahead** 人们猜测不到往后将发生什么；不知以后

怎样。 **one** 泛指任何人。 **guess** 猜；猜中；这里作“猜中”解。 **lay** lie 的过去式；**lie ahead** 在前面存在着，也就是将在今后出现或发生。

4 **It seemed tragically sensational** 这件事似乎使人悲痛地震动。It 指下面 when 引起的从句中所说的事情。

5 **the first Old Brookfeldian was killed in action** 第一个 Brookfield 校友阵亡。**Old Brookfeldian** 是“曾经在 Brookfield 学习过的人”，也就是“Brookfield 校友”；这里的 Old 没有“年老”的意思。 **in action** 在战斗中。

6 **Strange** = It is strange.

7 **in a way** 在某一点上；在某种程度上

8 **the sacrifices** ['sækrɪfaɪsɪz] **of one generation should so cancel out those of another** 一代的牺牲竟然如此不计另一代的牺牲。过去的一代曾为对法国作战而牺牲，现在的一代竟同法国结为联盟，对德国作战而牺牲。**those of another** = the sacrifices of another generation. **cancel out** 划掉；消去。

9 **Blades** [bleɪdz] 布雷兹，姓氏

10 **Head of School House** 校长住宅所在宿舍里的寄宿生头头

11 **in training for a cadetship** [kə'detʃɪp] 为当军官候补生而受训练

12 **What had all that history stuff to do with it, anyhow?** 毕竟所有那些历史上的东西跟这（现在的战争）有什么关系呢?

13 **Just old Chips with one of his queer ideas** 前面省去 It was。意思是：Chips 就是这样，这又是他的奇怪想法之一。

14 **Armies clenched in deadlock from the sea to Switzerland** ['swɪtsələnd].（双方）军队僵持在大西洋到瑞士之间（横贯法国的战线上）。**clenched** 是过去分词；被钳制住。**in deadlock** 僵持；陷于僵局；是习语。

15 **The Dardanelles** [ˌdɑːdə'nelz] 达达尼尔海峡（之战）。达达尼尔海峡在欧亚两洲之间。1915 年 4 月英法试图袭击达达尼尔，未获成功。Dardanelles 前面有 the。

16 **Gallipoli** [gə'lɪpəlɪ] 加里波利，达达尼尔海峡与爱琴海（Aegean Sea）之间的半岛，1915 年加里波利战役中英国海陆军大败。

17 **springing up** 涌现

18 **using the playing fields for sports and training** 用 Brookfield 的运动场进行体育活动和军事训练。

ment of Brookfield O.T.C.[1] Most of the younger masters gone[2] or in uniform[3]. Every Sunday night, in the chapel after evening service[4], Chatteris read out[5] the names of old boys killed[6], together with[7] short biographies. Very moving; but Chips, in the back pew[8] under the gallery[9], thought: They are only names to him[10], he doesn't see their faces as I do ...

1916. The Somme Battle.[11] Twenty-three names read out[12] one Sunday evening.

Towards the close of that catastrophic July[13], Chatteris talked to Chips one afternoon at Mrs. Wickett's. He was over worked and over worried[14] and looked very ill[15]. 'To tell you the truth[16], Chipping, I'm not having too easy a time here.[17] I'm thirty-nine, you know, and unmarried, and lots of people seem to think they know what I ought to do[18]. Also, I happen to be diabetic[19], and couldn't pass the blindest M.O.[20], but I don't see why I should pin a medical certificate on my front door[21].'

Chips hadn't known anything about this[22]; it was a shock to him[23], for he liked Chatteris.

---

1 **swift developments of Brookfield O.T.C.** Brookfield军官教练团的迅速发展。

O.T.C. = Officers' Training Corps [kɔːz].

2 **gone = were gone**（离校而）去。gone 是形容词。

3 **in uniform** ['juːnɪfɔːm] = **were in uniform** 穿着军装

4 **evening service** 夜礼拜

5 **read** [red] **out** 宣读

6 **old boys killed** 阵亡的校友。killed 是过去分词。

7 **together with** 连同

8 **back pew** 后座；pew 是教堂里的座位。

9 **gallery** 教堂的楼座

10 **They are only names to him** 他们（阵亡的校友）对他（Chatteris）来说，只是一些名字而已（并不认识他们）。

11 **The Somme** [sɒm] **Battle** 索姆河战役。索姆河在法国北部，流入英吉利海峡；1916 年、1918 年两次在此发生大战。

12 **read** [red] **out = were read out** 被宣读出来

13 **Towards the close** [kləʊz] **of that catastrophic** [ˌkætəˈstrɒfɪk] **July** 在生死关头的 7 月将近结束的时候。1916 年上半年德军进攻凡尔登（Verdun），巴黎告急，到 7 月始被击退。

14 **was over worked** ['əʊvə'wɜːkt] **and over worried** ['əʊvə'wʌrɪd] 劳累过度，忧虑过度。

15 **looked very ill** 看上去身体很不好。

16 **To tell you the truth** 老实对你说；作插入语。也说 To tell the truth。

17 **I'm not having too easy a time here** 我在这里日子不太好过。这里的 having 有"享有"、"经历"的意思。

18 **seem to think they know what I ought to do** 似乎认为他们知道我应该做什么（指认为他应该入伍）。

19 **happen to be diabetic** [ˌdaɪəˈbetɪk] 恰巧患糖尿病

20 **couldn't pass the blindest M.O.** 通不过最眼瞎的军医；即使最糊涂的军医也检查得出来，不会认为合格。**M.O.** = medical officer.

21 **I don't see why I should pin a medical certificate on my front door** 我不知道为什么必须（即"我认为不必"，也即"我总无需"）在我前门别上一张（因糖尿糖不能服役的）医学证明。

22 **this** 指 Chatteris 所讲的情况。

23 **it was a shock to him** 这（Chatteris 所讲的情况）对 Chips 是一个震动；这使 Chips 震惊。

The latter continued: 'You see how it is — Ralston filled the place up with young men[1], all very good, of course — but now most of them have joined up and the substitutes[2] are pretty dreadful[3], on the whole. They poured ink down a man's neck in prep[4] one night last week — silly fool[5] — got hysterical. I have to take classes myself, take prep for fools like that[6], work till midnight every night, and get cold-shouldered as a slacker on top of everything[7]. I can't stand it[8] much longer. If things[9] don't improve next term I shall have a breakdown[10].'

'I do sympathize with you,' Chips said.

'I hoped you would.[11] And that brings me to what I came here to ask you[12]. Briefly[13], my suggestion is that — if you felt equal to it and would care to — how about coming back here for a while[14]? You look pretty fit[15], and, of course, you know all the ropes[16]. I don't mean a lot of hard work for you — you needn't take anything strenuously[17] — just a

1 **filled the place up with young men** 把这个地方（Brookfield）塞满了年轻人；都请了些青年教师。

2 **substitutes** ['sʌbstitju:ts] 代课老师

3 **pretty dreadful** 很糟的。**pretty** 副词，= very。 **dreadful** 原义“可怕的”，

这里作“糟透的”解。两个都是口语。

4 **They poured ink down a man's neck in prep** 在预备课上他们把墨水倒在一个人的脖子里。 **They** 泛指“有人”。

5 **silly fool** 傻瓜（指被倒墨水的人）

6 **take prep for fools like that** 替代那样的傻瓜去主持预备课。 **like that** 那样的；是习语，这里作定语，修饰 fools。这个习语也可作状语用。

7 **get cold-shouldered as a slacker on top of everything** 在这一切之上（最难受的是），还被人视为逃避兵役的人而受到冷待。 **slacker** 一般作“懒汉”、“逃避职责的人”解。 **on top of** 在……之上；除……之外。

8 **stand it** 忍受现在的处境

9 **things** 情况

10 **have a breakdown**（身体或精神）垮掉

11 **I hoped you would.** = I hoped (that) you would sympathize with me. 我原来就是希望你同情我。

12 **that brings me to what I came here to ask you** 那个（希望）使我想到来这里请求你做的事。what 是关系代词，= that which；它既是主句中 to 的介词宾语，又是从句中 ask 的直接宾语（you 是间接宾语）。

13 **Briefly** 简单地说

14 **if you felt equal to it and would care to — how about coming back here for a while** 假如你觉得身体吃得消，而且又高兴的话，你回到这儿（学校）来（工作）一段时间怎么样？ felt 和 would care 都是虚拟语气，表示假设。 **equal to** 胜任的；经受得起的；to 是介词。 **it** 指后面的 coming back here for a while, care to = care to come back here for a while. **how about**（你以为）……怎么样？ **for a while** 一段时间（可长可短）；是状语短语。严格说来，my suggestion is that 后面不能接 how about …，可以改用 you might come back here for a while。

15 **pretty fit** 很健康

16 **know all the ropes** 熟悉（Brookfield 的）全部情况。 **know the ropes** 知道内情，是习语。

17 **needn't take anything strenuously** ['strenjʊəslɪ] 不必紧张地做什么事。 **take** 这里有“对待”、“处理”的意思。

few odd jobs here and there, as you choose[1]. What I'd like you for more than anything else is not for the actual work you'd do[2], though that, naturally, would be very valuable[3] — but for your help in other ways[4] — in just *belonging* here[5]. There's[6] nobody ever been more popular than you were, and are still[7] — you'd help to hold things together[8] if there were any danger of them flying to bits[9]. And perhaps there is that danger ...'

Chips answered, breathlessly and with a holy joy in his heart[10]: 'I'll come ...[11]'

1 **just a few odd jobs here and there, as you choose** = I mean just a few odd jobs … 我的意思是，随你高兴在各方面做一些零星的活儿。 **odd jobs** 零星工作。**here and there** 各处，是习语。

2 **What I'd like you for more than anything else is not for the actual work you'd do** 我甚于一切地寄希望于你的，不是你将做的实际工作。这里首先要弄清 more than anything 是状语短语，修饰 'd (= should 或 would) like，而不是 for 的介词宾语（for 的介词宾语是 What）。另外，按照语法，句中 not for the actual work 中的 for 是多余的，如 What I'm looking for is not *for* that book. 中的第二个 for 是多余的；但在较长的句子里，英美人常会有类似错误，后面 but *for* your help in other ways 中的 for 也是多余的。

3 **though that, naturally, would be very valuable** 虽然那（actual work）自然是非常有价值的。 **would be** 是虚拟语气，表示假如你做实际工作的话。

4 **in other ways** 在其他方面；用其他方式

5 **in just *belonging* here** 就在于归属这里；就在于回到学校里来作为学校的一员。 **in** 与上面 in other ways 的 in 并列，进一步说 ways 的内容。

6 **There's** = There has.

7 **you were, and are still** = you were popular, and are still popular.

8 **hold things together** 维持（Brookfield 的）局面

9 **danger of them flying to bits** 局面崩垮的危险。**them** 也可用 their，= things('). **flying to bits** 飞散成碎片；崩溃。

10 **breathlessly and with a holy joy in his heart** 气喘吁吁、满怀崇高的喜悦地

11 **I'll come ...** = I'll come back to Brookfield.

第十四章

内容提要

契普斯每天上午到学校，教几堂拉丁语和罗马史课。依旧是那些老课文，依旧是讲些老笑话，却都意外地成功。他仿佛是个重返舞台的红角儿。他也帮助处理一些问题；还讲了许多新的笑话。

1918年，校长查特里斯去世，契普斯再度代理校长。每逢星期天晚上，由他宣读阵亡校友名单。有一天，他在读名单时，忽然提到了原来布鲁克菲尔德的德语老师施特弗尔，说他在西线阵亡了，并表示惋惜。契普斯怎么把敌人的名字也读在一起呢？但大家也只是惊讶而已。

布鲁克菲尔德操场上正进行着劈刺训练。他对来自陆军部的一位将军说：“劈刺是庸俗的杀人方法。”一时传为佳话。

14

He still kept on his rooms with Mrs. Wickett[1]; indeed[2], he still lived there; but every morning, about half past ten, he put on his coat and muffler[3] and crossed the road to the School. He felt very fit[4], and the actual work was not taxing[5]. Just a few forms in Latin and Roman History — the old lessons — even the old pronunciation[6]. The same joke about Lex Canuleia[7] — there was a new generation that had not heard it, and he was absurdly gratified by the success it achieved[8]. He felt a little like a music-hall favourite returning to the boards after a positively last appearance[9].

They all said how marvellous it was that he knew every boy's name and face so quickly. They did not guess[10] how closely he had kept in touch from across the road[11].

He was a grand success altogether[12]. In some strange way he did, and they all knew and felt it, help things[13]. For

1 **kept on his rooms with Mrs. Wickett** 继续在 Mrs. Wickett 处租屋居住。 **on** 是副词，表示“继续”。

2 **indeed** 固然（表示让步，常和 but 搭配，这里就是一例）

3 **muffler** ['mʌflə] 围巾

4 **fit** 健康的

5 **the actual work was not taxing** 实际所做的工作并不繁重。 **taxing** 形容词；“使人疲劳”的意思。

6 **Just a few forms in Latin and Roman History — the old Lessons — even the old pronuciation.**（承接上文）他的实际工作就是担任几个班级的拉丁语和罗马史课，还是些老课文，甚至所教的读音也是老读音。原文没有谓语，是名词句。

7 **Lex Canuleia** 见第六章。

8 **he was absurdly** [əb'sɜːdlɪ] **gratified** ['grætɪfaɪd] **by the success it achieved** [ə'tʃiːvd] 它（笑话）所取得的成功（引起哄堂大笑）使他可笑地得意起来。

9 **felt a little like a music-hall favourite** ['feɪvərɪt] **returning to the boards after a positively last appearance** 觉得有点像在确实的最后演出之后重上舞台的游艺场红星。 **music-hall** 在美国指音乐厅；在英国指表演歌舞和杂耍的剧场，这种剧场在美国称 vaudeville ['vəʊdəvɪl] theater（或 house)。music hall 这里作定语，故在两词间加连字号。 **boards** 复数；舞台。

10 **guess** 猜中；想得到

11 **how closely** ['kləʊslɪ] **he had kept in touch from across the road** 他（住在学校对面）隔着马路（和学校）保持何等密切的联系。**kept in touch (with)** 保持（和……的）接触。

12 **He was a grand success altogether**。总的来说，他是取得极大成就的人；总之，他大获成功。**success** 成功的人（或事物）。

13 **In some strange way he did, and they all knew and felt it, help things** 他确实不可思议地对（学校的）情况有帮助——这一点他们（全校师生）全都知道，全都感觉得到。 **and they all knew and felt it** 是插入语。 **did help** 确实有助于；did help 是 helped 的着重式，did 要重读。

the first time in his life he felt *necessary*[1] — and necessary to something that was nearest his heart[2]. There is no sublimer feeling in the world[3], and it was his at last[4].

He made new jokes, too — about the O.T.C. and the food-rationing system[5] and the anti-air-raid blinds[6] that had to be fitted on all the windows[7]. There was a mysterious kind of rissole[8] that began to appear on the School menus[9] on Mondays, and Chips called it '*abhorrendum*[10]' — 'meat to be abhorred[11]'. The story went round[12] — heard Chips's latest?[13]

Chatteris fell ill[14] during the winter of '17, and again, for the second time in his life[15], Chips became Acting Head[16] of Brookfield. Then in April, Chatteris died, and the Governors asked Chips if he would carry on 'for the duration[17]'. He said he would[18], if they would refrain from appointing him officially[19]. From that last honour, within his reach at last, he shrank instinctively[20], feeling himself in so many ways[21] unequal to it[22]. He said

---

1 **he felt *necessary*** 他觉得自己是被需要的（Brookfield 少不了他）。

2 **necessary to something that was nearest his heart** 为他心上最亲切的东西（指 Brookfield 公学）所需要。

3 **There is no sublimer feeling in the world** 天下没有更崇高的感觉；感觉自己为心上最亲切的东西所需要是最珍贵的。

4 **it was his at last** 它（这种无比崇高的感觉）终于为他所有。

5 **food-rationing system** 粮食配给制

6 **anti-air-raid blinds** 防空窗帘

7 **fitted on all the windows** 装在所有的窗上

8 **a mysterious** [mɪsˈtɪərɪəs] **kind of rissole** [ˈrɪsəʊl] 一种莫名其妙的法国肉饼。**rissole** 用肉或鱼和面包屑等制成的腊肠状食物；原来是法语。

9 **the School menu** [ˈmenjuː]（Brookfield）学校的菜单

10 ***abhorrendum*** 拉丁语，是“望而却步”的意思。

11 **meat to be abhorred** [əbˈhɔːd] 讨厌的肉（作者用以译释 *abhorrendum*）

12 **The story went round** 这个笑话传开了。 **story** 有“轶事”、“传说”、“报道”等许多解释，不一定是“故事”。 **went round**（消息等）流传，是习语。

13 **heard Chips's latest?** = have you heard Chips's latest joke? 你听到了 Chips 的最新笑话吗？其实这话应放在引号里，因为这不是作者在问，而是引用 Brookfield 师生的问话，小说里常用这种写法，读来显得生动。

14 **fell ill** 病倒

15 **in his life** 他一生中

16 **Acting Head** 代理校长

17 **if he would carry on 'for the duration'** 他是否愿意“在整个非常时期里”坚持（担任代理校长）下去。 **carry on** 坚持下去；on 是副词。 **for the duration** 指在战争等的整个非常时期里；这是一个战时常用语，所以放在引号内。

18 **he would** = he would carry on 'for the duration'.

19 **refrain from appointing him officially** 并不正式任命他（为校长）。

20 **From that last honour, within his reach at last, he shrank instinctively** 他本能地躲闪那终于伸手可得的最后的荣誉（指校长职务）。 **From that last honour** 状语短语，修饰 shrank；shrank 是 shrink 的过去式，介词用 from。 **within his reach at last** = which was within his reach at last.

21 **in so many ways** 在那么许多方面

22 **unequal to it** 不配那最后的荣誉；不能胜任校长职务。

to Rivers[1]: 'You see, I'm not a young man and I don't want people to — um — expect a lot from me[2]. I'm like all these new colonels and majors you see everywhere — just a wartime fluke.[3] A ranker, that's all I am really.[4]'

1917, 1918. Chips lived through it all[5]. He sat in the headmaster's study every morning, handling problems, dealing with plaints and requests[6]. Out of vast experience had emerged a kindly, gentle confidence in himself.[7] To keep a sense of proportion, that was the main thing.[8] So much of the world was losing it[9]; as well keep it where it had, or ought to have, a congenial home[10].

On Sundays[11] in the chapel it was he who now read out the tragic list[12], and sometimes it was seen and heard that he was in tears over it[13]. Well, why not? the School said[14]; he was an old man; they might have despised anyone else for the weakness[15].

One day he got a letter from Switzerland, from friends there; it was heavily censored[16], but conveyed some news. On the following Sunday, after the names and biog-

1 **Rivers** Sir John Rivers，校董会主席，见第十一章。

2 **expect a lot from me** 对我有许多期望。

3 **I'm like all these new colonels** ['kɜ:nəlz] **and majors you see everywhere — just a war-time fluke** [flu:k] 我像你看到的所有这些新（当上）的上校、少校们一样，只是个战时的幸运儿。 **fluke** 侥幸的成功；是口语，有时也作"意外的挫折"解。**you see** = whom you see.

4 **A ranker, that's all I am really.** 其实我只是一个士兵出身的军官。这是"A ranker is all I am really."在口语中着重的讲法，= All I am is really a ranker.

5 **lived through it all** 全都撑过来了。

6 **dealing with plaints and requests** 处理（师生们提出的）诉苦和请求。

7 **Out of vast experience had emerged a kindly, gentle confidence in himself** 从广泛的经验中产生了一种亲切温柔的自信。这是倒装句，= A kindly, gentle confidence had emerged out of vast experience.

8 **To keep a sense of proportion, that was the main thing.** 保持分寸感，那是主要的事情。这句子用不定式短语做主语，that 是多余的，用 that 是为了强调语气。

9 **So much of the world was losing it** 世界上那么多的人正在失去分寸感。**the world** 世界上的人们，作单数用，所以前面用 much 而不用 many。

10 **as well keep it where it had, or ought to have, a congenial** [kən'dʒi:njəl] **home** 在分寸感原来有的——或应该有的——适当存在之处，还是把它在那里保持下来。 **as well** 还是；大可。

11 **On Sundays** 在每星期日

12 **tragic list** 悲伤的名单，指阵亡战士的名单。

13 **he was in tears over it** Chips 在读名单时流着眼泪。 **in tears** 是习语；前面说 was seen and heard，看到的是流泪，听到的是哭声。 **it** 指 list。

14 **Well, why not? the School said.** = 'Well, why not?' the School said. **the School** 全校师生；学校里的人们。

15 **they might have despised anyone else for the weakness**（如不是 Chips 而是）换了其他任何人的话，他们会瞧不起那个人的软弱表现的；别人哭了，会被轻视，但 Chips 老了，大家原谅他。they 代替 the School（全校师生）。

16 **was heavily censored** ['sensəd] 经过重重检查

raphies of old boys[1], he paused a moment and then added[2]:

'Those few of you who were here before the War will remember Max Staefel, the German master[3]. He was in Germany, visiting his home, when war broke out. He was popular while he was here, and made many friends[4]. Those who knew him will be sorry to hear that he was killed last week, on the Western Front[5].'

He was a little pale when he sat down afterwards, aware that he had done something unusual[6]. He had consulted nobody about it[7], anyhow; no one else could be blamed. Later, outside the chapel, he heard an argument:

'On the Western Front, Chips said.[8] Does that mean he was fighting for the Germans?[9]'

'I suppose it does.[10]'

'Seems funny, then, to read his name out with all the others.[11] After all, he was an *enemy*.'

'Oh, just one of Chips's ideas, I expect[12]. The old boy still has 'em[13].'

Chips, in his room again[14], was not displeased by the

---

1 **after the names and biographies of old boys** 在（宣读阵亡的）校友名字和

传略之后

2 **added** 接下去说

3 **will remember Max Staefel, the German master** 总记得那位德语教师 Max Staefel 吧。Staefel 是 Chips 的同事，德国人，1914 年回德国，见第十二章末。**will** 这里表示推测，有“可能”、“总”的意思。

4 **made many friends** 交了许多朋友。 **make friends** 交朋友；是习语。 **make friends with somebody** 与某人交朋友。

5 **Western Front** 西线。第一次世界大战中，德国西面对法国的战线为“西线”，东面对俄国的战线为“东线”。德国作家雷马克（Remarque）著有描述西线战争的小说《西线无战事》。

6 **aware that he had done something unusual** 觉得自己做了一件异乎寻常的事（指在宣读校友阵亡战士名单时，讲了在当时是敌人的德语老师“不幸阵亡”）。aware 是表语形容词，修饰 He。

7 **He had consulted with nobody about it** 他不曾同别人商量过这件事（指能不能通报德语教师阵亡）。 **had consulted** 用过去完成时，表示“事先商量过”。

8 **On the Western Front, Chips said.** = 'On the Western Front,' Chips said.

9 **Does that mean he was fighting for the Germans?** 那（指“On the Western Front”那句话）是说他（Staefel）在为德国人作战吗?

10 **I suppose it does.** = I suppose it means he was fighting for the Germans. 我想这（指“On the Western Front”一语）是说他在为德国人作战。

11 **Seems funny, then, to read his name out with all the others.** 那么，把他的名字（Max Staefel）和所有其他名字一起宣读出来，好像很滑稽。**Seems funny** = It seems funny；口语中省去了引起实际主语（不定式 to read ...）的虚词 It。

12 **just one of Chips's ideas, I expect** = I expect (that) it is just one of Chips's ideas 我想这（把德国人 Staefel 的名字和其他校友的名字一起宣读）只是 Chips 的诸多（特别的）想法之一。 **expect** 想；认为；是口语。

13 **'em** = them 指 ideas。

14 **in his room again** 回到房间里

comment[1]. Yes, he still had 'em — those ideas of dignity and generosity that were becoming increasingly rare in a frantic world[2]. And he thought: Brookfield will take them, too, from me; but it wouldn't from anyone else[3].

Once, asked for his opinion of[4] bayonet practice being carried on near the cricket pavilion[5], he answered with that lazy, slightly asthmatic intonation[6] that had been so often and so extravagantly imitated[7]: 'It[8] seems — to me — umph — a very vulgar way of killing people.'

The yarn[9] was passed on[10] and joyously appreciated[11] — how Chips had told some big brass hat from the War Office that bayonet fighting was vulgar[12]. Just like Chips. And they found an adjective for him — an adjective just beginning to be used: he was pre-War[13].

1 **was not displeased by the comment** 并没有被这评论弄得不愉快。 **not displeased** 是 pleased 的另一种讲法，含有“倒是愉快的”的意思。**the comment** 指上文师生们的议论。

2 **those ideas of dignity and generosity** [ˌdʒenəˈrɒsɪtɪ] **that were becoming increasingly rare in a frantic world** 那些在疯狂的世界里变得越来越难得的尊严和宽容的思想。that = which。这个名词词组是它前面的 'em (= them) 的同位语。

3 **Brookfield will take them, too, from me; but it wouldn't from anyone else** Brookfield 也将从我身上继承尊严和宽容的思想；但它不会从任何其他人身上继承这些。

4 **asked for his opinion of**（他）被问到他对于……的看法。这里 asked for 也可说 asked。

5 **bayonet** [ˈbeɪənɪt] **practice being carried on near the cricket pavilion** [pəˈvɪljən] 在板球场看台附近进行（用刺刀的）劈刺练习。being (carried on) 在语法上作为分词和动名词都可以；英国语法家 H. W. Fowler 称为 fused participle。

6 **asthmatic** [æsˈmætɪk] **intonation** 气喘病造成的音调

7 **extravagantly** [ɪksˈtrævɪgəntlɪ] **imitated** 被过分地模仿的；模仿得过分的

8 **It** 照语法，应指上面的 bayonet practice（劈刺练习），实际是指在战争中拼刺刀，即下节所说的 bayonet fighting。

9 **yarn** [jɑːn] 奇谈；也作“故事”解；是口语。

10 **was passed on** 被传述

11 **joyously appreciated** [əˈpriːʃɪeɪtɪd] 大受欣赏

12 **how Chips had told some big brass hat from the War Office that bayonet fighting was vulgar** Chips 怎样对陆军部来的某位高级军官说拼刺刀是恶俗的。这是个名词性从句，与 the yarn 同位。 **brass hat** 高级将领，高级军官；是俚语；也延伸作“大亨”解。

13 **pre-War** 战前的；指第一次世界大战以前的，意即只有第一次世界大战以前人们才会对用刺刀劈杀大惊小怪，视为恶俗。

第十五章

内容提要

契普斯正在上拉丁语课，忽然炮声隆隆，高射炮弹在头顶嘶嘶呼啸。有些学生惊慌了。可是契普斯照样讲课，照样讲笑话。他说：“新的杀人武器抹杀不掉千百年来有意义的东西。”他叫学生译释一段拉丁课文，学生翻译出来，正好是“日耳曼人是这样进行战斗的。”契普斯又在开玩笑，满堂大笑。契普斯成了传奇人物。

1919年11月11日，第一次世界大战结束。契普斯在去学校参加庆祝活动时受了凉，第二天患支气管炎病倒了，一直卧病到圣诞节之后。事实上，他在11月11日那天晚上已经提出了辞呈。他的代理校长的职务生涯结束了。

15

And once, on a night of full moonlight, the air-raid warning[1] was given while Chips was taking his lower fourth in Latin[2]. The guns began almost instantly[3], and as there was plenty of shrapnel[4] falling about outside[5], it seemed to Chips that they might just as well stay where they were[6], on the ground floor of School House. It was pretty solidly built and made as good a dug-out as Brookfield could offer[7]; and as for a direct hit[8], well[9], they could not expect to survive that, wherever they were[10].

So he went on with his Latin[11], speaking a little louder amidst the reverberating crashes of the guns[12] and the shrill whine of anti-aircraft shells[13]. Some of the boys were nervous; few were able to be attentive[14]. He said gently: 'It may possibly seem to you, Robertson[15] — at this particular moment in the world's history — umph — that the affairs of Caesar in Gaul[16] some two thousand years ago — are —

1 **air-raid warning** 空袭警报

2 **was taking his lower fourth in Latin** 正在给他的四年级上学期班级上拉丁语课。

3 **The guns began almost instantly**（刚发出警报，）高射炮（火）几乎立即开始。

4 **plenty of shrapnel** ['ʃræpnəl] 许多弹片。 **shrapnel** 弹片的集称，是不可数名词。

5 **falling about outside** 在学校外面四处掉落下来。about 和 outside 都是副词。

6 **might just as well stay where they were** 还是呆在原地不动的好。

7 **made as good a dugout** ['dʌgaʊt] **as Brookfield could offer** 成为 Brookfield 所能提供的最好的防空洞。 **made** 变成；成为；是过去式，与 was built 并列，不是与 built 并列的过去分词。

8 **as for a direct hit** 至于直接击中

9 **well** 语气助词，没有具体意义。

10 **they could not expect to survive** [sə'vaɪv] **that, wherever they were** 无论他们是在哪里，也不能指望被直接击中还能活命。 **that** 指 direct hit。

11 **went on with his Latin** 继续讲授他的拉丁语。

12 **reverberating** [rɪ'vɜːbəreɪtɪŋ] **crashes of the guns** 震荡的炮声

13 **shrill whine of anti-aircraft shells** 高射炮弹尖厉的呼啸声

14 **few were able to be attentive** 没有几个（学生）能集中思想（听课）。

15 **Robertson** ['rɒbətsn] 罗伯森，（一个学生的）姓氏

16 **the affairs of Caesar** ['siːzə] **in Gaul** [gɔːl] Gaius Julius Caesar（凯撒，公元前 100—44），古罗马政治家、将军、历史家，于公元前 58—51 年攻占高卢（Gaul）。这里所指的是 Chips 教的拉丁语课文中谈到这件事。 **affairs** 事态；情况；用复数，并不作“多桩事件”解。affairs 作这个解释时，前面不用冠词 the，如 investigate affairs。这里句中用 the，是因为 affairs 后有 of Caesar in Gaul，专指凯撒攻占高卢的情况。

umph — of somewhat secondary importance[1] — and that — umph — the irregular conjugation of the verb "*tollo*" is — umph — even less important still[2]. But believe me — umph — my dear Robertson — that is not really the case[3].' Just then there came a particularly loud explosion — quite near. 'You cannot — umph — judge the importance of things — umph — by the noise they make[4]. Oh, dear me[5], no.' A little chuckle. 'And these things — umph — that have mattered — for thousands of years — are not going to be — snuffed out — because some stink merchant — in his laboratory — invents a new kind of mischief.[6]' Titters of nervous laughter[7]; for Burrow[8], the pale, lean, and medically unfit science master[9], was nicknamed the Stink Merchant. Another explosion — nearer still. 'Let us — um — resume our work. If it is fate that we are soon to be — umph — interrupted, let us be found employing ourselves in something — umph — really appropriate.[10] Is there anyone who will volunteer to construe[11]?'

Maynard[12], chubby, dauntless, clever, and impu-

---

1 **of somewhat secondary importance** 或多或少是次要的

2 **that—umph—the irregular conjugation of the verb "*tollo*" is — umph —**

even less important still 拉丁动词 *tollo* 的不规则变化甚至更不重要。这个 that- 从句同前面一个 that- 从句并列。 ***tollo*** 拉丁语，有“举起、接收、教育、搬开”等许多意义。

3 **that is not really the case** 实际情况并不如此

4 **You cannot — umph — judge the importance of things — umph — by the noise they make** 你不能用发出声音的大小来判断事物的重要性。they make = that(或 which) they (= things) make.

5 **Oh, dear me** 噢，哎呀。dear me 也作 dear，是感叹词。

6 **And these things — umph — that have mattered — for thousands of years — are not going to be — snuffed out — because some stink merchant — in his laboratory — invents a new kind of mischief** ['mɪstʃɪf]. 几千年来关系重大的事物，不会因为哪个搞化学的家伙在他的试验室里发明了一种新的捣鬼的东西而被抹杀。句中许多破折号都只是表现说话时气喘吁吁的停顿或拖长声音。 **mattered** 有重大关系；事关重要。 **snuff** 原是“剪（烛）花；掐灭(蜡烛）”的意思，转义为“扼杀、消灭”； **snuff out** 消灭掉，抹杀。because 与前面 not 呼应，是“并不因为……而……”的意思，如 You should not despise him because he has made a mistake. 你不应该因为他犯了个错误而轻视他；不是“因为他犯了个错误，所以你不应该轻视他”的意思。stink merchant 中的 **stink** 由“臭气”转指“化学”； **merchant** 由“商人”转指“搞某一行当的人”。 **mischief** 这里指为害人类的东西。

7 **Titters of nervous laughter** 嗤嗤的胆怯的笑声。因为外面在轰炸，学生们害怕，所以笑也是胆怯的。

8 **Burrow** ['bʌrəʊ] 巴罗，姓

9 **medically unfit science master** 体检不合格（因而不能服兵役）的自然科学教师。

10 **If it is fate that we are soon to be — umph — interrupted, let us be found employing ourselves in something — umph — really appropriate** [ə'prəʊprɪɪt]. 假如命中注定我们就要被打断（被炸死），让我们被人们发现正在做真正恰当的事情（在坚持上课）。注意：fate 前无任何限定词。

11 **volunteer** [ˌvɒlən'tɪə] **to construe** [kən'stru:] 自愿分析和解释句子。

12 **Maynard** ['meɪnəd] 梅纳德，姓氏

dent[1], said: 'I will, sir.'

'Very good. Turn to page forty and begin at the bottom line.'

The explosions still continued deafeningly[2]; the whole building shook as if it were being lifted off its foundations[3]. Maynard found the page, which was some way ahead[4], and began shrilly[5]:

'*Genus hoc erat pugnae* — this was the kind of fight — *quo se Germani exercuerant* — in which the Germans busied themselves[6] — Oh, sir, that's good — that's really very funny indeed, sir — one of your very best[7] ...'

Laughing began, and Chips added[8]: 'Well — umph — you can see — now — that these dead languages — umph — can come to life again[9] — sometimes — eh? Eh?'

Afterwards they learned[10] that five bombs had fallen in and around Brookfield[11], the nearest of them just outside the School grounds[12]. Nine persons had been killed.

The story was told, retold, embellished.[13] 'The dear old boy never turned a hair[14]. Even found[15] some old tag[16] to illustrate[17] what was going on.[18] Something in Caesar

1 **impudent** ['ɪmpjʊdənt] 冒失的

2 **deafeningly** ['defnɪŋlɪ] 震耳欲聋地

3 **shook as if it were being lifted off its foundations**（建筑物）震得仿佛将被从地基上掀起来。 **as if** 仿佛；后面动词用虚拟语气。 **off** 在这里是介词。

4 **some way ahead** [ə'hed] 再往前些；还要翻过去些。如原来翻在第 10 页，现要翻到第 20 页，汉语说“在后面”，英语说“ahead”。

5 **began shrilly** 开始尖声地（朗读和解释）

6 ***Genus hoc erat pugnae* — this was the kind of fight — *quo se Germani exercuerant* — in which the Germans busied themselves** 斜体是拉丁语，破折号后是英语解释，意思是：“这是日耳曼人进行的一种战斗。” **Germans** 日耳曼人；妙在现代的德国人在英语里也叫 Germans。

7 **one of your very best** 你最妙最妙的笑话之一。very 用在形容词最高级前，加强语气。这里 best 用作名词，作“最好的东西（或人）”解。

8 **added** 进而说；接着说

9 **come to life again** 重新苏醒过来；复活

10 **learned** 获悉

11 **had fallen in and around Brookfield**（炸弹）掉在 Brookfield 及其周围。下文说最近的一枚炸弹就掉在校园外面，由此看来，这里这个 Brookfield 当指包括村庄在内的 Brookfield。见第二章开头，学校后面是它附属的小村庄。

12 **the nearest of them just outside the School grounds** = the nearest of them (bombs) falling just outside the School grounds.

13 **embellished** [ɪm'belɪʃt] 被添加细节；被添油加醋

14 **turned a hair** 动声色；这是习语，只用于否定式，如 never（或 not) turn a hair。

15 **Even found** = He even found

16 **old tag** 古老的简短引语

17 **illustrate** ['ɪlʌstreɪt] 说明

18 **what was going on** 在进行着的事情（指当时在进行的第一次世界大战）。

about the way the Germans fought.[1] You wouldn't think there were things like that in Caesar[2], would you? And the way Chips laughed[3] ... you know the way he *does* laugh[4] ... the tears all running down his face[5] ... never seen him laugh so much[6]...'

He was a legend[7].

With[8] his old and tattered gown, his walk that was just beginning to break into a stumble[9], his mild eyes peering over the steel-rimmed spectacles[10], and his quaintly humorous sayings[11], Brookfield would not have had an atom of him different[12].

November 11th, 1918.[13]

News came through[14] in the morning; a whole holiday was decreed[15] for the School, and the kitchen staff[16] were implored[17] to provide as cheerful a spread as wartime rationing permitted[18]. There was much cheering and singing and a bread fight[19] across the Dining Hall. When Chips entered in the midst of the uproar[20] there was an in-

---

1 **Something in Caesar about the way the Germans fought** 凯撒著作中有些关于德国人作战的话。其实凯撒的历史著作中是说日耳曼人的战争；见前注。the way = the way in which.

2 **You wouldn't think there were things like that in Caesar** 你不会想到凯撒的

著作中有那样的东西。

3 **And the way Chips laughed** 还有 Chips 笑的腔调（说话人一样样描述当时情景）。

4 **the way he *does* laugh** 他确实这样笑。 ***does*** 斜体；重读；注意用现在时，把当时的情景讲得如在眼前一样。

5 **the tears all running down his face** 眼泪满面地淌下来。这是独立结构，修饰 *does* laugh。

6 **never seen him laugh so much** 从没有看见他这样大笑过。never seen 前面省去 You have, We have 或 One has。

7 **legend** ['ledʒənd] 传奇人物

8 **With** 后接 his old and tattered gown 和 his walk, his mind, his quaintly humorous sayings 四个并列的介词宾语。这个有四行长的介词短语修饰后面 Brookfield would not have had an atom of him different 中的 him。

9 **break into a stumble** 随时跌倒

10 **peering over the steel-rimmed spectacles** 从钢丝边眼镜上面凝视着的；分词短语，修饰 eyes。

11 **quaintly humorous sayings** 奇妙的幽默话

12 **Brookfield would not have had an atom** ['ætəm] **of him different.** Brookfield 不会愿意他（在这些特征方面）有丝毫的变更。 **different** 是 have had 的宾语补足语。

13 **November 11th, 1918** 是第一次世界大战的停战日。

14 **News came through** 消息传来

15 **a whole holiday was decreed** 宣布放假一整天

16 **kitchen staff** 全体炊事人员。staff 是集合名词。

17 **were implored** 被恳求。叫炊事房备一餐好菜，本来无需"恳求"，但在战时配给制限制下，要他们备好菜，需要他们想想办法，所以有"恳求"的意思。

18 **provide as cheerful a spread as war-time rationing permitted** 供应一顿战时配给制容许下最使人欢欣的丰盛菜肴。 **spread** 丰盛的酒席；宴会，是口语。

19 **bread fight** 用面包相互投掷

20 **in the midst of the uproar** 在喧闹中

stant hush[1], and then wave upon wave of cheering[2]; everyone gazed on[3] him with eager, shining eyes, as on a symbol of victory. He walked to the dais[4], seeming as if he wished to speak[5]; they made silence for him[6], but he shook his head after a moment, smiled, and walked away again.

It had been a damp, foggy day, and the walk across the quadrangle to the Dining Hall had given him a chill[7]. The next day he was in bed with bronchitis[8], and stayed there[9] till after Christmas[10]. But already, on that night of November 11th, after his visit to the Dining Hall, he had sent in his resignation[11] to the Board of Governors[12].

When school reassembled after the holidays[13] he was back at Mrs. Wickett's. At his own request[14] there were no more farewells or presentations, nothing but[15] a handshake with his successor[16] and the word 'acting' crossed out on official stationery[17]. The 'duration'[18] was over.

1 **instant hush** 顿时的肃静

2 **then wave upon wave of cheering** 接上面 there was；然后是一阵又一阵的欢呼。

3 **gazed on** 注视；也作 gaze at。

4 **dais** ['deɪɪs]（大厅一端的）台。教室的讲台也叫 dais。

5 **seeming as if he wished to speak** 看上去好像他想说话。

6 **made silence for him** 安静下来让他（讲话）

7 **had given him a chill**（散步）使他着了凉

8 **was in bed with bronchitis** 因患支气管炎而卧床

9 **stay there** 一直卧在床上

10 **till after Christmas** 直到圣诞节过后。till 和 after 是两个介词叠用。介词叠用的例子还有，如 from under the bed 等。

11 **sent in his resignation** [ˌrezɪg'neɪʃən] 递交他的辞职信

12 **Board of Governors** 校董会

13 **school reassembled** ['riːə'sembld] **after the holidays** 全校师生在圣诞节假日结束后重新到校。

14 **At his own request** 依照他自己的要求

15 **nothing but** 除……之外什么也没有；只有；接上面 there were；照理 nothing but 前面应该用 there *was*，但这里因前面有 farewells or presentations，已用了 there *were*，后面不再重复而改用 there *was*.

16 **successor** 继任者（又来了一位新任校长）

17 **the word 'acting' crossed out on official stationery** 公务信笺等上面划去"代理"一词。（前一时期 Chips 任代理校长，所以公务信笺上印有"代理"字样。）the word ... 与 a handshake 并列，都是 but 的介词宾语。

18 **The 'duration'** 这段"（非常）时期"，见第 193 页注释 17。

第十六章

内容提要

1929年后，契普斯年逾八十，不再出门远行，只在风和日丽的日子到学校去走走。但是他仍常常在家里款待客人。

1930年，他立了遗嘱，遗产除一部分遗赠救济机关和维克特夫人外，其余捐赠给学校，用于设立一项公开奖学金。

战后的十年，全世界大动乱、大变化，而契普斯却安于变化不大的布鲁克菲尔德的生活。

1931年，1932年，人们把他看成是能够未卜先知的“万宝全书”，什么问题都要问他。他们不但期望他的回答，而且还准备着他把回答点缀成笑话。

同学们喜欢跟他开玩笑，有时故意引他说笑话，引出新的笑话来当新闻传播。

16

And now, fifteen years after that[1], he could look back upon it all with a deep and sumptuous tranquility[2]. He was not ill, of course — only a little tired at times, and bad with his breathing[3] during the winter months. He would not go abroad[4] — he had once tried it[5], but had chanced to strike the Riviera during one of its carefully unadvertised cold spells[6]. 'I prefer — um — to get my chills — umph — in my own country[7],' he used to say, after that[8]. He had to take care of himself[9] when there were east winds, but autumn and winter were not really so bad; there were warm fires[10], and books, and you could look forward to[11] the summer. It was the summer that he liked best[12], of course; apart from[13] the weather, which suited him, there were the continual visits of old boys[14]. Every weekend some of them motored up to Brookfield[15] and called at his house. Sometimes they tired him, if too many came at once[16]; but he did not really mind[17]; he could always rest and sleep afterwards.

1 **fifteen years after that** 在那个情况（指前一章末所讲 1918 年第一次世界大战结束，Chips 辞去代理校长职务）过去 15 年之后（即 1933 年）。

2 **look back upon it all with a deep and sumptuous** [ˈsʌmptjʊəs] **tranquility** [træŋˈkwɪlɪtɪ] 用一种深沉和悠闲的宁静回顾这一切。**look back upon** 也作 look back to，回顾。**it all** all 修饰 it，= all of it，但用作宾语时，多用 it all。**sumptuous** 奢侈的，豪华的；这里是“优哉游哉”的意思。

3 **bad with his breathing** 呼吸困难，如气喘

4 **go abroad** 到外国去

5 **tried it** = tried going abroad.

6 **chanced to strike the Riviera** [ˌrɪvɪˈeərə] **during one of its carefully unadvertised cold spells** 正好碰到里维耶拉在广告中特意避而不提的一次寒潮。**chanced** 偶然发生；碰巧；后接不定式。**strike** 碰到。**Riviera** 地中海沿岸的游览休养胜地；前面有 the。**carefully unadvertised** 特意不做广告宣传的。**cold spells** 寒潮；spell 是某种天气的一段持续时间。

7 **I prefer — um — to get my chills — umph — in my own country** 我（要着凉也）宁愿在本国着凉（不要在国外着凉）。

8 **after that** 在那次出国旅行之后

9 **take care of himself** 当心自己；照顾自己

10 **warm fires** 暖热的炉火

11 **look forward to** 盼望；这里的 to 是介词。

12 **liked best** 最喜欢

13 **apart from** 除了……之外

14 **continual visits of old boys** 常有校友来访。**continual** 频繁的。比较：**continuous** 连续不断的，不间断的；**continued** 着重“被使得连续不断的”。

15 **motored up to Brookfield** 乘（或驾驶）汽车到 Brookfield。这里 up 和 to Brookfield 都修饰 motored；不是习语 up to。

16 **too many came at once** 同时来了太多的校友；太多的校友一起来访。**at once** 同时；此处不作“立刻”解。

17 **did not really mind** 并不真怎么介意（太多校友同时来访而使他疲劳）。

And he enjoyed their visits — more than anything else in the world that was still to be enjoyed[1]. 'Well, Gregson[2] — umph — I remember you — umph — always late for everything[3] — eh — eh? Perhaps you'll be late in growing old — umph — like me[4] — umph — eh?' And later, when he was alone again and Mrs. Wickett came in to clear away the tea things[5]: 'Mrs. Wickett, young Gregson called — umph — you remember him, do you? Tall boy with spectacles. Always late. Umph. Got a job with the — umph — League of Nations[6] — where — I suppose — his — um — dilatoriness — won't be noticeable[7] — eh?'

And sometimes, when the bell rang for call-over, he would go to the window and look across the road and over the School fence and see, in the distance, the thin line of boys filing past the bench[8]. New times, new names ... but the old ones still remained[9] ... Jefferson, Jennings, Jolyon, Jupp, Kingsley[10] Primus, Kingsley Secundus, Kingsley Tertius[11], Kingston[12] ... where are you all, where have you all gone to[13]?... Mrs. Wickett, bring me a cup of tea just before prep, will you, please?

The post-War decade swept through with a clatter of change and maladjustments[14]; Chips, as he lived through

1 **he enjoyed their visits — more than anything else in the world that was still to be enjoyed** 他对他们的来访感到很有乐趣，胜于他当时（年老了）还能够享受的世界上任何其他乐趣。more 修饰前面的 enjoyed。

2 **Gregson** ['gregsn] 格雷格森，姓氏

3 **always late for everything** 做什么事都迟一步；前面省去 you were。

4 **late in growing old — umph — like me** 像我一样，老起来也迟。（如别人 60 岁就老了，他到 80 岁也不老。）

5 **clear away the tea things** 收拾茶具

6 **Got a job with the—umph—League** [li:g] **of Nations** 在国际（机构）中得到一份工作。Got = He got. 注意：get a job with 用介词 with。**League of Nations** 国际联盟，1920 年成立，1946 年解散。

7 **where — I suppose — his — um — dilatoriness** ['dɪlətərɪnɪs] **won't be noticeable** 在那里（国际联盟），我猜他的拖拉作风不会被人注意。（讽刺国际联盟办事本来就是拖拖拉拉的。）

8 **look across the road and over the School fence and see, in the distance, the thin line of boys filing past the bench** 隔着马路、越过学校的围栏眺望，看远处学生排着稀疏的纵队走过（老师站在或坐在那儿点名的）长凳。**in the distance** 指望得见或听得见的远处。

9 **the old ones still remained** 老姓氏还在（被 Chips 记着）

10 **Jefferson** ['dʒefəsn], **Jennings** ['dʒenɪŋz], **Jolyon** ['dʒɒljən], **Jupp** [dʒʌp], **Kingsley** ['kɪŋzlɪ] 都是学生的姓氏

11 **Tertius** ['tɜːʃjəs] 第三（同姓同学中年龄或在校时间居第三位的）。Primus（第一），Secundus（第二）。

12 **Kingston** ['kɪŋstn] 金斯顿，姓氏

13 **where are you all, where have you all gone to?** 是 Chips 的口吻，下一句同。下一句也是 Chips 说的话。

14 **The post-War decade swept through with a clatter of change and maladjustments** ['mælə'dʒʌs*t*mənts] 战后的十年（1919—1929，泛指 20 世纪 20 年代前后）像暴风雨般过去了，充满着变化和失调的骚动。

it[1], was profoundly disappointed when he looked abroad[2]. The Ruhr[3], Chanak[4], Corfu[5]; there was enough to be uneasy about in the world[6]. But near him, at Brookfield, and even, in a wider sense[7], in England, there was something that charmed his heart[8] because it was old — and had survived[9]. More and more he saw the rest of the world as a vast disarrangement[10] for which England had sacrificed enough[11] — and perhaps too much. But he was satisfied with Brookfield. It was rooted in things that had stood the test of time and change and war[12]. Curious, in this deeper sense, how little it *had* changed.[13] Boys were a politer race[14]; bullying was nonexistent; there was more swearing and cheating[15]. There was a more genuine friendliness between master and boy[16] — less pomposity on the one side, less unctuousness on the other[17]. One of the new masters, fresh from Oxford[18], even let the Sixth[19] call him by his

---

1 **lived through it** 熬过这十年

2 **looked abroad** 看看国外

3 **The Ruhr** [rʊə]（德国的）鲁尔区。1923 年，法国因德国不能如期交纳作为战后赔款的煤和木材，派兵进驻德国的主要工业区鲁尔区，引起德国工人罢工，1924 年法军撤出。注意：Ruhr 前有 The。

4 **Chanak** [tʃə'nɑːk] 也称 Kale Sultanie，恰纳卡莱，是达达尼尔海峡亚洲海岸的商业城市和要塞，第一次世界大战中于 1915 年受英国海军轰击。

5 **Corfu** [kɔː'fjuː] 科孚，希腊西北部大岛，第一次世界大战后，希腊国内外争纷不止。

6 **there was enough to be uneasy about in the world** 世界上有够多的使人担心的事情。

7 **in a wider sense** 在更广泛意义上

8 **charmed his heart** 使他醉心

9 **because it was old — and had survived** 因为它（指上面的 something）古老，而且（经过大战）幸存下来。

10 **More and more he saw the rest of the world as a vast disarrangement** 他越来越觉得世界上（除英国之外）其余的地方是一大片混乱。

11 **for which England had sacrificed enough** 英国已经为它牺牲够多的了。照语法讲，which 当是指 disarrangement。照意思看，应是指 the rest of the world。

12 **was rooted in things that had stood the test of time and change and war** 扎根于经受了时间、变迁和战争考验的种种事物之中。

13 **Curious, in this deeper sense, how little it *had* changed.** Brookfield 真正发生了的变化是多么少，这在更深刻的意义上说来是稀奇的。**Curious** = It was curious，**It** 引起 "how..." 名词从句。

14 **Boys were a politer race** 学生们(在战后)变得更文明了。**race** 原义"人种"，这里作"一批人"解。

15 **bullying** ['bʊlɪɪŋ] **was nonexistent; there was more swearing** ['sweərɪŋ] **and cheating** 霸凌是不存在了；但骂脏话和作弊多起来了。(暗指学生实际上变得更调皮了。)

16 **genuine** ['dʒenʊɪn] **friendliness between master and boy** 师生之间真挚的友好。master 和 boy 都是可数名词，对称时虽用单数可以省去冠词。

17 **less pomposity** [pɒm'pɒsɪtɪ] **on the one side, less unctuousness** ['ʌŋktjʊəsnɪs] **on the other** 一方面（教师方面）架子比过去小，另一方面（学生方面）虚伪的殷勤也少了。**on the other** = on the other side.

18 **fresh from Oxford** ['ɒksfəd] 刚从牛津大学毕业的

19 **the Sixth** 六年级（学生们）

Christian name[1]. Chips didn't hold with that[2]; indeed, he was just a little bit shocked. 'He might as well — umph — sign his terminal reports — umph — "yours affectionately" — eh — eh?[3]' he told somebody.

During the General Strike of 1926[4] Brookfield boys loaded motor vans with foodstuffs[5]. When it was all over[6] Chips felt stirred[7] emotionally as he had not been[8] since the War. Something had happened, something whose ultimate significance had yet to be reckoned[9]; but one thing was clear: England had burned her fire in her own grate again[10]. And when, at a Speech Day function[11] that year, an American visitor laid stress on[12] the vast sums that the strike had cost the country[13], Chips answered: 'Yes, but — umph — advertisement — always *is* costly[14]?'

'Advertisement?'

'Well, wasn't it — umph — advertisement — and very fine advertisement — too? A whole week of it[15] — umph — and not a life lost — not a shot fired[16]! Your country would have — umph — spilt more blood in — umph — raiding a single liquor saloon[17]!'

---

1 **call him by his Christian** ['krɪstʃən] **name** 直呼他的教名。 **Christian name**

也称 first name，given name，如 James Hilton 中的 James。直呼 James，当然没有称 Mr. Hilton 客气，但更亲切。

2 **hold with that** 赞同那种做法（指用教名称呼教师）

3 **He might as well — umph — sign his terminal reports — umph — "yours affectionately" — eh — eh?** 他不妨在期终报告上签"你亲爱的"，是不是？这里用陈述句，在末后加上疑问词 eh，表示疑问；实际上这是反问，Chips 不赞成这样做。**He** 指上文的 One of the new masters。**yours affectionately** 是在给亲友写信时使用的 complimentary closing（信结尾的客套语），用以签在学校的文件上当然不合适。**might as well ...**（要是上面所说的事是合适的，那么）……也是合适的了。

4 **the General Strike of 1926** 1926 年的总罢工。1926 年英国煤矿资本家用停工威胁工人，引起全国总罢工。

5 **loaded motor vans with foodstuffs** 把各种食物装上卡车。（因总罢工而由学生帮忙搬运食物。）**motor van** 卡车；是英国称法，= truck。

6 **it was all over** 总罢工全部结束。

7 **stirred** 激动的；是过去分词，作表语。

8 **had not been** 后面省去 stirred emotionally。

9 **had yet to be reckoned** ['rekənd] 还有待估计（目前还估计不出）

10 **England had burned her fire in her own grate again** 英国已经重又在它自己的炉中燃起火来了；英国已经开始恢复正常。

11 **Speech Day function** 授奖典礼日的集会

12 **laid stress on** 把重点放在……上；强调

13 **the vast sums that the strike had cost the country** 罢工使国家（英国）付出的巨大金额（的代价）

14 **advertisement — always *is* costly** 广告总是费用很高。这话的含义见下文 Chips 自己的解释。always is 比 is always 语气重。

15 **A whole week of it** 整整一个星期的罢工

16 **not a life lost — not a shot fired** = not a life was lost — not a shot was fired 没有死一人，没有放一枪。

17 **Your country would have — umph — spilt more blood in — umph — raiding a single liquor** ['lɪkə] **saloon** [sə'lu:n] 在你们的国家（美国）……单单是袭击一家供应私酒的沙龙……呃……就会流更多的血。这是虚拟句，含有"假如发生袭击沙龙事件"的意思。 **spilt** 是 spill 的过去分词。 **spilt blood** 造成流血。

Laughter ... laughter ... wherever he went and whatever he said, there was laughter. He had earned the reputation of[1] being a great jester, and jests were expected of him[2]. Whenever he rose to speak at a meeting, or even when he talked across a table[3], people prepared their minds and faces for the joke[4]. They listened in a mood to be amused[5] and it was easy to satisfy them. They laughed sometimes before he came to the point.[6] 'Old Chips was in fine form[7],' they would say, afterwards. 'Marvellous the way he can always see the funny side of things[8]...'

After 1929, Chips did not leave Brookfield — even for Old Boys' dinners in London[9]. He was afraid of chills, and late nights began to tire him too much.[10] He came across to the School, however, on fine days; and he still kept up a wide and continual hospitality in his room[11]. His faculties were all unimpaired[12], and he had no personal worries of any kind. His income was more than he needed to spend, and his small capital, invested in gilt-edged stocks, did not suffer when the slump set in[13]. He gave a lot of his money away[14] — to people who called on him with a hard-luck story[15],

1 **earned the reputation of** 赢得……的声誉

2 **jests were expected of him** 随时期待他说笑话。这里的 of 有时也用 from，但用 of 普遍。

3 **talked across a table** 隔着桌子说话；在餐桌（或茶桌等）上跟桌子对面的人说话。

4 **prepared their minds and faces for the joke** 心理上和面部（表情上）都做好听笑话的准备。

5 **in a mood to be amused** 在等待被逗笑的心情下

6 **They laughed sometimes before he came to the point.** 他（说笑话）还没有说到关子上，他们就笑了。**come to the point** 到紧要关头；是习语。

7 **in fine form** 兴致好；也作 in great form。

8 **Marvellous** ['mɑːvɪləs] **the way he can always see the funny side of things.** = It is marvellous the way he can always see … 他怎么总是能够看到事物有趣的一面，真是奇妙。 **the way** 是习语，= how。从语法上讲，It 引起 the way, the way 后省去 in which。the way 甚至可以起连词的作用，如：The way he works, he must be an old hand. 看他工作的样子，他一定是个老手。

9 **even for Old Boys' dinners in London** 甚至在伦敦举行的校友聚餐会也（不去参加）。for 承接前面的 leave。

10 **He was afraid of chills, and late nights began to tire him too much.** 他怕风寒，深更半夜里也开始感到不堪疲劳。注意：chill 是可数名词。

11 **kept up a wide and continual hospitality in his room** 继续在他房里广泛和频繁地招待客人。

12 **His faculties** ['fækəltɪz] **were all unimpaired** 他的官能全都没有损坏。

13 **his small capital, invested in gilt-edged** ['gɪlt-edʒd] **stocks, did not suffer when the slump set in** 当不景气到来时，他投资购买金边证券的小额资本没有受到损失。**gilt-edged stocks**，也作 gilted stocks，金边证券。原先政府发行的有价证券是金边的，因此最有保证的证券称“金边证券”。 **the slump** 指 1929 年整个资本主义世界经济危机到来，股票暴跌。**set in** 开始；到来；是习语。

14 **gave a lot of his money away** 他捐掉很多钱。 **gave away** 送掉；分发。 **a lot of** 许多；后面可数、不可数名词都可以接。

15 **called on him with a hard-luck story** 来看 Chips，向他诉说不幸的遭遇（求他援助）。

to various School funds[1], and also to the Brookfield mission[2]. In 1930 he made his will[3]. Except for legacies to the mission and to Mrs. Wickett, he left all he had to found an open entrance scholarship to the School.[4]

1931 ... 1932 ...

'What do you think of Hoover, sir?[5]'

'Do you think we shall ever go back to gold?[6]'

'How d'you feel about things in general[7], sir? See any break in the clouds?[8]'

'When's the tide going to turn[9], Chips, old boy[10]? You ought to know, with all your experience of things[11]?'

They all asked him questions, as if he were some kind of prophet and encyclopaedia combined[12] — more even than that, for they liked their answer dished up as a joke[13]. He would say:

'Well, Henderson[14], when I was — umph — a much

---

1 **various School funds** 各种学校基金（指 Brookfield 筹集的各种基金）

2 **Brookfield mission** Brookfield（在伦敦东部贫民区）办的救济机关（见第六章）

3 **made his will** 立遗嘱

4 **Except for legacies** ['legəsɪz] **to the mission and to Mrs. Wickett, he left all he**

had to found an open entrance scholarship to the School. 除了遗赠给那个救济机关和 Mrs. Wickett 的财物之外，他把（其余）所有的一切都捐出，用以设立一项这所学校（Brookfield）的公开入学奖学金。**Except for** 一般情况下作“除了因为……”解，与 except（除了…）不同；但 except 用在句首时须作 except for。换言之，这里的 Except for = Except。**legacies** 遗产（一般指动产）。**left all had** = left all that he had 把他所有的一切留给。注意：an open entrance scholarship（美国 Little, Brown 版作 open scholarship）to the School 一语中用介词 to。

5 **What do you think of Hoover** ['hu:və]**, sir?** 先生，你认为胡佛怎么样？ Herbert Clark Hoover (1874—1964) 胡佛，1929—1933 年任美国总统。

6 **Do you think we shall ever go back to gold?** 你看我们今后会有一天恢复金本位制吗？这句问句和前面一句、后面两句都是人家问 Chips 的，不是对话。由于 1929—1933 年资本主义世界的经济危机，英国在 1931 年 9 月放弃了金本位制。

7 **things in general** 总的情况

8 **See any break in the clouds?**。你看有情况好转的希望吗？ **See** = Do you see.

9 **When's the tide going to turn** 这潮流几时会转变？意即“现在世界不景气（或动乱）的情况几时会好转？”**When's** = When is.

10 **old boy** 在本书中多作“校友”和“老头儿”解；这里是招呼用语，犹如我们说“老朋友”。

11 **You ought to know, with all your experience of things.** 凭你这么多阅历、经验，你应该知道。注意：with all 连用时，with 常作“尽管……”、“虽有……”解；这里 with 是“有着”、“凭着”的意思；两种用法正好相反。

12 **some kind of prophet** ['prɒfɪt] **and encyclopaedia** [en,saɪkbləʊ,pi:djə] **combined** 某种预言家和百科全书的混合体；既能预见未来，又是万宝全书，无所不知。**combined** 是过去分词，修饰 prophet and encyclopaedia。

13 **liked their answer dished up as a joke** 喜欢他们（所得到）的回答听来妙趣横生，像个笑话。 **their answer** 一般是“他们所作出的回答”，这里是“他们所得到的回答”，把他们得到的回答据为己有了。 **dished** 这里是过去分词；dish up 是习语，原是“上（菜）”的意思，这里是“把（论点）有滋有味地说出来”。

14 **Henderson** ['hendəsn] 亨德森，姓氏

younger man — there used to be someone[1] who — um — promised people ninepence for fourpence[2]. I don't know that anybody — umph — ever got it[3], but — umph — our present rulers seem — um — to have solved the problem of how to give — umph — fourpence for ninepence[4].'

Laughter.

Sometimes, when he was strolling about the School, small boys of the cheekier kind would ask him questions, merely for the fun of getting Chips's 'latest' to retail[5].

'Please, sir, what about the Five Year Plan?[6]'

'Sir, do you think Germany wants to fight another war?'

'Have you been to the new cinema, sir? I went with my people the other day.[7] Quite a grand affair for a small place like Brookfield.[8] They've got a Wurlitzer[9].'

'And what — umph — on earth — is a Wurlitzer?'[10]

'It's an organ, sir — a cinema organ[11].'

'Dear me ... I've seen the name on the hoardings[12], but I always — umph — imagined — it must be some kind

1 **there used to be someone**（过去）常常有人

2 **promised people ninepence** ['naɪnpəns] **for fourpence** ['fɔːpəns] 允诺给人 9 便士，以回报他所给出的价值 4 便士的劳力（或货物）。pence 是 penny 的复数形式。penny 有两个复数形式：pennies 指一个个便士钱币，pence 指金额。过去英国币制 1 镑 (pound) 等于 20 先令 (shilling), 1 先令等于 12 便士；1971 年币制改革，1 镑等于 100 便士，取消先令。在表示便士的数额时，2 到 12 便士，还有 20 便士，数字和 pence 连写，其余分开写。

3 **I don't know that anybody — umph — ever got it** 我不知曾有任何人拿到过它（指 9 便士）；据我所知，一个人也没有拿到过。

4 **our present rulers seem — um — to have solved the problem of how to give — umph — fourpence for ninepence** 我们现在的统治者们似乎已经解决怎样给人 4 便士，以换得他给出的价值 9 便士的劳力（或货物）；即该给 9 便士却给 4 便士。（讽刺统治有方）

5 **merely for the fun of getting Chips's 'latest' to retail** （问 Chips 问题）只是为了要听到 Chips 的最新笑话去传播。Chips's 'latest' 的用法同前面看到 Chips's best 一样，都是把形容词最高级当名词用。 **retail** 原义“零售”，这里作“传播”解，很形象化。

6 **what about the Five Year Plan?**（你认为）（苏联 1928 年开始的）五年计划怎么样？ **what about ...?**（征求意见或打听消息时用）……怎么样？

7 **I went with my people the other day.** 前两天我同家里人一起去。 **my people** 我的家人（尤指父母）。 **the other day** 最近过去的某一天，即前几天。

8 **Quite a grand affair for a small place like Brookfield.** 对于像 Brookfield 这样的小地方说来，（新电影院）是个宏伟设施。Quite 前省去 It（新电影院）is。 **affair** 在口语中可作“事物”、“东西”解。

9 **Wurlitzer** ['wɜːlɪtsə] 沃利策商标名，代指影院风琴。

10 **And what — umph — on earth — is a Wurlitzer?** 沃利策到底是什么？前面三段引语都是人家对 Chips 说的。这一句开始，Chips 与提问者对话。

11 **organ** 风琴。 **cinema organ** 影院里用的风琴。

12 **I've seen the name on the hoardings** 我在广告牌上看到过这个名字（指 Wurlitzer）。 **hoardings**（利用空地、工地等的板围所做的）广告牌；是英式英语。

of — umph — sausage ...[1]'

Laughter ... Oh, there's a new Chips joke[2], you fellows, a perfectly lovely one. I was gassing to the old boy about the new cinema[3], and[4] ...

1 **I always — umph — imagined — it must be some kind of — umph — sausage** ['sɒsɪdʒ，美国人也读作 'sɔːsɪdʒ] 我一直认为那 (Wurlitzer) 一定是一种什么香肠。主句中是过去式 (imagined)，其宾语从句也应该用过去式，这叫做时态的连续 (sequence of tense)，但 must 没有过去式，除必要时用 had to 或其他方式表示外，一般仍用 must。

2 **Chips joke = Chips's joke** 后者是一般的表现法，前者已把“Chips 的笑话”作为一个独立概念，仿佛成了一个固定词组。

3 **I was gassing to the old boy about the new cinema.** 我讲的关于新电影院的事，是跟老头儿开玩笑的。 **gas** 吹牛，说废话；这是口语。

4 **Oh, there's ... and ...** 这两句是学生说的话，照理应加引号，但在现代文艺作品中常用作者叙述的口吻写出，不用引号。

第十七章

内容提要

契普斯八十五岁那年（1933年）冬天，因为身体不适躺在家里。医生也嘱咐他在这样的天气不要出门。

忽然有一个新学生来访。房东维克特太太那天不在家，契普斯亲自出去开门。年少的新生名叫林福德，他说："是契普斯先生叫我来看他。"同学们让新生把契宾先生的绰号契普斯当作真名，并骗他找上门来，那已成为传统的玩笑。契普斯明知孩子上了当，却招待如仪，开还给他们一个玩笑。

契普斯和林福德谈了半天，又送他到门口。回到屋里，契普斯突然发现自己动弹不得——他太累了，仰倒在椅子上。

17

He sat in his front parlour[1] at Mrs. Wickett's on a November afternoon in thirty-three[2]. It was cold and foggy, and he dare not go out[3]. He had not felt too well[4] since Armistice Day[5]; he fancied he might have caught a slight chill during the Chapel service[6]. Merivale had been that morning for his usual fortnightly chat.[7] 'Everything all right?[8] Feeling hearty?[9] That's the style[10] — keep indoors this weather[11] — there's a lot of flu about[12]. Wish I could have your life for a day or two[13].'

His life ... and what a life it had been! The whole pageant of it swung before him[14] as he sat by the fire that afternoon. The things he had done and seen[15]; Cambridge in the sixties[16], Great Gable on an August morning[17]; Brookfield at all times and seasons throughout the years. And, for that matter[18], the things he had *not* done, and

1 **front parlour** ['pɑːlə] 前客厅，相当于中国的客堂。

2 **thirty-three** (19)33 年

3 **dare not go out** = dared not go out. dare 作情态动词，主要用在否定、疑问或条件句中，且现在式可用以表示过去。

4 **had not felt too well** 觉得身体不太好

5 **Armistice** ['ɑːmɪstɪs] **Day** 第一次世界大战停战日，即 1918 年 11 月 11 日。后来将 11 月 11 日定为停战纪念日。（现在英国在离 11 月 11 日最近的星期日举行纪念，称为 Remembrance Sunday 或 Remembrance Day，美国把 11 月 11 日称为 Veterans Day。）

6 **Chapel service** 在学校附属的小教堂里举行的礼拜仪式

7 **Merivale had been that morning for his usual fortnightly chat.** Merivale 医生（见第一章）那天早上在，是来（跟 Chips）做他每两星期一次的惯常闲谈的。

8 **Everything all right?** = Is everything all right?

9 **Feeling hearty?** = Are you feeling hearty? **hearty** 健壮的。

10 **That's the style** 这样才对；正该如此

11 **keep indoors this weather** 这个天气不要出门。 **this weather** 前面省去 under 或 in，作状语短语。

12 **there's a lot of flu** [fluː] **about** 流感很流行。 **flu** influenza [ˌɪnflʊ'enzə] 的简略语，流行性感冒，是口语。 **about**（疾病）流行；是副词。

13 **Wish I could have your life for a day or two.** 但愿我能过一两天你的生活。口语中 I wish 和 I hope 常说成 Wish 和 Hope。

14 **The whole pageant** ['pædʒənt] **of it swung before him** 它（Chips 一生）壮丽的行列在他面前悠然行进；一件件往事依次在他眼前浮现，有如一个壮丽的行列。

15 **The things he had done and seen** 他做过和见过的种种事情（下面一一列举）。The things 后面省去 which 或 that。

16 **Cambridge** ['keɪmbrɪdʒ] **in the sixties**（19 世纪）60 年代的剑桥大学，Chips 当时在那里念书。

17 **Great Gable on an August morning** 某个 8 月早晨的大山墙。Chips 在那里遇到 Katherine，见第四章。

18 **for that matter** 至于那个；这里指“至于做过没做过、见过没见过”。

would never do now that he had left them too late[1] — he had never travelled by air[2], for instance, and he had never been to a talky show[3]. So that he was both more and less experienced than the youngest boy at the School might well be[4]; and that, that paradox of age and youth, was what the world called progress[5].

Mrs. Wickett had gone out, visiting relatives in a neighbouring village; she had left the tea things ready on the table[6], with bread and butter and extra cups laid out in case anybody called[7]. On such a day, however, visitors were not very likely[8]; with the fog thickening hourly[9] outside, he would probably be alone.

But no. About a quarter to four a ring came[10] and Chips, answering the front door[11] himself (which he oughtn't to have done[12]), encountered a rather small boy wearing a Brookfield cap[13] and an expression of anxious timidity[14]. 'Please, sir[15],' he began, 'does Mr. Chips live here?'

'Umph — you'd better come inside[16],' Chips answered.

---

1 **the things he had *not* done, and would never do now that he had left them too late** 他没有做过、而且因他迟迟未做而往后也永远不会做的种种事情。the things he had *not* done … = there were the things which (或 that) he had *not* done … **now that** 既然；由于；是复合连词，有时单用 now。

2 **travelled by air** 乘飞机旅行

3 **had never been to a talky show**（美国 Little, Brown 版作 talkie-show）从没去看过一场有声电影。 **talky = talkie** 有声电影；是口语。 **show** 演出；放映；节目。

4 **So that he was both more and less experienced than the youngest new boy at the School might well be** 所以他的经验既比学校里最小的新生可能有的经验多，又比他们可能有的经验少。 **might well be** = might well be experienced 很可能有经验的。

5 **and that, that paradox** ['pærədɒks] **of age and youth, was what the world called progress** 那个情况（指分号前所说的情况）——老年和少年之间的矛盾——就是世人所谓的进步。**that paradox of age and youth** 是前面一个 that 的同位语。 **paradox** 自相矛盾的话（或事物）；似是而非的话。

6 **she had left the tea things ready on the table** 她（出去前）已把茶具放好在桌子上。

7 **extra cups laid out in case anybody called** 以备有人来访而摆着的额外的茶杯。 **laid** 这里是 lay 的过去分词；laid out 修饰 cups。 **in case** 以防（万一）；以备。

8 **visitors were not very likely** 不太像会有客人来

9 **thickening hourly** 一小时比一小时更加浓起来

10 **a ring came** 门铃响了

11 **answering the front door** 应声开前门

12 **which he oughtn't to have done** 这事（应门）他不该做（却已做）

13 **Brookfield cap** Brookfield 校帽

14 **an expression of anxious timidity** [tɪ'mɪdɪtɪ] 局促不安的表情；这是 wearing 的宾语。 **wearing an expression of** 带着……的表情。

15 **Please, sir** 先生，请问。**Please** 不单作“请”解，也可表示“请问”。 **sir** 对陌生人或上司等的尊称。学生来访，不知开门的就是 Chips，所以称 sir。

16 **you'd better come inside** 你最好还是到里面来；你里面来吧。**'d better** = had better，也可以说 = would better，但后者现在不大用；had better 是习语，口语中也有省去 had 的，如 You better come inside 或 Better come inside。

And in his room a moment later[1] he added: 'I am — umph — the person you want.[2] Now what can I — umph — do for you?[3]'

'I was told you wanted me[4], sir.'

Chips smiled. An old joke — an old leg-pull[5], and he, of all people, having made so many old jokes in his time, ought not to complain[6]. And it amused him to cap their joke, as it were, with one of his own[7]; to let them see that he could keep his end up, even yet[8]. So he said, with eyes twinkling: 'Quite right, my boy, I wanted you to take tea with me. Will you — umph — sit down by the fire? Umph — I don't think I have seen your face before[9]. How is that?[10]'

'I've only just come out of the sanatorium, sir[11] — I've been there since the beginning of term with measles[12].'

'Ah, that accounts for it[13].'

Chips began his usual ritualistic blending of tea from the different caddies[14]; luckily there was half a walnut cake with pink icing in the cupboard[15]. He found out[16] that the

---

1 **a moment later** 过了一会儿

2 **I am — umph — the person you want.** 我就是，呃，你要找的人。

3 **what can I — umph — do for you?** 我能为你做什么？你有什么事找我？这是问人有什么事的惯用语，如营业员问顾客要买什么东西，也常用此语。

4 **you wanted me** = you wanted me to come 或 you wanted to see me.

5 **leg-pull** 愚弄；从习语 pull somebody's leg 生成的名词。

6 **he, of all people, having made so many old jokes in his time, ought not to complain** 在所有的人当中，他最不应该抱怨（人家给他开玩笑），因为他在学校执教时开过那么多已成为旧闻的玩笑。**of all ...** 在所有的……偏偏。**make a joke** 讲笑话，开玩笑。 **in his time** 在他的一生中；在他工作于某处期间。

7 **it amused him to cap their joke, as it were, with one of his own** 自己来开个玩笑，可以说是盖过他们开的玩笑，这使他感到有趣。 **cap** 盖罩；胜过。 **as it were** 可以说是；仿佛；是习语。注意：不要和 as it was（is 的过去式）混淆，那是"实际上；既然如此"的意思。**his own** = his own jokes.

8 **could keep his end up, even yet** 即使现在还能够精神饱满地对付对手。**keep one's end up** 是习语；也可作 keep up one's end。

9 **I don't think I have seen your face before** 是 I think I haven't seen your face before 的意思，但习惯上用前一说法。

10 **How is that?** 那是怎么回事？（指 Chips 以前没有见过他。）

11 **I've only just come out of the sanatorium** [ˌsænəˈtɔːrɪəm], **sir** 我刚刚出疗养院，先生。此时这学生已知道这位老师是 Mr. Chips，但仍称他 sir，那是学生对老师、下属对上司的尊称。

12 **I've been there since the beginning of term with measles** 我学期一开始就因生麻疹住在那里（疗养院里）。注意：term（学期）前没有 the；这个 the 往往省去，如 Term is over（学期结束了）。

13 **that accounts for it** 那（因病住在疗养院）说明了这问题（何以 Chips 从没见过他的问题）；原来如此。 **account for** 是……的原因。

14 **his usual ritualistic** [ˌritjʊəˈlɪstɪk] **blending of tea from the different caddies** 他像往常一样有一定仪式似的从不同的茶罐里（舀出茶叶）配制茶。

15 **luckily there was half a walnut** [ˈwɔːlnət] **cake with pink icing in the cupboard** [ˈkʌbəd] 幸好橱里有半块粉红色糖霜的胡桃蛋糕。 **cupboard** 碗橱；食品橱，在英国也指一般小橱。

16 **found out** 弄明白

boy's name was Linford[1], that he lived in Shropshire[2], and that he was the first of his family at Brookfield[3].

'You know — umph — Linford — you'll like Brookfield — when you get used to it[4]. It's not half such an awful place — as you imagine.[5] You're a bit afraid of it — um, yes — eh? So was I, my dear boy — at first.[6] But that was — um — a long time ago. Sixty-three years ago — umph — to be precise[7]. When I — um — first[8] went into Big Hall and — um — I saw all those boys — I tell you[9] — I was quite scared. Indeed — umph — I don't think I've ever been so scared in my life[10]. Not even when — umph — the Germans bombed us[11] — during the war[12]. But — umph — it didn't last long — the scared feeling, I mean[13]. I soon made myself — um — at home.[14]'

'Were there a lot of other new boys that term[15], sir?' Linford asked shyly.

---

1 **Linford** ['lɪnfəd] 林福德，姓氏

2 **Shropshire** ['ʃrɒpʃɪə] 英国西部的一个郡（shire ['ʃaɪə]；现在 shire 只用在地名中，单独说"郡"用"county"）

3 **he was the first of his family at Brookfield** 他是他家里第一个在 Brookfield（念书）的学生。

4 **get used to** [ju:s*t* tə] **it** 对它（Brookfield）习惯了。 **used** 是形容词，作“习惯的”解；这个 used to 中的 to 是介词。注意：不要同作动词过去式的 used 后接 to- 不定式相混淆。后者表示过去惯常的动作，如 He used to（也读作 [ju:s*t* tə]) come on Sundays. 他过去经常星期天来。

5 **It's not half such an awful place — as you imagine.** 这（Brookfield）决不是像你想象的那样可怕的地方。 **not half** 不到一半；一半也不到；这里进一步作“毫不”解。

6 **So was I, my dear boy — at first.** 我亲爱的孩子，我开始时候也是这样（也害怕）。So was I 承接上文 You're a bit afraid of it；这是一种惯用的句型。

7 **to be precise** 准确地说来；是插入语。类似的插入语有 to be frank（坦率地说），to sum up（总结起来说）等。

8 **first** 第一次（指 Chips 刚来到 Brookfield 任教的时候）

9 **I tell you** 我对你说；这也是插入语。

10 **in my life** 在我一生中

11 **Not even when — umph — the Germans bombed us** 承接上句，= I don't think I was so scared even when the Germans bombed us.

12 **the war** 这里专指第一次世界大战，所以美国 Little, Brown 版上 war 作 War。

13 **it didn't last long — the scared feeling, I mean** 它并没持续多久——我是说这种受惊吓的感觉。it 就是 the scared feeling。这一句如没有 I mean，写成 it didn't last long, the scared feeling 也可以，只是语气不同。这句话基本的结构是 the scared feeling didn't last long. **scared feeling** 突然受惊之感，这种过去分词的同类用例有 excited shout，amused look 等；这些过去分词实际上已具有形容词的性质，所以前面可以用 very 修饰。

14 **made myself — um — at home** 使自己泰然。**at home**（像在自己家里一样）自由自在。

15 **Were there a lot of other new boys that term** 那个学期还有许多其他新学生吗？（Linford 还以为 Chips 当时也是新学生，不知道他是新教师，所以这样问。）

'Eh? But — God bless my soul[1] — I wasn't a boy at all — I was a man — a young man of twenty-two! And the next time you see a young man — a new master — taking his first prep in Big Hall — umph — just think — what it feels like[2]!'

'But if you were twenty-two then, sir ...'

'Yes? Eh?'

'You must be — very old — now[3], sir.'

Chips laughed quietly and steadily to himself[4]. It was a good joke.

'Well — umph — I'm certainly — umph — no chicken.[5]'

He laughed quietly to himself for a long time.

Then he talked of[6] other matters, of Shropshire, of schools and school life in general, of the news in that day's papers[7]. 'You're growing up into — umph — a very cross sort of world[8], Linford. Maybe it will have got over some of its — umph — crossness — by the time you're ready for it.[9] Let's hope so — umph — at any rate[10] ... Well ...' And with a glance at the clock he delivered himself of his old familiar formula[11]. 'I'm — umph — sorry — you can't stay ...'

At the front door he shook hands[12].

'Good-bye, my boy.'

And the answer came, in a shrill treble[13]:

1 **God bless my soul** 照字面解，是"愿上帝赐福给我的灵魂"，实际上它只是一句口头禅，有感叹词的作用，犹如说："天哪"，表示惊奇等，也作 Good bless me.，God bless my life. 等。照语法讲，这是个表示愿望的虚拟句，bless 是虚拟语气，所以不用 blesses。

2 **what it feels like** 那（年轻的新教师在大礼堂上第一堂预备课）是什么感觉？ **feels like** 感觉到像……（如摸上去什么感觉等）。

3 **You must be — very old — now** 承接上面 if you were twenty-two then；如果你那时候是 22 岁，现在一定很老了。 **must** 谅必，肯定；不是"必须"。

4 **laughed quietly and steadily to himself** 平静而沉着地暗自好笑。

5 **I'm certainly — umph — no chicken** 我当然不是什么小伙子了；我当然老了。 **chicken** 本是"小鸡、小鸟"，转义为"年轻人"。注意这里的 no 用法，比较：He is not a scholar. 他不是学者。He is no scholar. 他不是什么学者，甚至字也不大识。

6 **talked of** 谈到；谈论关于……

7 **news in that day's papers** 那天报上的新闻。**papers** = newspapers，前面介词用 in。

8 **You're growing up into — umph — a very cross sort of world** 你正在逐渐长大，进入一个很棘手的世界。 **a sort of** 和 a kind of 一样，后面虽用单数的可数名词，但不加冠词。

9 **Maybe it will have got over some of its — umph — crossness — by the time you're ready for it.** 也许在你（长大了）准备进入这个世界的时候，它已经把一些棘手问题克服了。 **got over** 克服；熬过；over 是介词。 **by the time** 到那个时候之前。

10 **at any rate** 无论如何；不管世界实际上怎样发展

11 **delivered himself of his old familiar formula** 说出大家熟知的他的老公式。（他招待同学到一定时间，总说："I'm sorry you can't stay"；已成为公式。）**delivered himself of** 把肚里的（话）说出来。

12 **he shook hands** = he shook hands with Linford。也可以说 they shook hands。

13 **shrill treble** 尖厉刺耳的声音。 **treble** ['trebl] 在音乐上指最高部音；高音。

'Good-bye, Mr. Chips.'

Chips sat by the fire again, with those words echoing along the corridors of his mind[1]. 'Goodbye, Mr. Chips ...' An old leg-pull, to make new boys think that his name was really Chips[2]; the joke was almost traditional[3]. He did not mind[4]. 'Good bye, Mr. Chips ...' He remembered that on the eve of his wedding day[5] Kathie had used that same phrase[6], mocking him gently for the seriousness he had had in those days[7]. He thought: Nobody would call me serious today, that's very certain ...

Suddenly the tears began to roll down his cheeks — an old man's failing[8]; silly[9], perhaps, but he couldn't help it[10]. He felt very tired; talking to Linford like that had quite exhausted him[11]. But he was glad he had met Linford. Nice boy[12]; would do well[13].

Over the fog-laden air came the bell for call-over, tremulous and muffled.[14] Chips looked at the window, greying into twilight[15]; it was time to light up[16]. But as soon as he began to move he felt that he couldn't[17]; he was too tired; and anyhow, it didn't matter[18]. He leaned back in his

1 **those words echoing along the corridors** ['kɔːrɪdɔːz] **of his mind** 那些字眼（指 Good-bye, Mr. Chips）沿着他心灵的走廊回响着；在心中回荡。

2 **An old leg-pull, to make new boys think that his name was really Chips = It was an old leg-pull to make ...** 让新来的学生们以为他的名字真叫 Chips，这是个愚弄人的老花样。

3 **the joke was almost traditional** 这个玩笑几乎已成为传统（每学期新生入学，都要被开这个玩笑）。

4 **did not mind** 不介意（学生用 Mr. Chips 这绰号来称呼他，而不正式称呼他 Mr. Chipping）

5 **on the eve of his wedding day** 他结婚日的前夕。 **eve** 指前一天晚上，也指前一天整天。

6 **that same phrase** 同样的用语，指"Good-bye, Mr. Chips." **phrase** 不单指"习语"或语法上的"短语"，它也作"用语"、"措辞"等解。

7 **mocking him gently for the seriousness he had had in those days** 由于他当时的一本正经而嘲弄他。当时 Chips 很严肃、古板，Kathie 特地在结婚前夕分手时用绰号称呼他，跟他开玩笑。

8 **old man's failing** 老人的弱点

9 **silly** 愚蠢的；傻的。这里是说流泪是愚蠢的，因而 = that was silly。

10 **couldn't help it** 不能自禁；禁不住流泪

11 **exhausted** [ɪg'zɔːstɪd] **him** 使他精疲力尽

12 **Nice boy** = He was a nice boy. 这是 Chips 在想。

13 **would do well.** = he would do well. 他会有出息。这也是 Chips 在想。

14 **Over the fog-laden air came the bell for call-over, tremulous** ['tremjʊləs] **and muffled.** 颤抖而沉闷的点名钟声透过浓雾弥漫的空气传送过来。这句子因状语短语 Over the fog-laden air 放在句首，所以 the bell ... 和 came 主谓倒装。**muffled**（声音）被压抑（得不响亮）的。

15 **greying into twilight** ['twaɪlaɪt]（窗口）渐渐灰暗，进入黄昏。 **twilight** 既指黄昏、暮色，又指黎明，曙光；总之是半明半暗。

16 **light up** 点起灯来

17 **he couldn't** = he couldn't move.

18 **it didn't matter** 这（因过分疲劳而不能动）并不要紧

chair[1]. No chicken[2] — eh, well — that was true enough. And it had been amusing about Linford[3]. A neat score off the jokers who had sent the boy over.[4] Good-bye, Mr. Chips[5] … odd, though, he should have said it just like that[6]...

1 **leaned back in his chair** 往后仰靠在椅子上

2 **No chicken = He was no chicken** 他老了

3 **it had been amusing about Linford** 关于 Linford 的事使他觉得有趣。 **it** 泛指刚才发生的事情。

4 **A neat score off the jokers who had sent the boy over.** 彻底击败了开玩笑叫这个学生来访的人。A neat score 前面省去 He had made。make a score off sb. 驳倒某人；占某人上风。

5 **Good-bye, Mr. Chips** Chips 在回想 Linford 告别时说的话。

6 **odd, though, he should have said it just like that** 但是奇怪，他恰好就是那样说的。"Good-bye, Mr. Chips." 恰恰是他和 Katherine 结婚前夕两人告别时 Katherine 所说的，Chips 觉得奇怪。**odd** = It was odd. **though** 这里是副词，作"但是"、"然而"解。

第十八章

内容提要

维克特太太从外面回来，发现契普斯昏倒在椅子上。待契普斯苏醒过来的时候，医生、校长、维克特太太等好多人围在他床边。契普斯在半昏迷状态，一生的往事在脑海中迷糊地回旋。一幕幕的情景，一个个的形象，此起彼伏。钟声、笑声、炮声、点名时一串串的名字……融合成一支和谐的乐曲。

契普斯听见床边有人在说："可怜这老朋友一生孤独；没有结过婚，没有孩子。"他得意地含笑回答道："不……我有……我有成千成万的孩子……都是男孩。"

一会儿，契普斯安详地睡去了。可爱的契普斯就这样与世长辞了。

18

When he awoke, for he seemed to have been asleep[1], he found himself in bed[2]; and Merivale was there, stooping over him and smiling. 'Well, you old ruffian[3] — feeling all right?[4] That was a fine shock you gave us[5]!'

Chips murmured, after a pause, and in a voice that surprised him by its weakness[6]: 'Why — um — what — what has happened?[7]'

'Merely that you threw a faint.[8] Mrs. Wickett came in and found you[9] — lucky she did[10]. You're all right now. Take it easy.[11] Sleep again if you feel inclined.[12]'

He was glad someone had suggested such a good idea. He felt so weak that he wasn't even puzzled by the details of the business[13] — how they had got him upstairs, what Mrs. Wickett had said, and so on. But then, suddenly, at the other side of the bed, he saw Mrs. Wickett[14]. She was

1 **for he seemed to have been asleep** 因为他似乎睡着过。这个并列从句插在这里解释 When he awoke。When he awoke 修饰 he found himself in bed。

2 **found himself in bed** 发现自己卧在床上

3 **you old ruffian** ['rʌfjən] 你这个老混蛋。 **ruffian** 原意为"流氓"，这里 old ruffian 是对老朋友的戏称。

4 **feeling all right?** = Are you feeling all right? 你感觉还好吗?

5 **a fine shock you gave us** 你让我大吃一惊。 **fine** 可怕的；是不正式用法。shock 后省去 that 或 which。

6 **surprised him by its weakness** 其声音之微弱使他惊异。

7 **Why — um — what — what has happened?** 怎么——发生什么事啦? **Why** 这里是感叹词，表示惊奇。

8 **Merely that you threw a faint.** 仅仅是你昏过去了一会儿。**Merely** = It is merely that... **threw a faint** 昏倒一下。像 a faint 前动词用 throw 之类的搭配（collocation），纯粹是习惯，必须处处注意并熟记。

9 **found you** = found you in a faint 发现你昏倒了。

10 **lucky she did** = It was lucky that she did; did = found you in a faint.

11 **Take it easy.** 从容；不要紧张；这是习语。

12 **Sleep again if you feel inclined.** 假如你觉得要睡，就再睡。**inclined** = inclined to sleep (again); inclined 是过去分词。也可看作是形容词，作"倾向于……的"、"想要……的"解。

13 **wasn't even puzzled by the details of the business** 甚至对于这件事（指昏倒）的细节也不感到困惑。 **business** 事物（常指使人讨厌的或无价值的事物）。下面 how ... 和 what ... 便是列举细节。

14 **at the other side of the bed, he saw Mrs. Wickett**（Chips 正在和床这一边的 Dr. Merivale 说话，）他发现 Mrs. Wickett 在床的另一边。

smilling. He thought: God bless my soul, what's she doing up here?[1] And then, in the shadows behind Merivale, he saw Cartwright[2], the new Head (he thought of him as 'new'[3], even though he had been at Brookfield since 1919), and old Buffles[4], commonly called 'Roddy[5]'. Funny, the way they were all here[6]. He felt: Anyhow, I can't be bothered to wonder why about anything[7]. I'm going to go to sleep.[8]

But it wasn't sleep, and it wasn't quite wakefulness, either[9]; it was a sort of in-between state[10], full of dreams and faces and voices. Old scenes and old scraps of tunes[11] — a Mozart trio that Kathie had once played in[12] — cheers and laughter and the sound of guns — and over it all, Brookfield bells, Brookfield bells[13]. 'So you see, if Miss Plebs wanted Mr. Patrician to marry her ... yes, you can, you liar …[14]' Joke ... Meat to be abhorred[15] ... Joke ... That you, Max?[16] Yes, come in.[17] What's the news from the Fatherland[18]? ... *O mihi praeteritos*[19] ... Ralston said I was slack and inefficient — but they couldn't manage without me.[20]

---

1 **what's she doing up here?** 她在这里楼上干什么？ **up** 在楼上；上文已说到 Chips 昏倒后被抬到楼上睡下。

2 **Cartwright** ['kɑ:trait] 卡特赖特，姓氏

3 **thought of him as 'new'** 把他看作“新的”。

4 **old Buffles** ['bʌflz] 老巴福尔斯。old 首字母小写，指老年的。

5 **Roddy** ['rɒdɪ] 教师 Buffles 的绰号，可能是从 rod（打学生的鞭子、棍棒）演化出来的。

6 **Funny, the way they were all here.** = It was funny the way they were all here. the way 后面省去 in which，相当于 how。

7 **I can't be bothered to wonder why about anything** 我对任何事情都不能烦心去猜想为什么。 **why** 在这里作名词用，作 wonder 的宾语。

8 **I'm going to go to sleep.** 我将睡着。 **go to sleep** 入睡；睡着；比较：**go to bed** 上床去睡。

9 **it wasn't sleep, and it wasn't quite wakefulness, either** 这不是睡着，也不是真正的醒。这两个 it 都指 Chips 当时所处的状态。

10 **a sort of in-between state** 一种（在睡着和醒着之间的）中间状态

11 **Old scenes and old scraps of tunes** 旧时的情景和旧时乐曲的片断。以下列举 Chips 半昏迷中的零乱印象。

12 **Mozart trio that Kathie had once played in** = Mozart trio in which Kathie had once played. Kathie 曾经参加演奏的莫扎特的三重奏，见第 86 页。

13 **and over it all, Brookfield bells, Brookfield bells** 在（乐曲声、喝彩声、笑声、炮声）这一切之上还有 Brookfield 的一阵阵不断的钟声。这里 it 统指上述一片混杂的声音。"Brookfield bells"重复，表示声声不绝。

14 **"So you see, if Miss Plebs wanted Mr. Patrician to marry her … yes, you can, you liar …"** 见第 72 页。

15 **Meat to be abhorred** 见第 192 页。

16 **That you, Max? = Is that you, Max?** 是你吗，麦克斯？ **Max** Max Steafel，是 Brookfield 的德语教师，已在第一次世界大战中战死，见第十四章。

17 **Yes, come in.** 是啊，进来。（当是 Chips 在半昏迷状态中看见 Max 出现在面前。）

18 **Fatherland** 祖国；这里指德国。称德国人的祖国，常用 Fatherland，此字来源于德语 *Vaterland*。

19 ***O mihi praeteritos …*** 见第 168 页。

20 **Ralston said I was slack and inefficient — but they couldn't manage without me.** 见第 146 页。 **couldn't manage without me** 没有我（学校）办不下去；少不了我。

... *Obile heres ago fortibus es in aro*[1] ... Can you translate that, any of you? ... It's a joke ...

Once[2] he heard them talking about him in the room.

Cartwright was whispering to Merivale. 'Poor old chap — must have lived a lonely sort of life, all by himself[3].'

Merivale answered: 'Not always by himself. He married, you know.'

'Oh, did he?[4] I never knew about that.'

'She died. It must have been — oh, quite thirty years ago. More, possibly.[5]'

'Pity. Pity he never had any children.[6]'

And at that[7], Chips opened his eyes as wide as he could[8] and sought to attract their attention[9]. It was hard for him to speak out loud[10], but he managed to murmur something[11], and they all looked round[12] and came nearer to him.

He struggled, slowly, with his words[13]. 'What — was that — um — you were saying — about me — just now?[14]'

Old Buffles smiled and said: 'Nothing at all[15], old chap — nothing at all — we were just wondering when you were going to wake out of your beauty sleep.[16]'

1 ***Obile heres ago fortibus es in aro*** 拉丁语，意思是“Obilus（人名），我要坚强者作继承人，你应当努力耕作”。也有人解释说，此话是以拉丁文发音的方式拼写的英语，“Oh Billy, here is a go: forty buses in a row.”

2 **Once**（在半昏迷中）一度

3 **all by himself** 完全单独地，一直都是一个人。 **by oneself** 单独地，独自；是习语。all 作状语。

4 **did he?** 照语法，承应上文，= Did he marry?

5 **More, possibly.** = It was possibly more than thirty years ago. 这里是讲 1933 年的事；Katherine 死于 1898 年（见第八章末），实际上是 35 年前。

6 **Pity. Pity he never had any children.** 真可怜！可怜他从来没有过孩子。第一个 Pity = That's a pity 或 What a pity。第二个 Pity = It's a pity that。

7 **at that** 一听到这句话

8 **opened his eyes as wide as he could** 尽量睁大他的眼睛。 **wide** 这里是形容词，作 eyes 的宾语补足语，有“张足”的意思。**as he** = as he could open his eyes.

9 **sought to attract their attention** 想要引起他们的注意；要他们听他说话。sought（seek 的过去式）后接不定式，表示“企图”;这种用法较文也较旧。

10 **speak out loud** 高声说出话来

11 **managed to murmur something** 终于低声说了些什么。managed 后接不定式。表示“设法做成”。

12 **looked round** 掉过头看（因为他们原在离 Chips 较远处窃窃私语，现在听见他在低声说话，都掉头来看他。）

13 **struggled, slowly, with his words** 缓慢地、费劲地说话。说出每一个字都要费很大劲，所以用 struggled（挣扎）。

14 **What — was that — um — you were saying — about me — just now?** = What was that that you were saying … 刚才……你们……呃……在说我……什么? **just now** 刚才；是习语；也作“此刻”、“马上”解。

15 **Nothing at all** = We were saying nothing at all (about you). 这是骗骗 Chips 的。

16 **beauty sleep** 午夜前的酣睡

'But — umph — I heard you — you *were* talking about me ...'

'Absolutely nothing of any consequence[1], my dear fellow — really, I give you my word[2] ...'

'I thought I heard you — one of you — saying[3] it was a pity — umph — a pity I never had — any children[4] ... eh? ... But I have, you know ... I have ...'

The others smiled without answering, and after a pause Chips began a faint and palpitating chuckle[5].

'Yes — umph — I have,' he added, with quavering merriment[6]. 'Thousands of 'em ... thousands of 'em ... and all boys[7] ...'

And then the chorus sang in his ears in final harmony[8], more grandly and sweetly than he had ever heard it before[9], and more comfortingly too ... Pettifer, Pollett, Porson, Potts, Pullman, Purvis, Pym-Wilson, Radlett, Rapson, Reade, Reaper, Reddy[10] Primus ... come round me now, all of you, for a last word and a joke[11] ... Harper, Haslett, Hatfield, Hatherley[12] ... my last joke ... did you hear it? ... did it make you laugh? ... Bone, Boston, Bovey, Bradford, Bradley, Bramhall-Anderson[13] ... wherever you are, whatever

1 **Absolutely nothing of any consequence** ['kɒnsɪkwəns] = We were talking of absolutely nothing of any consequence 我们绝对没有讲什么要紧的事。

2 **I give you my word** 我向你保证。

3 **I thought I heard you saying** 我好像听见你们在说。 **I thought I heard** 我原来以为我听到；我刚才好像听到。 **hear you saying** 有"偶然听到你们正在说"的意思。

4 **it was a pity — umph — a pity I never had — any children** I never had 前面省去 that。

5 **began a faint and palpitating** ['pælpɪteɪtɪŋ] **chuckle** 开始一阵微弱而颤抖的低声的笑。

6 **added, with quavering merriment** 带着颤抖的愉快接下去说（愉快却又带着颤抖）

7 **thousands of 'em... and all boys**（我有）成千上万的孩子，都是男孩子。**'em** = them (children).

8 **the chorus** ['kɔːrəs] **sang in his ears in final harmony** 合唱的歌声以最后的和谐在他耳边升起（Chips 临终前的感受）。

9 **more grandly and sweetly than he had ever heard it before** 比他过去曾听到过的合唱歌声更雄壮、更甜美。

10 **Pettifer** ['petɪfə], **Pollett** ['pɒlɪt], **Porson** ['pɔːsn], **Potts** [pɒts], **Pullman** ['pʊlmən], **Purvis** ['pɜːvɪs], **Pym-Wilson** ['pɪm'wɪlsn], **Radlett** ['rædlɪt], **Rapson** ['ræpsn], **Reade** [riːd], **Reaper** ['riːpə], **Reddy** ['redɪ] 都是学生的姓氏。

11 **come round me now, all of you, for a last word and a joke** 你们大家现在都到我身边来，听我说最后一句话，再讲一个笑话。all of you 是插入的呼唤语。

12 **Harper** ['hɑːpə], **Haslett** ['heɪzlɪt 或 'hæzlɪt], **Hatfield** ['hætfiːld], **Hatherley** ['hæðəlɪ] 都是学生的姓氏。

13 **Bone** [bəʊn], **Boston** ['bɒstən], **Bovey** ['buːvɪ, 'bəʊvɪ 或 'bʌvɪ], **Bradford** ['brædfəd], **Bradley** ['brædlɪ], **Bramhall-Anderson** ['bræmhɔːl'ændəsn] 都是学生的姓氏。

has happened, give me this moment with you[1] ... this last moment ... my boys ...

And soon Chips was asleep[2].

He seemed so peaceful that they did not disturb him to say good night[3]; but in the morning, as the School bell sounded for breakfast, Brookfield had the news[4]. 'Brookfield will never forget his lovableness,' said Cartwright, in a speech to the School. Which was absurd[5], because all things are forgotten in the end[6]. But Linford, at any rate, will remember and tell the tale[7]: I said good-bye to Chips[8] the night before he died ...

1 **wherever you are, whatever has happened, give me this moment with you** 无论你们在哪里，无论发生了什么，这一刻让我和你们在一起吧。

2 **Chips was asleep** Chips 睡着了。

3 **did not disturb him to say good night** 不去打扰他向他道“晚安”告别。Good night 是晚上分别时用语。比较：Good evening 晚上好（在晚上会面时和分别时都可以用）。

4 **had the news** 得到消息（Chips 逝世的消息）。

5 **Which was absurd** 这话是荒谬的。Which 指校长 Cartwright 说“Brookfield will never forget his lovableness.”

6 **in the end** 最后；最终

7 **remember and tell the tale** 记住并讲述这件事。**tale** 不一定是“故事”，这里就作“经历过的事情”解。

8 **said good-bye to Chips** 对 Chips 道了“再会”；向 Chips 告别。

契普斯先生年表

伊丽莎白时代 (1558 — 1603) 年间 Brookfield 公学创立。

(Brookfield ... was an old foundation; established in the reign of Elizabeth. 第 2 章 / 第 20 页)

1840 年 Wetherby 来到 Brookfield，任校长。

(Wetherby, who came in 1840, restored its [Brookfield's] fortunes somewhat. 第 2 章 / 第 22 页)

1848 年 Chips 生；其正式姓氏为 Chipping，Chips 是他的绰号。

(Born in 1848, ... 第 1 章 / 第 8 页；

"You are a young man, Mr. Chipping … 第 1 章 / 第 10 页)

1867 年前后 Chips 19 岁前后，在剑桥大学学习。

("… sixty-seven, when you were up at Cambridge." 第 6 章 / 第 76 页)

1869 年，21 岁 在 Melbury 任教一年。

(Chips had put in for Brookfield [1870 年，见下条] after a year at Melbury. 第 1 章 / 第 8 页)

1870 年，22 岁 开始在 Brookfield 任教。

("We began here … in 1870. 第 11 章 / 第 150 页；

"I was ... a young man of twenty-two!" 第 17 章 / 第 240 页)

同年，校长 Wetherby 去世，Meldrum 接任。

(Chips could even remember Brookfield in Wetherby's time ... 1870 ... He remembered that day of his preliminary interview [with Wetherby] ... 第 1 章 / 第 8 页；

Wetherby ... died during the summer vacation. 第 1 章 / 第 10 页；

"Mr. Meldrum came here, and that was thirty-eight years ago." 第 11 章 / 第 150 页 [这话是 Chips 在和 Ralston 争吵时说的；争吵发生在 1908 年，见后。])

1880 年，32 岁 Chips 已在 Brookfield 任教十年。

(About 1800, after he had been at Brookfield a decade, 第 2 章 / 第 24 页)

1888 年，40 岁 Chips 已扎根于 Brookfield，乐于在 Brookfield 的教书生涯。

(At forty, he was rooted, settled, and quite happy. 第 2 章 /24 页)

1896 年，48 岁 春，任舍监。

(Spring — the spring of 1896. He was forty-eight ...

He had just been appointed housemaster: 第 5 章 / 第 44 页)

暑期，到湖泊区度假，遇 Katherine Bridges。

(During the summer vacation, he went up to the Lake District... One day, climbing on Great Gable, he noticed a girl waving excitedly from a dangerous-looking ledge. 第 4 章 / 第 44 页；Her name was Katherine Bridges. 第 4 章 / 第 48 页)

Katherine 年方二十五，与 Chips 相爱，两人于同年秋季开学前在伦敦结婚。

(She was twenty-five — young enough to be Chips's daughter. 第 4 章 / 第 48 页）

Within a week they were head over heels in love, ... they were married in London a week before the beginning of the autumn term. 第 4 章 / 第 54 页）

1897 年，49 岁 维多利亚女王在位六十周年大庆，Brookfield 放假一天。

(He remembered the Diamond Jubilee; there had been a whole holiday at Brookfield. 第 10 章 / 第 132 页）

在 Katherine 建议下，Brookfield 所办救济机关的儿童来到 Brookfield 比赛踢足球。

(It was Katherine who suggested that a team of the mission should come up to Brookfield and play one of the School's elevens at Soccer. 第 6 章 / 第 74 页；

"... this is eighteen-*ninety*-seven — not *sixty*-seven ..." 第 6 章 / 第 76 页）

1898 年，50 岁 Chips 成为全校教职员的首席。

(At fifty, he was doyen of the staff. 第 2 章 / 第 24 页）

同年 4 月 1 日，Chips 的爱妻 Katherine 和初生婴儿同日死去。

(They had died on the same day, the mother and the child just born, on April 1st. 1898. 第 8 章 / 第 106 页）

Chips 从比较舒适的大楼住所迁回单身宿舍。他曾想辞去舍监一职，校长挽留了他。

(Chips changed his more commodious apartments in School House for his old original bachelor quarters. He thought at first that he would give up his housemastership, but the Head persuaded him otherwise；第 9 章 / 第 110 页；

He was fifty. 第 9 章 / 第 110 页）

1900 年，51 岁 校长 Meldrum 突患肺炎去世；Chips 暂时代理校长，直到年轻的新校长 Ralston 就任。

(In 1900 old Meldrum ... died suddenly from pneumonia; and in the interval before the appointment of a successor, Chips became Acting Head of Brookfield ... 第 10 章 / 第 126 页；

... they brought in a mere youngster of thirty-seven ... 第 10 章 / 第 126 页；

...Ralston, the new head ... 第 10 章 / 第 128 页）

1908 年，60 岁 新任校长 Ralston 很年轻，实际上 Chips 成了 Brookfield 的化身。

(At sixty, under a new and youthful Head, Chips *was* Brookfield. 第 2 章 / 第 24—26 页）

Ralston 要 Chips 退休，Chips 大怒，发生争吵。全校支持 Chips。

(… in 1908, when he [Chips] had just turned sixty, came Ralston's urbane ultimatum. "Mr. Chipping, have you ever

thought you would like to retire?" 第 11 章 / 第 140—142 页；
And then the row with Ralston. 第 11 章 / 第 140 页；
The amazing result was a spontaneously outburst of sympathy and partisanship ... 第 11 章 / 第 156 页）

[按第 11 章 / 第 148 页上 Ralston 对 Chips 说："... your Latin and Greek lessons are exactly the same as they were when I began here ten year ago". 实际上 Ralston 来到 Brookfield 任校长是在 1900 年（见前），至此只有八年，不到十年。他说"十年"，可能是约数，也可能是作者误计。]

1910 年，62 岁　英王爱德华七世逝世，Brookfield 停课半天，举行礼拜。

(A May morning, ... "... His Majesty King Edward the Seventh died this morning ... There will be no school this afternoon, but a service will be held in the Chapel at four-thirty." 第 10 章 / 第 128 页）

1911 年，63 岁　Ralston 离职；Chatteris 接任校长。

(And in 1911 Ralston left ... His successor was a man named Chatteris, ... 第 12 章 / 第 164 页）

1913 年，65 岁　Chips 退休。

(And in 1913, when he turned sixty-five, he retired. 第 2 章 / 第 26 页）

同年 7 月，Bookfield 欢送 Chips，会上 Chips 称在校服务 42 年。

(At that final end-of-term dinner, in July 1913, Chips received farewell presentations and made a speech ... he mentioned that he had been at Brookfield for forty-two years. 第 12 章 / 第 166 和 168 页)[按 Chips 于 1870 年来到 Brookfield（见前），到 1913 年退休，实有 43 年。42 年是误计。]

8 月，去德国 Wiesbaden 疗养，住德语老师 Staefel 家。

(August 1913. Chips went for a cure to Wiesbaden, where he lodged at the home of the German master at Brookfield, Herr Staefel. 第 12 章 / 第 172 页)

9 月，德国回来，移居 Mrs. Wickett 家。

(In September, when term began, Chips returned and took up residence at Mrs. Wickett's. 第 12 章 / 第 172 页)

1914—1918 年，66—70 岁 第一次世界大战。

(The War years. 第 13 章 / 第 178 页)

1916 年，68 岁 校长 Chatteris 因患糖尿病，不能服役，工作有难处，要求 Chips 回到学校，Chips 应允。

(1916 ... Chatteris talked to Chips ... "… I happen to be diabetic, and couldn't pass the blindest M. O., but I don't see why I should pin a medical certificate on my front door." 第 13 章 / 第 182 页；

"… how about coming back here for a while? ..." ... Chips answered ... "I'll come …" 第 13 章 / 第 184 和 186 页)

1917—1918 年，69—70 岁 Chatteris 于 1917 年冬病倒，翌年 4 月去世；Chips 再度代理校长。

(Chatteris fell ill during the winter of '17, and again, for the the second time in his life, Chips became Acting Head of Brookfield. Then in April [1918] Chatteris died, and the Governors asked Chips if he would carry on "for the duration". He said he would if they would refrain from appointing him officially. 第 14 章 / 第 192 页)

1918 年，70 岁 11 月 11 日，消息传来，大战结束；Brookfield 放假一天。

(November 11th, 1918. News came through in the morning; a whole holiday was decreed for the School. 第 15 章 / 第 208 页)

同日，Chips 提出辞呈。第二天患支气管炎，一直卧床到圣诞节后。

(The next day he was in bed with bronchitis, and stayed there till after Christmas. But already, on that night of November 11th, ... he had sent in his resignation to the Board of Governors. 第 15 章 / 第 210 页)

1919 年，71 岁 Cartwright 任新校长。

(... Cartwright, the new Head (... he had been at Brookfield since 1919), … 第 18 章 / 第 250 页)

1926 年，78 岁 英国总罢工；Brookfield 学生帮助装运食物，Chips 深有感触。

(During the General Strike of 1926, Brookfield boys loaded motor vans with foodstuffs. 第 16 章 / 第 220 页)

1929 年后，80 岁后 Chips 不再离开 Brookfield 出门，连在伦敦举行的校友聚会也不参加：怕受寒，怕晚睡太累。

(After 1929, Chips did not leave Brookfield — even for Old Boys' dinners in London. He was afraid of chills, and late nights began to tire him too much. 第 16 章 / 第 222 页）

1930 年，82 岁 立遗嘱，除一部分遗赠外，尽捐余款设立公开的入学奖学金。

(In 1930, he made his will. Except for legacies to the mission and to Mrs. Wickett, he left all he had to found an open entrance scholarship to the School. 第 16 章 / 第 224 页）

1931—1932 年，83、84 岁 人们把 Chips 当作预言家和百科全书，各种问题都要问他。

(1931 ... 1932 ... They all asked him questions, as if he were some kind of prophet and encyclopaedia combined — more even than that, for they liked their answers dished up as a joke. 第 16 章 / 第 224 页）

1933 年，85 岁 11 月，Chips 感觉不适，以为是在停战纪念日做礼拜受了点凉。

(He sat in his front parlour at Mrs. Wickett's on a November afternoon in thirty-three ... He had not felt too well since Armistice Day; he fancied he might have caught a slight chill during the chapel service. 第 17 章 / 第 232 页）

某日下午，忽有新同学 Linford 来访，Chips 亲自应门，亲自送客到门口，又受凉；且谈话过多，使他疲惫不堪。

(About a quarter to four a ring came, and Chips, answering the front door himself (which he oughtn't to have done), encountered a rather small boy ... 第 17 章 / 第 234 页；

"I'm — umph — sorry — you can't stay ..." At the front door he shook hands. 第 17 章 / 第 240 页；

He felt very tired; talking to Linford like that had quite exhausted him. 第 17 章 / 第 242 页)

Chips 昏倒，虽经救醒，实处于半昏迷状态，终于在无数往事的回忆中溘然长逝。

("Merely that you threw a faint ... Take it easy. Sleep again if you feel inclined." 第 18 章 / 第 248 页；

But it wasn't sleep, and it wasn't quite wakefulness, either; it was a sort of in-between state, full of dreams and faces and voices. Old scenes and old scraps of tunes ... 第 18 章 / 第 250 页；

And soon Chips was asleep. 第 18 章 / 第 256 页；

... he died ... 第 18 章 / 第 256 页)

人们总是易忘的，只有那个新同学 Linford 将永远记得，他曾在隔夜向 Chips 告别。

(... all things are forgotten in the end. But Linford, at any rate, will remember and tell the tale: I said good-bye to Chips the night before he died. 第 18 章 / 第 256 页

"Good-bye, Mr. Chips ..." 第 17 章 / 第 242 页)

图书在版编目(CIP)数据

再会，契普斯先生 /(英)詹姆斯・希尔顿著；
葛传槼，俞亢咏注解．—上海：上海译文出版社，2017.8（2024.3重印）
ISBN 978-7-5327-7393-0

Ⅰ.①再… Ⅱ.①詹… ②葛… ③俞…
Ⅲ.①长篇小说−英国−现代 Ⅳ.①I561.45

中国版本图书馆 CIP 数据核字(2016)第 253355 号

James Hilton
Good-Bye, Mr. Chips

再会，契普斯先生
[英]詹姆斯·希尔顿　著　　葛传槼　俞亢咏　注解
责任编辑/金宇　装帧设计/张志全工作室

上海译文出版社有限公司出版、发行
网址：www.yiwen.com.cn
201101　上海市闵行区号景路159弄B座
江阴市机关印刷服务有限公司印刷

开本 787×1092　1/32　印张 8.75　插页 5　字数 154,000
2017年8月第1版　2024年3月第4次印刷

ISBN 978-7-5327-7393-0/I·4506
定价：48.00元